UNNATURAL

ERICA ROSEN MD TRILOGY : BOOK 1

DEVEN GREENE

Black Rose Writing | Texas

ISBN: 978-1-68433-608-1
PUBLISHED BY BLACK ROSE WRITING
www.blackrosewriting.com

Printed in the United States of America
Suggested Retail Price (SRP) $19.95

Unnatural is printed in Georgia Pro

*As a planet-friendly publisher, Black Rose Writing does its best to eliminate unnecessary waste to reduce paper usage and energy costs, while never compromising the reading experience. As a result, the final word count vs. page count may not meet common expectations.

To my husband, Glen, with love.
For your infinite encouragement and support.

UNNATURAL

CHAPTER 1

Exiting the restroom where I'd been unsuccessful in removing the vomit stain from the front of my white coat, I'd barely taken two steps before my physician's assistant spotted me.

"There you are, Dr. Rosen. You're in room nine next. Here's a clean coat."

"Thank you, Martha, you read my mind." I shed my soiled coat, grabbed my stethoscope and other items from the pockets, and tossed the garment to my assistant. She handed me a clean white coat which I slipped on, all without missing a step as I strode toward room nine. We'd done this drill many times, synchronizing our moves for maximum efficiency. I often imagined my coat-switching exercise must be similar to refueling a jet in the sky. After I'd filled my pockets with the items in my hands, Martha removed my nametag from the dirty coat and handed it to me. I attached it to the upper pocket on my clean coat with the alligator clip. "Who's the patient?"

Martha smiled and held out a clipboard for me. "Evan Fields and his mom. Forearm laceration."

Continuing to walk, I grabbed the clipboard. "Thanks." Martha started to speak, but I interrupted her. "I know, I know. Room nine."

Martha, a stout woman in her late thirties with short brown hair and a pasty complexion, slowed down, letting me approach the waiting patient on my own. When I reached the door to room nine, I knocked twice to let Evan and his mom know I was about to enter, then stopped. Obvious waste of time, I reminded myself. I slowly opened the door to the small, cluttered exam room, the familiar Shrek poster the first thing that greeted me. Pushing the door farther, I saw Evan sitting on the firetruck exam table, his mother seated in one of the two adult-size chairs. The two children's chairs were empty.

As usual, my jaw tightened a bit upon seeing the computer terminal, like the others found in every exam room. It sat innocently enough on a small table with a faux wood top near the sink. The best thing one might say about the computer is that it united all physicians practicing in the clinic and in clinics and hospitals across the country. Male, female, black, white, brown, tall, short, progressive, conservative, they all hated the computer, the bearer of the despised Electronic Health Record, or EHR. After two years in the clinic, you'd think I would be used to it, but I wasn't. I still resented its intrusion into the time I spent with my patients and their parents. Instead of having a comfortable discussion with that now almost passé element known as eye contact, I needed to spend most of my appointment time sitting before the terminal, typing. Resigned to postponing my long-planned ax attack of the computer, I logged in and confirmed Martha had made sure all the necessary information, such as patient's name and age, parents' names, address, insurance, and reason for visit, was up to date.

Evan and his mom looked at me and smiled while I signed "Hello." They each responded with a reciprocal sign. Both Evan and his mother are profoundly deaf. I was the only clinic doctor or staff of any sort proficient in American Sign Language, so it was always up to me to take care of the severely hearing-impaired patients, something I enjoyed.

Evan was holding a bloody washcloth over his left forearm. His mother was signing furiously, informing me that Evan had fallen while climbing a tree, and cut his arm on the sprinkler below. I signed to Evan, requesting to take a look. He peeled away the washcloth, revealing a ragged two-inch gash on the lateral aspect of his forearm. I conveyed that I needed to clean the area and put in a few stitches.

I left the room to get a suture kit, returning a few minutes later to find Evan sitting on his mother's lap. "He's afraid," she signed.

I explained it only hurt a few seconds when I injected the numbing medicine, and when we were done, I'd give him a dollar bill he could use at the dollar store a few blocks away. That's all the encouragement Evan needed. I anesthetized the area, cleaned it, and put in five stitches. When I was done, Evan's mom signed that she was proud he was so brave. I spread antibiotic over the wound and handed the boy a crisp dollar bill—one of six I had in my pocket. Most days I needed at least three to coax my patients into submission for various procedures.

I broke away to sit on the stool facing the dreaded computer so I could enter information about the visit. I usually spoke to my patients as I typed, often just small talk. My inability to sign while I typed made me hate the EHR even more. After I finished typing, I instructed Evan and his mom how to care for his injury. Mother and son motioned their thanks, I handed Mom a printed set of wound care instructions, gestured goodbye, and backed out of the room.

Martha wasted no time in finding me. "Five-year-old girl and her mom in room four for kindergarten physical. New patient. Good luck with that one. Mom has heavy accent. Chinese, I think."

The UC San Francisco pediatric clinic was always busy. In addition to the myriad clerks, physician's assistants, nurses, and doctors rushing through the halls, there were the patients and their entourages. Each small visitor was accompanied by a parent, sometimes two, often with one or more siblings or a grandparent. Between the ages of two and eight, patients and siblings frequently ran through the hallway, not mindful of anyone or anything in the way.

Making my way to room four, I dodged three-foot-high twins running in front of their mother, the colorful LEDs on the soles of their shoes flashing erratically while they laughed and bumped into the legs of strangers. According to the clock above the clerk's station, it was 11:30 a.m. Two patients behind already, I picked up my pace, brushed back the stray hairs that had escaped my low ponytail, noticed the name tag on my coat that read "Erica Rosen, MD, Pediatrics," was crooked, and knocked on the door of room four.

From within, I heard the muffled voice of a young woman. I barely heard, "Come in."

I straightened my name tag before opening the door, glancing up in time to see the clinic director, Dr. Gabe Lewis, turn the corner and walk in my direction. As usual, his white coat was clean and pressed, his hair looked ready for a photo shoot, and he looked more like a TV doctor than a real one.

Avoiding eye contact, I pushed hard on the door and entered. The door slammed behind me.

"Hello, Ms. Chen," I said, consulting the clipboard. "I'm Dr. Rosen."

I gazed around the familiar room with torn posters of SpongeBob SquarePants, The Little Mermaid, and Minions. The two adult-size chairs were empty. An attractive, thin young Asian woman with short hair sat in one of the little chairs, a small child on her lap with its face buried in her chest. The child had straight shoulder length shiny black hair.

Damn. Martha didn't get the kid stripped down to her underwear. Only took her shoes and socks off.

The woman seemed nervous, unable to speak for a few seconds. When she finally spoke, it was with a heavy Chinese accent. "This Wang Shu, Doctor. I Ting. His mother."

"Pleased to meet you," I said, happy my roommate, Daisy, had exposed me to her parents and their heavy Mandarin accents countless times. Over the years, I had developed an ear for understanding their speech.

"Hello, Wang Shu," I said in my winning pediatrician's voice, smiling. "How are you today?"

The child didn't move. "He shy," Ting said.

Knowing Asians pronounce "he" and "she" the same in their native tongue, the inappropriate gender reference didn't surprise me.

"I understand you're here today to have Wang Shu's kindergarten physical form filled out."

"*Shi*. Yes." Ting reached into her purse and handed me a two-page form, folded in thirds.

I took a moment to examine the form. It looked familiar, resembling many I had filled out previously. I sat facing the computer and checked the EHR. Other than the patient's name, age, address, and mother's name, her chart was blank. It wasn't unusual to have patients with no medical insurance. "Has Wang Shu had her vaccinations?" I asked.

"Shi, yes. Everything. He have very good medical care. The best."

"I'm glad to hear that. Do you have some documentation?"

Ting looked at me blankly.

"Papers that list her vaccinations."

"We come from China. He get them there. I not have papers, but I know he get everything. Very excellent medical care."

"Wang Shu doesn't start school for over a month. Can you have the information sent to you?"

"No. Not possible."

"You must have shown documentation when you moved here. How long have you been in this country?"

"Two month."

"You speak English very well for someone who's been here such a short time."

"I study hard."

"Since it was only two months ago, you should still have the documentation of vaccination you showed to pass the health inspection when you came here."

"I not find it."

"If you don't get the documentation, we'll need to revaccinate her. Without proof of vaccines, she can't go to school."

"Oh. He no like more vaccine. But no choice."

This woman seemed intelligent, clearly educated enough to speak English and know about vaccines. But something didn't seem right. "I have to ask you this," I said in a gentle tone so as not to alarm her. "Did you enter the US illegally?"

Ting burst into tears.

I grabbed a tissue and handed it to her. "It's okay. You can tell me. I won't report you. But if you came here illegally, I'm going to insist that Wang Shu also have a TB test."

"Okay, we not legal, but I know he not have TB," Ting said, her tears now a slow trickle. "He very healthy, never around people with TB."

"She still needs the test. I can't put other children at risk."

"No, no," Ting said, still sniffling. "He have BCG vaccine."

The BCG vaccine is given to protect people from TB in countries like China that have a high incidence of the disease. When a TB skin test is given to people who have had a BCG vaccine, the test is often falsely positive. I turned to the child.

"Now, Wang Shu, I have to examine you," I said, wondering if the child understood a word I was saying. "Don't worry, it won't hurt."

I got up from my seat at the computer, picked up Wang Shu and placed her on the exam table. For the first time, her tiny face was exposed as she looked straight at me. Black hair cut into short, straight bangs across her forehead. Light olive skin. Typical Asian features, with a small nose and epicanthal folds in upper eyelids. I almost gasped. Light blue eyes. What I was seeing was not possible.

CHAPTER 2

A blue-eyed Chinese person? Genetically impossible. And yet, there she was. She looked one hundred percent Asian like her mom. Was it possible she had Scandinavians in her family tree, with eye color being all that was left of those foreign genes?

"My, what beautiful eyes you have," I remarked. Wang Shu looked at me blankly.

"He no speak English," her mother said.

"Where'd she get her blue eyes? Is her father Caucasian?"

"No. He Chinese. And he dead."

"I'm sorry to hear that." Ting looked nervous and started to tear up again. Wanting to avoid more waterworks, I changed the subject.

"I'm sure it's stressful moving to a new country. Both for you and your child."

Ting nodded.

"I'll need to examine her. Could you help her take off her shirt and pants? You can leave her underpants on."

"Please," Ting begged. "Keep his clothes on. Nurse try to take off clothes, but Wang Shu get very upset. He no like doctors. Or nurses."

With Ting starting to tear up again and Wang Shu staring at me, her body almost frozen in fear, I acquiesced against my better judgment. "Okay, I can examine her under her clothes."

"Thank you."

I offered Wang Shu one of the dollars from my pocket, but she ignored it.

"She no understand," Ting said. "No use money in China. Pay for everything with phone."

Unable to bribe her, I steeled myself for some resistance as I listened to Wang Shu's heart, lungs, and bowel sounds through her clothes, palpated her thyroid, liver, and spleen, and checked her reflexes. I quickly lifted her shirt to inspect her skin, front and back, then examined both feet, looking for signs of poorly fitted shoes or other problems. Wang Shu seemed tense the whole time. I anticipated a problem with the next part of the exam, intentionally leaving it for the end. I laid her down and quickly pulled her pants down to examine her external genitals. Wang Shu became hysterical. I saw what I needed in less than two seconds and pulled her pants back up, but the damage had been done. Wang Shu was inconsolable as Ting grabbed her, held her in her arms, and spoke to her quietly in their native tongue.

I felt like shit. All I could do was look on helplessly. The crying finally stopped, and Ting sat with her child on her lap, Wang Shu's face again buried in her chest.

"I'm sorry I upset your daughter so much, but I needed to do a full exam."

"I understand." Ting said a few words to her daughter in Chinese, then turned to me. "I tell him I buy him treat when we leave. He be okay."

"I'm happy to say that your daughter appears to be very healthy. I want to order a blood test for thalassemia, if you don't mind, because it's so common in the Chinese population." We routinely test Asian children for thalassemia, a genetic disease resulting in decreased hemoglobin production, with varying degrees of anemia.

"No thalassemia. Blood fine. Test in China. He get excellent care there. Maybe too much care. Make him very upset."

"I'm not sure how good the testing is there," I said.

"Very good thalassemia test in China."

"I'd feel better if you could show me some documentation."

"Cannot get papers from China."

I was struck by the story unfolding. This child had excellent medical care in China, according to Mom. Yet she couldn't get any documentation. She was here illegally. The child's father was dead. Maybe he was a political figure in China. It wouldn't be a stretch to imagine he was executed, and she fled with her child, fearing governmental reprisals.

"Have you applied for political asylum?" I asked.

"I cannot. I not a political."

"But if your husband, or Wang Shu's father was, and you came here because you were afraid of your government, you could apply."

Ting's eyes started to fill with tears. "Wang Shu father no enemy of government. The government love him. He no dead. He dead to me."

As the conversation grew stranger by the moment, I was intrigued, curious about this woman's story. But I was already behind. Other patients were waiting.

"If you need the name of a good immigration attorney, Lisa at the reception desk can make some recommendations." I started typing as I spoke. "In the meantime, I'm ordering vaccines, a test for thalassemia, and a chest X-ray, instead of the TB skin test we usually do, since she had a BCG vaccine. Once those are done, you'll be notified, and you can come back to pick up your school form."

Typing into the computer, I swore under my breath—the EHR was hung up, preventing me from proceeding. Finally, when the damn thing had regained its composure, it gave me a hard time for ordering an X-ray to rule out TB instead of the more economical skin test. Despite it being common to rule out TB with an imaging study rather than a skin test in people from countries where the BCG vaccine is often administered, I was going around in circles trying to explain this to the computer. One more bad experience with the EHR to add to my list of hundreds. I eventually managed a workaround, requesting the X-ray to look for a lung mass, with a freehand comment to rule out TB. I hit send and prepared to say my goodbyes before hightailing it to my next patient.

"It was a pleasure to meet you, Ms. Chen," I said, standing. "I look forward to seeing you on your next visit. Martha will be in to assist—"

"Another question, Doctor. Another question," Ting interrupted.

Her insistence surprised me, although it wasn't uncommon for patients, or their parents in the case of pediatrics, to wait until a visit is almost over to bring up an issue of grave concern.

"I worry about Wang Shu."

The waterworks started again. Was I ever going to get out of there? "Now, now, Ms. Chen. Tell me your concern. Like I said, your daughter seems healthy, so there's probably nothing to worry about."

I handed her the box of tissues from which she removed several to blow her nose. "I worry about Wang Shu because he suppose to be boy." Once she blurted out the last words, she cried uncontrollably, her whole body shaking.

Doing my best to hide my disapproval of what I assumed was a negative attitude towards having a girl, I said, "Why do you say that? You should be happy with your beautiful, healthy daughter." I expected her to describe a ritual she had performed, or an herbal concoction she had taken, to assure the birth of a boy.

It took minutes before Ting could speak. "They do genetic test before he born. He a boy. Then he born, and he a girl."

I sank back onto the stool opposite the computer. What had been a strange visit was entering Twilight Zone territory. If what she just told me was true, the adorable little girl sitting in front of me had the genetic makeup of a male. I knew of a rare condition, complete androgen insensitivity syndrome, in which genetically male individuals are born with a complete lack of testosterone receptors on tissue, rendering them unable to respond to the male hormone, testosterone. Because of this, affected people look and develop like females in every way, except they are infertile, lacking a uterus and ovaries. This is not usually diagnosed until the person reaches late puberty with no sign of a normal menstrual cycle.

"How old are you, Ms. Chen?" I asked. To me, she looked to be in her late twenties. An age so young genetic testing is not typically done without a family history of an inherited disorder.

"Thirty."

"You were only around twenty-five when you were pregnant. Why did you have genetic testing? Is there a heritable disease in your family? Or the father's? Did you have a problem with another pregnancy?"

"No. The test done to be safe."

"Did it show any abnormalities?"

"I no think so. They not tell me everything. But they tell me is boy."

I couldn't have been more confused, but from my exam, this was definitely a girl. At least from the outside. There was no way I was going to do a pelvic exam on this child. I started typing on the computer. "I'm referring Wang Shu to the genetics department. She may have a rare condition that causes genetically male people to appear female. Unfortunately, they are unable to have children, but can otherwise live normal lives as females."

I swore under my breath some more when the EHR rejected my referral multiple times until I finally logged out and back in again. Success, at last. I didn't look forward to the argument I knew I would have about this with Gabe. The tightwad clinic director kept a close eye on the budget and also happened to be the man I was romantically involved with until two days ago when I'd decided to call it quits. I hadn't told him about the calling it quits part yet.

CHAPTER 3

It was 8:00 p.m. when I opened the door to my apartment, a fifth-floor, two-bedroom, two-bath unit in a modern high-rise South of Market. I'd known my roommate, Daisy Wong, since we were in the sixth grade. After a year of fierce competition to be the best at everything in our class academically, we pretty much tied for that honor—she being slightly better at math and grammar, I slightly better at science and social studies—and became BFFs.

"I thought you were going to start getting home earlier," Daisy chided me.

"I meant tomorrow."

"You're going to kill yourself with the work hours you keep. One day, you'll keel over and—"

"Not all of us can be part of the chosen few who get paid big bucks to write code from home."

"You're lucky I have some leftover lasagna you can heat up if you're hungry."

"How about if I'm famished?" I was already looking through the refrigerator for said lasagna and found it in the vegetable crisper. I placed the comfort food in the microwave for three minutes and turned, noticing a vase of red roses on the kitchen table. "Who are those from?" I asked.

"I was wondering how long it would take you to spot them. You don't really have to ask, do you?"

"I called it, didn't I? A dozen roses two days after our last blowout fight."

"Well? Are the roses going to work again, or are you going to tell that misogynist asshole, gorgeous on the outside while rotten to the core on the inside, to go fuck himself?"

"This time he really did go too far. I'm going to tell him to go fuck himself."

"It's about time. This time, I hope you mean it, girl."

"Say, why don't you take these flowers and put them in your room?"

"No problem. They're beautiful, even if they're a gift from the devil himself."

"C'mon, now. He's not that bad."

"Are you going to wimp out on me again? If you don't dump him this time—"

"Don't worry, I'm going to do it."

"When? You have to tell me when."

"After I finish all the lasagna."

"How much after? Five minutes? Five months?"

"You won't leave me alone till I do it, will you?"

"You see right through me."

"How about I send him a text?"

"How 'bout you call him on the phone, thank him for the flowers, and then tell him to go fuck himself?"

"Don't forget, he's still my boss."

"Oh, that."

*

The lasagna was good. Or maybe it wasn't. I ate it so fast there wasn't enough time for the taste to register. I sat at the desk in my bedroom, a half-empty glass of Cabernet in front of me, and stared at my cell phone. I needed to do this. Sure, it would be awkward at work. He could try to fire me, but he would know I'd have his ass in a sling, our hospital having strict rules against retaliatory firings. San Francisco is nothing if not a bastion of liberal values, including #MeToo support. I loved my job, but if it got too awkward, I could always find work elsewhere. Jobs for physicians can be hard to fill in the city, because of the high cost of living. At the time, paying over two thousand a month for my share of the rent didn't bother me. I'd finished my residency and fellowship two years earlier, was single, with no kids or financial obligations except repayment of school loans. I was planning to seriously consider saving for a house at some future date. At least nine hundred thousand for a dump here in SF. But at the time I was young, carefree, and living the life.

I pressed "Gabe" on my phone and waited.

"Did you like the flowers?"

It was just like Gabe to act as if nothing had happened after sending me a bouquet following a major argument. "They're very pretty."

"Say, what's all this shit you ordered on one of your patients? Including a genetics referral for complete androgen insensitivity syndrome? Do you have any idea how rare that is and how much money you've wasted by ordering that work-up? You should thank me for approving the testing so you wouldn't be embarrassed. But really—"

"So, I should thank you for not publicly humiliating me, merely berating me privately."

"Now that you mention it, yeah. I'm doing you a favor, but don't think that because you're fucking the boss, you can do whatever you want."

"Listen, you condescending jerk, I ordered that referral based on my sound medical judgment, not a judgment based on the bottom line. I plan on continuing to depend on my medical acumen at work. I don't care if I'm no longer in the boss's favor. We are history. I've had it with you."

"Wow! I did not see that coming. I've never seen you so pissed off. Take a few more days to cool off."

"A few days won't change my mind. I shouldn't have let things go on for so long, with your yelling and bullying. But you crossed the line the other day when it got physical, and you twisted my arm. I still have a red mark from your grip. You've got a serious anger management issue. I'd suggest you see a therapist." I pressed "End," took a large gulp of the Cabernet, and felt much better.

I walked back to the living room where Daisy was sitting on the overstuffed beige couch, studying brochures offering tours of China.

"Thinking of taking one of those organized tours with a bus and everything?" I asked. "Where they tell you what time to get up, what to have for dinner, you walk around with a large group of rowdy Americans, and everyone stares at you?"

"Well, since Brian can't go with me on account of a conflict with his best friend's wedding, and you won't take time off from your fucking job to go with me, this seems like a reasonable second choice."

Brian was the latest of Daisy's revolving door of men. I figured she'd be dumping him soon because they'd been seeing each other for over three months. He was near his expiration date.

"Don't try to make me feel bad," I said.

"Why shouldn't I?"

"Because you should be proud of me." I paused for effect. "I did it," I said, smiling.

Daisy stood and gave me a high five.

CHAPTER 4

The next weeks at the clinic were awkward. I did my best to avoid Gabe, averting my eyes when we passed in the hall. I caught snippets of conversations when I passed by staff chatting in the hall.

"Did he dump her?"

"She couldn't have dumped him. Why would she?"

I carried on as if I hadn't heard but couldn't escape the feeling of being constantly scrutinized. I was board certified in pediatric intensive care and had spent a year working in the county pediatric ICU after finishing my training. Kids that sick took a toll on me, though, and I decided to switch to the clinic. I'd never regretted my decision, but I still worked several evening shifts each month in the peds ICU located in the adjacent building. If I worked there full time, I'd see Gabe and the other staff rarely, if at all. And make more money. I'd think about it.

Early one evening after the clinic was closed, I was reviewing my patients' lab values, and came across Wang Shu's results. No, she didn't have thalassemia, and she had no evidence of TB on her x-ray, all in agreement with what her mother had told me. Knowing her daughter had received the appropriate vaccines in our clinic, I signed the form for Wang Shu to start school. Ting could pick it up in the clinic at her convenience.

Three days later, I saw the geneticist's report, diagnosing Wang Shu with complete androgen insensitivity syndrome. Genetic studies had confirmed she was genetically male, and imaging studies had demonstrated anatomic findings diagnostic of the syndrome. Undescended testicles still in her abdomen, as found in this syndrome, would need to be surgically removed later due to the high incidence of malignancy that can arise when testes fail to descend into the scrotum during fetal development.

I imagined Gabe's face turning red and him punching a hole in a nearby wall when he got around to looking up that result, which I'm sure he would do soon if he hadn't already. So sad he couldn't shame me with evidence of my poor judgment and lack of budgetary concerns. Beyond that, I couldn't help but wonder. What were the chances of a blue-eyed Asian having complete androgen insensitivity syndrome? About zero.

I had an hour to kill before heading to the adjacent hospital for my scheduled eight-hour shift. I half dreaded it, and half looked forward to it. One thing was for sure: without it, I'd have a hard time coming up with the rent each month.

I called my mom who lived in a small apartment in Santa Monica. It had been a difficult five years for her. And for me. Five years earlier, my dad had succumbed to an E. coli infection brought on by eating tainted lettuce. As if that wasn't bad enough, three years ago, Cory, my older brother by two years, had died unexpectedly after being struck by a car. Born with cerebral palsy, he had walked with difficulty using braces and a crutch. Almost completely deaf, he was the reason I had learned sign language. I'm sure he never heard the car that sped around the corner and took his life. I still hadn't recovered.

Using sign language, whether at work or in a situation that occasionally arose when I was merely a civilian in public, reminded me of Cory, and made me feel connected in a positive way. The same could be said of all my encounters with disabled children, whether deaf, blind, wheelchair-bound, autistic, retarded, or any combination.

I knew my mom suffered as much as I did after our family's losses, but we rarely spoke of it. Too painful. Her mailbox was still labeled "Harold and Maya Rosen." After the usual pleasantries, the dreaded questioning began.

"And how is that handsome young man of yours, Gary, is it?"

"It's Gabe." I was surprised she'd forgotten his name. I'd been dating him for a while and my mother asked about him constantly. "Mom, I know you're not going to like this, but I warned you."

"Oh?" Her voice sounded weak.

"We broke up."

Silence. Followed by, "What happened? It can't be that serious. Make up with him. A nice Jewish boy like that—a doctor no less—they don't grow on trees."

"No, they don't, Mom. And he wasn't one. Not nice, anyway."

"You shouldn't be so critical. Nobody's perfect."

"He's far from perfect. I don't want to talk about it now. Please believe me. He's not son-in-law material."

"I don't know what to say."

"How about telling me you're sure I must have made the right decision?"

"I'm on your side, Erica. I love you, I want the best for you. It's just that sometimes I'm not convinced you know what's best for your future happiness. A career isn't everything."

"I realize you're trying to give me the best advice. But you don't know him like I do. Looks good on the outside. Believe me, I know that. But scratch beneath the surface, and there's some real ugliness there."

"I worry. Thirty-four years old and still single. You're running out of time. I want to be a grandmother."

"I know, Mom. This may come as a shock, but I don't have to be married for you to get your wish."

"Thanks for the education, Dear."

"I'm not ready for motherhood now. If and when I am, I'll figure out what to do."

"Well, you can't blame me for looking out for my beautiful, brilliant daughter who works too hard and doesn't eat right or get enough sleep. I wish your father was here. You'd listen to him."

"I'm listening to you, Mom. Gotta run."

Mother had a point, but I'd never admit it to her. I'd always been closer to Dad. An FBI agent involved in many famous cases, including the Unabomber, 9/11, and the Green River murders, I'd looked up to him ever since I could remember. When I was younger, I often fantasized about following in his footsteps. I glamorized living dangerously, fighting crime, going undercover, doing anything I could to put the bad guys away. Eventually, due mainly to my brother's condition, I decided to follow a career in medicine and help children in need. I'd never regretted that choice but sometimes wondered how different my life would be if I'd followed the other path. If my life would be more exciting, more rewarding.

*

I bought a bagel and a cup of coffee, large, at my favorite neighborhood coffee roaster, and started loading up on caffeine while I walked to the hospital for the start of my shift. I was in the peds ICU learning about the patients, when I heard a commotion approaching. A woman's cries were interspersed with shouts in an Asian-sounding language. I turned to see a small child on a gurney being pushed by two nurse's aides and a pediatric intensivist. Fluid flowed into the child's arm from an IV bag hung on an attached pole. Following closely behind was none other than Wang Shu's mother, Ting Chen, hysterical.

I figured something terrible had happened to Wang Shu. Had someone harmed her because she was different? A hate crime against a young child? I ran over to comfort Ting as the gurney was wheeled into the ICU.

I detected a modicum of relief in Ting's face when she recognized me. "Doctor! You help me, please. Someone try to kill my boy."

Her comment surprised me. Calling Wang Shu a boy was not appropriate for a child with her syndrome. The genetic counselor should have explained that to her. When I reached the gurney, I was stunned. It wasn't Wang Shu, but a younger child, a boy. He appeared semiconscious, moaning. The team transferred him to a bed and began hooking him up to monitor his heart rate, EKG, respiration, and oxygen saturation. I saw several sutured lacerations on his arms, legs, and chest. Bruising was evident and half his face was swollen.

"Is this your child?"

"This Kang, my son."

"I didn't realize you had another child. I'm terribly sorry he's been hurt. How old is he? What happened?"

"Kang, he three and half year old. He outside walking with me and his sister. A car come and try to run him over. Try to kill him. I know they do it on purpose."

Ting was unable to speak further through her tears. I located a box of tissues and handed it to her.

This woman intrigued me. She had secrets, secrets that led her to come to a foreign country with her two children, one of whom had a strange constitution. The other lay seriously injured—I didn't know how seriously—after being hit by a car. The latter seemed like terrible luck. Why did she think someone was intentionally trying to harm her child? Was she crazy, or was there an explanation buried in her mysterious past? My curiosity would have to wait until after her son was stabilized.

The team went through the motions of collecting blood and urine samples, then cleaning and bandaging Kang's minor wounds not taken care of in the emergency room. Ting insisted on inspecting all their ID badges despite being told to stay out of the way. One of the nurses approached me.

"I'm so glad you're here, Doctor. We asked for a Mandarin translator, but they're all busy elsewhere right now. None of us can understand this woman with her thick accent. You're so much better than we are in that area. She seems quite bizarre, checking everyone's identification. She did the same thing in the ER, I'm told. She keeps getting in our way while we're trying to stabilize her son. Can you ask her if she knows of any allergies or underlying medical conditions?"

I looked at Ting. "Does Kang have any allergies?"

"*Meiyou.* No allergy."

"Any medical conditions? Is he currently on any medications?"

"No medication."

"Any previous surgeries or medical conditions we should know about?"

Ting became agitated. "You need save my boy. No ask so much question. No surgery. He healthy boy before he hit by car."

I turned to the nurse and told her the boy had been healthy, with no allergies or previous surgeries. But I couldn't keep from thinking Ting was holding something back.

Ting cried with spurts of hysteria as radiology technicians wheeled in a portable X-ray machine. She insisted on examining the badges of the operators immediately upon their entrance to the ICU, matching their faces to the pictures.

I pulled Ting away to avoid exposure to the X-rays, while the technicians positioned film after film under Kang and took images of his entire body.

"They will come here to kill him," Ting screamed.

What's with this woman. "Where's Wang Shu? Is she in danger?" I wanted to see how far Ting's paranoia ran.

"He with a friend. Take good care of him. No, no. They no need to kill Wang Shu."

Did she think her son Kang was the target of assassins? Why not her daughter? She seemed nothing short of crazy.

CHAPTER 5

Other than Ting's hysteria, the pediatric ICU was relatively quiet that evening. I was able to sit with the distraught mother for a while and try to comfort her. Every time someone entered the unit, she jumped up to check the badge. Kang's lab and X-ray results started coming in. Two broken ribs and a hairline left radial fracture. Labs unremarkable. Vitals remained stable with good respiration, cardiac function, and oxygen saturation.

"Luckily, his bone fractures are limited. There was concern about his breathing because his respirations were rapid and shallow when he came in," I told Ting. "I'm not surprised to find that he has broken ribs. That makes breathing very painful. Fortunately, we know his breathing is adequate because his oxygenation is good and his pH is normal. The pH can go down when a patient isn't breathing enough." I paused to look over the latest lab results on a nearby computer terminal. "What's this? Probably lab error. Let me check."

Kang's venous blood gas was normal—almost. I considered ignoring it, an obvious lab error. Call me anal compulsive, but I couldn't let it go. I walked over to Brad and Fran, the two other doctors in the unit who were discussing the case.

"Did you see the low oxygen saturation on the venous blood gas?" I asked.

"Haven't seen it yet," Brad answered. "Let's take a look."

He and Fran followed me to the nearest computer terminal and studied the numbers.

"Could be a lab error. It's way too low. Doesn't make sense," Fran said. "Would only expect such a low venous oxygen sat if the patient's cardiac output was significantly decreased, which it isn't. His cardiac output is fine."

"Did they put the sample on ice when it was collected?" I asked.

"Don't know. We weren't there at the time," Fran answered.

I called the lab and was assured that the results were correct. The proper controls had been run, and no other unexpectedly low oxygen results had been reported in the last few hours.

"Maybe we should get another one, just to be sure," I told Brad. "Don't want the boy to run into trouble later because we didn't think of something."

"I can't imagine what that could be. But yeah, go ahead. I'm sure it'll come back normal, and we can forget about it."

I ordered a repeat venous blood gas and watched the respiratory therapist collect it ten minutes later, making sure the sample was placed in ice immediately. The therapist left the unit with the sample, the door swinging shut behind her. I glanced at Kang's monitor and confirmed that his vitals were still stable. He'd been sedated with morphine and Ativan and appeared to be asleep while fluid and antibiotics were pumped into his veins through the IV. I was getting ready to examine the patient in the next bed, a young girl with unstable diabetes, when my attention turned to a loud commotion.

Ting was yelling, "Call police! Call police!" She had pulled a gun out from I-don't-know-where and was pointing it at a young Asian man in surgical greens standing by the nursing station, hands raised. The man remained calm, laser-focused on Ting.

Brad ran over to me. "That lady's nuts. She pulled that gun from behind her back. Must have had it inside her pants. Can you talk to her? She obviously likes you best."

My medical education was sorely lacking when it came to handling patient family members with guns. I slowly approached Ting, holding my right arm up, as if it could stop a bullet coming my way. "Ting," I said softly. "Please put the gun away. Let's talk about this. You don't want to hurt anyone, do you?"

"He come to kill my son! He come to kill Kang!"

Despite her excited state, she held the gun steady, still aimed at the man with raised arms. Ill-equipped to be a hostage negotiator, I turned to Brad and asked him to call the police. "Already done," he whispered. "Try to stall for time until they get here."

"There's probably some mistake," I said to Ting.

"No mistake. Look. See, name tag have different face.

"No one can look as long as you have a gun pointed at him."

"Someone look. I no shoot."

The staff looked from one to the other. Finally, Brad spoke. "Okay, I'll check. But you'd better not shoot me," he said, looking at Ting.

Brad walked slowly toward the man in question. "Now I'm just going to look at the identification badge." Brad's voice was loud and deliberate as he bent forward, his right arm reaching towards the nametag.

With lightning speed, the Asian man reached into his pocket with his left hand and produced a knife with a four-inch blade. Using his right hand, he grabbed Brad's outstretched arm, twirled him around and bent his arm at the elbow, pulling it up by the wrist behind his back. When the motion had stopped, the blade tip of the knife in the assailant's left hand was positioned at Brad's carotid artery. Brad remained silent, straining to look down at the knife near his neck, less than a quarter inch away from ending his life.

"No one move or this man die," the man yelled in a heavy Chinese accent. He shouted several words at Ting in Mandarin, the tone threatening. Ting yelled in response as the man backed away toward the door with Brad facing us, still at knifepoint, now with beads of sweat visible on his forehead.

When the intruder and his hostage were within a few feet of exiting, the doors to the unit flew open, and two uniformed police officers entered, guns drawn.

"Back up, or he die," the knife-wielding man yelled.

Still holding their guns, the officers retreated sideways, allowing the intruder to exit the peds ICU with his terrified hostage.

The officers spoke into their shoulder microphones, telling colleagues approaching to proceed with caution, and noting it wouldn't be safe to chase the man in the crowded hospital hallways. After a few back and forth comments, they left the unit in pursuit of Brad and his abductor.

The staff remained silent, stunned expressions all around. I quietly asked Ting if she knew how to fire her gun. "Yes, I see on TV," she said.

"You'll have to get rid of it. You can't have a gun in here."

She reached behind her, presumably returned the gun to where she had hidden it, and showed me both her hands, gun-free. Since it was now away and out of sight, I decided to ignore the fact that she had a weapon, at least for the moment. I wasn't going to wrestle it away from her.

Five long minutes later, Brad returned to the ICU looking dazed, a small amount of blood dripping down the side of his neck where the knife had nicked him. He sat in one of the chairs by the nurse's station, placed his face in his hands, and wept. Several nurses comforted him.

A few minutes later, he raised his head and spoke. "That was no ordinary man. The way he overcame me so quickly. Clearly, that guy is an expert in martial arts. I'm not saying that to save face. That guy is well-trained."

"How'd you get away?" I asked.

"When we got outside the stairway in the East wing, he pushed me to the floor and ran down the stairs. Or up the stairs. I'm not sure." He looked at Ting. "Who was that? Do you know him? What's going on?"

"I not know him. But I know he sent to kill Kang. You see his badge, right?"

"You're right. The picture was a different person. David Fang, a phlebotomist. Why do you think someone wants to kill your son?"

Ting cried out. "I cannot say. I cannot say."

"I'm calling the lab to speak to David Fang," Brad said.

"I'll see if we can get someone up here to guard Kang," I told Ting.

"Thank you," she said. "I no leave here without him. I stay until he all better."

"David Fang didn't show up to work today," Brad said, hanging up the phone at the nurse's station. "He didn't call in sick, either. Very unusual for him, I was told."

We were all thinking the same thing. That man had gotten David Fang's name tag to gain access to the unit, and David was now missing. I was overcome with a desire to run out of the unit and hunt down the man who had invaded the sanctity of the peds ICU. How dare he? I wanted to be a superhero. But I couldn't. I had responsibilities to my patients. And I knew I wouldn't be able to catch and arrest someone, certainly not someone trained in martial arts and armed with a knife.

Two police officers, different from those we had seen earlier, entered the unit and approached Ting. "Ma'am, you cannot have a weapon in here. Where'd you put it?"

I could see Ting weighing the consequences of her next move. I hoped she would turn the gun over peacefully. After what seemed like an eternity, she said, "It toy gun. A joke." She slowly reached behind and pulled out a pistol. Her fingers held the grip, allowing the gun to dangle harmlessly.

One of the officers grabbed it. After examining the gun, he placed it in a bag he removed from a pocket. "Even though it's a toy, I have to keep it as evidence. It's not a good idea to go around showing off look-alike guns. Someone could get hurt."

They spent the next three hours questioning us individually about the altercation, devoting most of their time to Brad. I think I was the only one who noticed that the toy gun Ting showed the police was not the same weapon she'd pointed at the intruder. I wasn't sure the first one was real, but I suspected it was. I said nothing about it to the police.

After the officers completed their interviews, one of them spoke to all of us together. "Unfortunately, the suspect got away, but fortunately, no one was seriously hurt. There may be images of him on video cameras. One of our inspectors is checking on that now. We're arranging to have an officer stationed here for now while we investigate. Thank you all for your cooperation. Please call me if you think of anything else."

After the officer had finished passing out his card, a nurse took me aside. "That venous blood gas is back, Doctor," she said. "I think you'll want to see it."

I walked to the nearest computer terminal and brought up the results. Oxygen saturation: 20%. Too low. Identical to the original result. That was no lab error. That was a lab result that made no sense. What was I missing?

CHAPTER 6

Kang improved quickly. I visited him almost daily during my lunch hour at the clinic. Ting remained by his side the whole time he was hospitalized, checking everyone's ID badge, day or night. I'd heard that David Fang, the missing phlebotomist, had never returned to work, wasn't in his apartment, and was officially a missing person. His disappearance was being investigated, and I feared the worst. Not everyone was convinced the intruder had been sent to assassinate Kang, but it was difficult to imagine why a random Chinese-speaking criminal without a specific target wanted access to the peds ICU. Enough to murder Mr. Fang, as I feared he had, to get his ID badge. With an armed guard stationed at the peds ICU entrance, no more incidents occurred during Kang's stay. I wasn't sure if the guard would be permanent—that was up to the powers that be—but the staff, especially Brad, enjoyed the extra security.

Six days after being admitted, Kang was discharged. I was able to break away from the clinic to attend the party the peds ICU staff threw for him and Ting in the break room. This mother and child had captured the hearts of the entire ICU staff.

Aside from minor facial swelling, visible bruises all over his body, a cast on his left arm, and occasional wincing from residual rib pain, Kang looked and acted like a normal three-and-a-half-year-old. Both Ting and her son ate generous portions of vanilla ice cream. Neither ate cake, probably because of unfamiliarity with the strange food.

When Kang opened a box containing an official San Francisco Giants T-shirt, he smiled broadly and put it on. "Baseball," he said. The only English word I'd heard him say. The head nurse presented him with three tickets to a Giants game, to take place a month later. Kang was exhilarated. "Baseball! Giants!" he said over and over.

"You can take your mom and your sister to the game," the nurse said.

Ting looked uncomfortable. "Thank you, everybody," she said softly, looking down.

I hugged them both before they left and told Ting to make a clinic appointment for Kang so I could check that he was healing properly.

"I cannot bring him back," she said. "I need move or they kill him. Before, I worry they steal him, take him back to China. But now I know they think easier to kill him. We must hide."

Doubtful Ting would let her son go to the baseball game, I regretted the gift of the tickets. That would be one uncomfortable conversation she'd have with Kang later. "Where will you go?" I asked. "I want to be sure you and your children are okay. How can I find you?"

"Dr. Rosen, I not trust many people. You very nice. I trust you. Still, I cannot say where I go."

I handed her my card and wrote my cell number on the back. "Please call me. I want to be sure you, Kang, and Wang Shu are doing okay. Call me right away if you or the children need help."

I'd never done that with a patient before, reached out like that. But the mystery, along with Ting's dedication to her children despite her difficult situation in a foreign land, compelled me. It was nice having something to occupy my mind, to keep my thoughts away from Gabe. I was missing him, and the good times we'd had both in and out of the sack. My emotional mind was telling me that perhaps I should give him another chance. But my logical mind was telling me, "No."

Despite Ting's assurance that Kang, like Wang Shu, had tested negative for thalassemia in China, I had sent a sample of his blood for testing. Two days after his discharge, the result came back. "Negative for thalassemia." Just like Ting had said. But that wasn't all the test found.

"Positive for unknown hemoglobin type." I'd never seen a report like that before.

Hemoglobin is a complex molecule carried by our red blood cells. It is responsible for transporting oxygen from our lungs to all our tissues, where the oxygen is released to meet our metabolic needs. Normal hemoglobin is perfectly designed to grab oxygen in the lungs, where it is relatively plentiful, and let go of it in the tissues that need it, where oxygen is at a lower concentration. Those with abnormal hemoglobin caused by a genetic mutation, like sickle cell disease, have different hemoglobin types with altered solubility and/or oxygen affinity. Kang had no normal hemoglobin. He had only an unusual hemoglobin, one different from any known common variant. What was going on?

Could this be why Kang's venous oxygen was so low? Kang's hemoglobin bound enough oxygen to deliver ample oxygen to his body's tissues, yet seemed to give it up to tissue more readily than normal hemoglobin. This allowed his peculiar hemoglobin to become more oxygen-depleted than usual, resulting in a lower than normal venous oxygen level. Like a car driven until the gas tank is practically empty would go farther than a car driven until the tank is only half empty, Kang's hemoglobin had less oxygen after one trip through the circulation than normal because it delivered more oxygen to his tissues. I reasoned that by allowing his tissues to extract more oxygen than normal, this strange hemoglobin could bestow his body with more endurance.

I spent the following weekend researching hemoglobin variants online and in the library. I found no such hemoglobin described. It's not every day when a physician in private practice thinks he or she has discovered something new. Now what? Should I publish this? Could I be sure Kang really had a unique type of hemoglobin, even though I couldn't find any evidence of it described previously?

I had an idea. First, I'd get Kang's remaining blood from the lab. Then I'd send it to a place that could analyze his hemoglobin in detail. The following Monday, I called the appropriate lab, located on the third floor of the hospital.

"Special Chemistry, Mike speaking."

"This is Dr. Rosen from pediatrics. Can you tell me how much is left of a sample sent two weeks ago from my patient, Kang Chen?"

I gave Kang's medical record number to Mike, who put me on hold while he went to check. "The sample's depleted, Doctor," he said when he returned.

"Damn. What happened? Don't you usually save your samples for three weeks?"

"Yes, we do typically save samples. I asked the tech who ran it. Seems the result was so unusual, she ran the test four times for confirmation. Got the same results each time but used up the specimen. Sorry."

Shit. Now what? Even if I chase Kang down, I'd hate to subject him to another blood draw simply to satisfy my curiosity. But there's the mom. She must be a carrier for this abnormal hemoglobin. I know she'll do anything for her child. I'll get her blood. It won't be one hundred percent abnormal, but the abnormal hemoglobin won't be hard to find at fifty percent.

Thinking about it further, something didn't seem right. Wang Shu was tested for thalassemia, and no abnormal hemoglobin showed up. Possible if both her mom and her dad had one normal gene and one abnormal gene each. Wang Shu could have gotten a normal gene from each parent and Kang an abnormal gene from each. Yet the chances of the mom and dad each having a copy of this abnormal gene, so rare it doesn't appear in the literature, had to be exceedingly low. Unless the parents are related. Whether Ting is related to the father or not, I needed to find her to start the process of characterizing this mysterious hemoglobin.

CHAPTER 7

The following weekdays were busy, but uneventful. I had Saturday off until my evening shift at the peds ICU started. I'd never made a house call before, but saw no way around it. Although Ting said she was going to move, I hoped she hadn't gotten around to it yet, or had changed her mind. With no phone number listed, I went to the address in her children's charts. It was in a small apartment building in Chinatown above a neighborhood grocery store selling exotic spices and foods, with ducks hanging by their feet, bags of seaweed, and jars of cardamom in the window. I felt conspicuous walking up the stairs and looking for her apartment. Even though I'd lived in San Francisco for over five years, I felt like a foreigner with my Caucasian features and curly brown hair, conscious of people staring at me and speaking loudly in Chinese, probably about me.

I found the apartment and knocked quietly. When no response was forthcoming, I banged louder and louder. A neighbor yelled at me in Chinese. She sounded angry, probably irritated by the noise. An old woman carrying groceries came along shortly.

"She not here," she said.

"Do you know where she is?"

"She move. Not here."

"Ting Chen? She moved? With her two children?"

"Last week. Or week before. No one live here."

"Do you know where she moved to?"

The old lady looked at me with distrust. "Nobody know. She gone."

I was disappointed, but not surprised. I needed that blood sample, though. Finding her would be difficult. Walking through Chinatown on the way back to my apartment, I thought I saw Ting at every turn, straight black hair not hard to find in the twenty square blocks comprising Chinatown. Even away from those densely populated sidewalks, many people looked like Ting from the back, or from a distance. Searching for her while walking around the streets was not going to yield the desired result. I needed to think of something else.

When I got home, a note from Daisy was on the kitchen table telling me her parents had stopped by around noon and taken her to lunch at a neighborhood restaurant. They wanted me to join them if I hadn't eaten yet. I always enjoyed visiting with Daisy's parents, but I wasn't hungry and instead decided to take a nap before I needed to show up for work. I was about to lie down when a police inspector called requesting a few minutes of my time. I invited her to meet me at the hospital fifteen minutes before my shift started. After the call, I fell asleep until my alarm woke me. Feeling refreshed, I combed my hair and headed to the hospital.

Dressed in a gray pantsuit with a white blouse, brown hair pulled into a bun, I figured the middle-aged woman for either a police officer or attorney as she walked into the hospital lobby. She must have seen a picture of me from our security department, because she walked up to me, showed me her badge, and introduced herself. She was the inspector I'd spoken to earlier.

"I have a few questions to ask you about the night one of your doctors was assaulted during your shift in the pediatric intensive care unit."

"No problem," I said, "but I was already questioned right after the event. I don't have more to add."

"I understand, and I know you're busy. But more questions have arisen. You see, the man who perpetrated the act was wearing the badge of David Fang. Mr. Fang hadn't been seen since. Last night his body was found by a jogger in an isolated area of Golden Gate Park. He'd been shot."

"That's terrible," I said. I didn't know Mr. Fang, but was sorry that what I had suspected had come to pass.

"Were you acquainted with Mr. Fang? Personally or professionally?"

"No. I may have seen him in the past if he came to draw blood while I was on duty, but until the incident, I wasn't familiar with him. I don't think I can be of help. Do you think his death is related to the occurrence in the peds ICU?"

"We're interviewing everyone related to the incident as well as all of Mr. Fang's acquaintances. At this time, we don't know, and we're keeping an open mind. But you're an intelligent woman. It's not hard to connect the dots."

CHAPTER 8

The baseball game. Just maybe, Ting would take Kang after all. It was worth a try looking for her there. Only three days away, the game was sold out. StubHub to the rescue. I bought the cheapest seat listed, sixteen bucks, for something in the nosebleed section. I asked the head nurse in the peds ICU where the seats she'd gotten for Kang were, but she couldn't remember. I pressed her. Told her I was going to the game and wanted to take the opportunity to talk to Kang's mom about a medication his sister was taking. The nurse told me the gift had been donated by someone from her church with season tickets and she would call her to find out. The next time I saw her, though, she had forgotten all about it.

"What time do you get home tonight?" I asked. "I'll call you."

"Must be really important to you."

"It is. Kang's mom missed the last appointment with her daughter and I may need to adjust medicine."

"I didn't know you were a baseball fan. Somehow, I can't picture it."

I called the nurse that night, and she told me the seat numbers. I finally had what I needed. The Giants played the next day, 1:10 p.m. I'd already canceled my afternoon appointments.

Game day was cloudy and cold, a typical summer day in San Francisco. Coming from work, I felt overdressed in my black pants, white blouse, and beige cardigan. A tourniquet, needle, and tube for collecting blood were in my purse, in case I was lucky enough to find Ting. I mixed in with the hordes of people heading to Oracle Park. The last few feet were the slowest. As I passed through the metal detector, I regretted not having told Ting she and her children would be safe at the baseball game—no guns or knives allowed. Maybe that would have encouraged her to take her kids.

Following my purse inspection, I entered the stadium. I had already memorized the seating chart and knew where to go. A half hour before game time, it took a good ten minutes to maneuver through the crowd to the appropriate section.

People, many dressed in the orange and black of the Giants, were milling around. Half the seats were still empty, as were the seats given to Kang. No need to panic yet. I watched the empty seats of interest for a while, dodging people who passed by. One fan spilled beer on my sweater, so I left to find a restroom to clean up. It was like walking through molasses, taking what seemed like an hour to reach the restroom. According to my watch, however, it had barely been six minutes. Fortunately, I didn't need to stand in the long line for a stall. I reached a sink and did my best to wash the beer off my sweater, leaving an unsightly wet spot. I hoped there would be no stain after the area dried.

By the time I made it back to the section, the seats I'd been watching were filled by a tall red-headed woman, clearly Caucasian, and two brown-haired kids wearing sunglasses. *Damn! Ting sold the tickets or gave them away.* I was about to leave when I noticed one of the children staring at me, getting the attention of the other. Then both kids looked at me while speaking to each other.

It hit me. I was looking at Kang and Wang Shu. The brown wigs and sunglasses had thrown me. But their size, complexion, mouths, and noses were the same. Kang was wearing the Giant's shirt we'd given him. The woman was definitely not Ting, but those were her kids. Until then, I hadn't realized how tense my neck and shoulders were. I let that dissipate. I didn't know where Ting was, but at least, I had a chance of finding her.

I figured the redhead was someone Ting trusted to take care of her children and keep them disguised, but I doubted she could communicate with either of them. My plan was to keep an eye on the trio and follow them out of the park, hopefully to Ting's new apartment. If I was lucky, they'd leave early. It was difficult standing, then walking around pretending to look for my seat, then standing some more. I didn't want someone checking my ticket and sending me away to my cheap section. Which is what happened in the third inning. I probably stuck out with my still-wet sweater, keeping my eyes on the kids despite three Giants on base, two out, and a count of three balls, two strikes. An usher checked my ticket and sent me back to where I belonged, a seat I hadn't seen yet. *Damn.*

I walked by several concession stands, then made my way back to the section I was surveilling. The usher was gone, but the redhead and kids were still there. I took up residence near the back of the section. I was bored and uncomfortable, but at least Kang seemed to be having the time of his life, jumping up and down with every play. Even Wang Shu sprang up occasionally. By the time the seventh inning stretch came around, I was starting to believe they wouldn't be leaving early. The score was tied, 2-2. I was dreading the possibility of extra innings.

I tried passing the time by reading my email and browsing articles from the New York Times on my iPhone. Despite the cloudy skies, glare from the sun made it difficult to read, so I gave up on that. I tried to remember how to count to one hundred in Spanish. Then French. The bottom of the ninth. Two away. Still 2-2. *Damn.* This game wasn't going to end. My hopes soared when the Giants' catcher hit a fly ball far into center field, looking like it was going to clear the fence. At the last moment, the opposing team's center fielder jumped high and caught it. Extra innings.

My stomach was growling. I hadn't eaten for hours, but I dared not leave to get food. The game could be over by the time I pushed through the crowd to the concession stand and returned. Bottom of the tenth. Still 2-2. The Giants' third baseman hit a line drive past the shortstop and was safe on first. A wild pitch allowed him to steal second. The next batter sealed the deal with a hit deep into right field allowing the man on second to make it home. Finally. Game over. Now I had to stay on my toes.

It was difficult to stand where I was as people pushed past me. The redheaded woman stood and straightened Wang Shu's wig which had become slightly askew. Then she said something to the children, and they spoke back to her. After several volleys of conversation, I concluded that this woman spoke Chinese. Unusual for a Caucasian, but not more astonishing than some of the other things involving Ting and her family.

As the crowd started to thin out, the Chinese-speaking redhead followed the two children to the aisle, bending slightly to keep one hand on Kang's shoulder. With a small group of people separating me from them, I tailed the red hair down several flights of stairs and out the doors of the stadium. They took Third Street in the direction of Market. After crossing Mission, no one was between them and me, so I kept my distance. Not trained in the ways of a private eye, I tried my best to remain inconspicuous.

Suddenly, the woman guided the children into an alleyway. Not sure what to do, I walked past the alley, stopped, and slowly, quietly, retraced my steps, peering around the corner building, expecting to see their backs as they cut through the backstreet. To my surprise, the redheaded woman was facing me, less than two feet away, with the children behind her.

"What do you want?" she asked accusatorially.

The woman had an accent I couldn't place. For a moment, I was at a loss for words. "I-I know you're not the mother of these children. I'm calling the police right now to report a kidnapping." I regretted what I said immediately. If this woman was a friend of Ting's, I didn't want to scare her off by calling the police. On the other hand, if she had abducted the kids, I could use the help of the police. Thing is, I doubted she had kidnapped them.

"Let's be honest here. The kids tell me you're their doctor."

"That's true," I said with some relief. "I want to talk to their mother. It's about abnormal lab results on one of them."

"As you can see, their mother isn't here."

"Please, can you take me to her? It's important. There are some odd findings with one of the children. I want to talk to her about it, but she moved before I could speak to her again."

The woman, appearing skeptical, pulled a phone from her pocket. Looking away from me momentarily, she pressed the phone screen a few times and waited. Then she began speaking. I couldn't understand a word. It was all Chinese.

The woman ended the call and looked at me for a moment. "I need to check you. Make sure you have no weapon."

"Sure," I responded. I must have looked surprised. The woman patted me down, front, back, and sideways. Then she rifled through my purse. Finally, she cracked a smile.

"Dr. Rosen, I'm Ebba Lindgren." She held out her hand. "Pleased to meet you."

We shook hands while she spoke to the children. Whatever she said made them excited. "I'll take you to see Ting if you promise never to divulge her whereabouts to a soul."

"I promise." I was convinced Ting wasn't a crazy woman with paranoid delusions, but I still didn't understand what was happening. Two children with strange medical findings, and two possible murder attempts on her son—one by car, another by an assassin in the hospital. I wasn't sure if Ebba was inclined to tell me anything, but I was going to try to find out.

"How do you know Ting, and how did you learn Chinese?"

"I'll let Ting tell you most of it. But I'll say this much. I lived in China for ten years. That's where I learned Mandarin. I was a coach for the Chinese Olympic track team after my days on the Norwegian Olympic team were over. I coached Ting. In her day, she was a star. Everyone in China knew her. For a while, she held the world record in the women's 1500-meter race. Everything that has befallen poor Ting is a consequence of that god-given talent of hers."

I was no closer to understanding the mystery around Ting than the first time I saw blue-eyed Wang Shu. I looked forward to my meeting.

CHAPTER 9

We walked in silence, Ebba leading the way with Kang and Wang Shu on either side, me following. Continuing up Third, we reached Market Street and made a left. Foot traffic was heavy, and I found it difficult to dodge the pedestrians, street peddlers, and beggars without losing them. At times, I almost stepped on people, probably high on drugs, lying on cardboard next to buildings. Crossing Powell, the density of beggars increased. The air was thick with the aroma of marijuana, a smell occasionally interrupted by the scent of tobacco. After walking almost a mile on Market, Ebbe turned right on Larkin. Several blocks later, past the public library, she made a series of quick turns down alleys until we arrived at a rundown four-story cement apartment building. It lacked any of the charm usually associated with the City by the Bay.

Using a key, Ebba opened the front door of the building and led our entourage up two flights of poorly lit stairs, down a dark hallway, to a gray door with a peephole, 218 stenciled in yellow paint underneath. Ebba knocked —three quick raps followed by two slow ones. The door opened, and Ting waved everyone inside. She was wearing blue sweatpants and a tank top, her hair slightly disheveled. Kang and Wang Shu each grabbed one of her legs.

The apartment reminded me of one of the sorrier places I'd lived in when I was an undergraduate at UC Berkeley. A small window at the far end let in whatever light wasn't blocked by the surrounding buildings. The wooden floor had at one time probably been charming but was currently so scratched and stained, it begged for carpeting. Five folding chairs, and an orange crate which served as a coffee table, furnished the living room. A folding card table, bare of chairs, stood in the eating area. I assumed some of the living room chairs were placed around the card table at mealtime.

Ebba reached up and grabbed a tuft of her hair. "This thing's killing me," she said, pulling off her wig and the underlying fishnet cap, exposing long blond hair pinned to the top of her head. "Now I feel so much better."

"Please sit, Dr. Rosen," Ting said, peeling her children from her legs. "I apologize my apartment so humble."

"Don't apologize. This reminds me of a place I lived in when I was younger."

"I appreciate your help for my children, especially Kang when he in hospital. Other doctors and nurses think I crazy, I worry so much about Kang's safety. I think maybe you believe me. Don't think I crazy."

Once I sat down, Ting and Ebba followed. Wang Shu sat on Ting's lap and buried her head in her mom's chest. Kang sat on the floor, playing with a plastic fire truck.

"I don't think you're crazy. The man who came into the peds ICU scared all of us. But why do you think he was after Kang? Why does someone want to hurt your son? He's merely a young child."

"First, you tell me why you look for me. Ebba say you have important medical information."

I felt out of place, awkward. I wanted a sample of her blood so I could characterize her son's strange hemoglobin variant. He seemed healthy, so this was more of an academic exercise. Of interest to the scientific community, to be sure, although probably of no interest to her. Real or imagined, she was concerned with life and death issues, not a mutation causing a shift in the hemoglobin oxygen-binding curve.

"We tested Kang's blood for thalassemia but didn't get the result back until after he'd left the hospital."

Ting became agitated. "Why you test him? I tell you, no thalassemia."

41

"We like to use our own lab to verify what people tell us. Sometimes they're wrong."

"I not wrong," Ting yelled, clearly agitated. "Why you here? What you find?"

Wang Shu wrapped her arms tightly around Ting's neck, pressing her head against her mother's face.

"Please don't be angry. No thalassemia, you're right. But we did find something else."

"What you find? Tell me," Ting said, looking around her daughter's head. "Stop taking so much time."

"Kang has abnormal hemoglobin. I'm not saying it's harmful, but—"

"I know, I know. You never see anything like it before." Ting started crying. Wang Shu went into a nearby room and brought her mother a tissue.

I was stunned. "You know about his hemoglobin?"

"Yes. That why they want kill him. So nobody find out," she shouted before completely breaking down in tears.

I looked at Ebba, hoping for an explanation, but none came. Ebba put an arm around Ting and murmured something to her in Chinese. Wang Shu slipped to the floor and left the room. When Ting regained her composure, Ebba said, "Why don't you tell her everything? Start at the beginning. Maybe she knows someone who might help."

Ting dried her eyes and stared at me. "What I tell you. You must promise to keep it secret. Can't tell anyone."

"I promise."

"Hard to know where to start."

"Take your time," Ebba said.

"I grow up in poor village, People's Republic of China. I have brother, Lim."

"I thought there was a limit of one child per family until recently."

"You right. But Lim my twin. Twin is okay to have two children. Me and Lim, we both love to run. Very fast. We get attention of Chinese government. Government think winning medals in Olympics very important, so they take care of children athletes. The government want take me and Lim to place where they give us everything we need and train us to be great runners. My parents very proud, very happy we will have great future as athletes for the people of China, so they approve.

"We live in special place for years, fifty kilometers from Beijing, in countryside. We are ten when we leave home. We both work very hard there. We go to school and rest of time we run, run, run. Lim very fast, very strong. He train special in four hundred-meter hurdle. Hold world record then. I very fast too. They train me to specialize in fifteen hundred meter. I hold world record for my age at fourteen, fifteen, sixteen. Ebba my coach then. She make me the best I can be. Me and Lim both very famous in China. Have wonderful life. Place to live, good food, medical care, even fancy clothes. People want meet us, touch us. We sad because we cannot get time off to visit parents, and they not have money to see us. Then they get sick and die from flu epidemic. We want to go to burial but cannot get permission. Government say too risky for us to go because of contagious disease in the area."

"That must have been very hard on you," I said.

"Yes. Very hard. But must train all the time. When I seventeen, Lim introduce me to teammate, Peng. He very fast. China's fastest one hundred-meter runner. I see him before and think he very cute. He become my boyfriend. We cannot spend a lot of time together because have to work hard, but see each other when we can. When I nineteen, shortly before I go to compete in my first Olympics, I have bad motorcycle accident. Break bones in ankle and leg. Lots of pain. They send me to best doctors. I have surgery and physical therapy. I cannot go to Olympics. Lim and Peng go, but they don't get medal. Lim get fourth place in hurdle, and Peng get fifth in one hundred-meter race. They still very young and expect to win gold in next Olympics.

"After I heal from accident, I train and train but never can run so fast again. No longer top Olympic material. No longer Olympic material at all. The government no longer like me. But Peng try to help me. He join Communist party. They like him a lot. He get me good job to help train athletes and work in office, where I get supplies and arrange medical care. Take care of whatever come up. Good pay, and I get nice apartment. But one condition. I must listen to what everyone say and report back to Communist Party. I must be spy. I not want to do that. Lim not like Communist Party. He tell me bad things about it. I have no interest in politics, but I not spy on my brother. I talk to Ebba. She want me help her coach full time, but Peng say I cannot be coach if I not spy."

"He sounds like a horrible person," I said, feeling like I should say something, but not wanting to slow Ting's narrative.

"Yes. I have big fight with Peng. He act like he own me. Tell me I have to do what he say. He hit me. Make me angry. I tell Lim, and he get very mad. My brother and I decide to leave training facility and get jobs in Beijing. We go to Beijing and get government jobs in bureaucracy. Life not bad. Then things change.

"Peng come find me in Beijing six years ago. At first, he very nice. He tell me he want me move to town in Sichuan province where he live. He no longer compete in Olympics. He think is more important to make sure China win the most Olympic medals in future games. He work on special training methods at new, modern government facility. He want me come see, then marry him and have children. He say if we make babies together, they grow up to be best runners in the world.

"I am in shock. I not want move. I not want marry him and have babies with him. If I have babies, I don't care if they good runners. I tell Lim. He agree with me. Very strange request. He not trust Peng. Lim in secret anti-government group. He hear Peng move up higher and higher in Communist Party. I tell Peng I not go because I like my job in Beijing so much. Two days later, in middle of night, I am kidnap and taken to secret facility in Sichuan province. They call it *Fengshou,* mean Great Harvest."

Tears welled up in Ting's eyes. Obviously, reliving this chapter of her past was painful. "I see you've survived quite a nightmare," I said. "Peng wouldn't take 'no' for an answer, so he kidnapped you to force you to marry him."

"Oh, no. Much worse. You have hard time believe what I learn, what happen next."

I looked at Ebba. She was nodding her head in agreement as Wang Shu walked in with a box of tissues and handed one to her mom.

CHAPTER 10

Ting looked helpless, clearly uncomfortable describing her painful past. She had descended a long way, from being a pampered elite athlete in China to living in fear in a strange country with very few resources. Escaping with her two children must have been difficult. She was lucky to have Ebba here. I felt compelled to help Ting, me being a superhero wannabe and all. My problems—student loans, an ex-boyfriend I was trying to avoid, a mother who wanted me to get married—seemed trivial compared to hers.

"Please continue," I said. "What was worse than being kidnapped by this man?"

"When they take me, they give me drug to make me sleep. I not know how long I sleep, but when I wake up, I in nice apartment. Have bedroom, kitchen, living room, bathroom. Nice furniture. Much better than this place. I don't know where I am, so I try leave but apartment door locked from outside. I cannot open door."

"Was it a prison?" I asked.

"Not official prison, but like prison. Soon, a man come to explain everything to me. The government make a plan to dominate Olympics. The Communist Party think that is way to make citizens so proud of our country and win respect of other countries. With such large population, China should have more medal than any other country, but had most medals only one time. China never win medal for one hundred meter, fastest man. China win medal here and there in track and field but party want to do much better. Not just track and field, other sport too. In past, some Chinese athletes test positive for drugs and must forfeit medals. Very humiliating. Although China have very sophisticated doping program, the government not to want to rely on that. The testing get better every year. Now China plan try something new. They grow super athletes."

"What do you mean by *grow*?"

"They use procedure. You call it gene editing of embryonic stem cells."

"Oh, my god! I can't believe they're thinking about performing gene editing on human embryos to improve their athletic performance."

"They do more than think about it," Ting responded, tears forming in her eyes.

"How? What genes are they changing? Are they doing this with the athletes in the next Olympics? I have so many questions."

"I have so many answers."

"I don't know where to begin."

"They not edit genes on athletes for next Olympics. This is long-term project. They making these athletes, like you say, *from scratch*. They very young now. First ones will be ready for two thousand thirty-two Summer Olympics."

"What you're saying is they've already changed the genes of embryonic stem cells at the one-cell stage, and they've created future super-athletes who are young children now."

"Right."

"That's preposterous! I read about a rogue Chinese scientist who tried making babies resistant to HIV using embryonic stem cell gene editing, but he was heavily criticized and arrested by the Chinese government. Worldwide, the scientific community has agreed not to do any gene editing of human embryonic stem cells. It's way too dangerous. It can potentially change all the genes in the body, and the changes, good or bad, are passed on to future children. There are no protocols for doing it safely."

"That why it very secret. They upset with that scientist because he do stupid editing for HIV protection, not for making athletes. He bring much bad attention to China. Don't want anyone to think they approve of editing genes in embryos to make live babies."

"I read a few years ago the Chinese government had approved of editing a gene in embryos that couldn't survive because of a defect unrelated to the gene being edited. They were at the early stages, proceeding very slowly and carefully, following international guidelines."

"That publicity stunt. What you call *get ahead of story*. They make that up in case someone hear about real program. A big lie. They have very advance gene-editing program for over five years."

My mind was racing. I chose my words carefully. "Have your children been affected by this in any way?"

Ting's reaction answered my question. She bent over and sobbed loudly. Wang Shu placed the box of tissue on her mother's lap as Ebba tried to console her.

Finally, Ting lifted her head and spoke. "Yes, all my children edited. All three of them."

"Three? I thought you had two."

"I have Kang and Wang Shu with me. Mingyu four-month-old. He still in China." Ting started crying again. After she calmed down enough to say, "I must get him," she burst into tears again.

"This is incredible," I said. I had to think for a moment before stating the obvious. "The hemoglobin. I suppose the strange properties could make someone a super athlete. Able to deliver more oxygen to tissue during times of high demand. Like so-called blood doping, where blood is transfused to deliver extra oxygen, a practice which is detected by Olympics screening methods."

"You very smart, Dr. Rosen," Ting said. "You figure out the advantage of the mutation in Kang's hemoglobin."

"How did they do this? I don't blame you Ting, but did they explain the possible dangers to you? The possibility of harmful mistakes in gene editing?"

"They explain nothing to me. I agree to nothing. They force me. I stay lock up in apartment. They give me medicine. Hold me down, inject me, force me take pills. Make me very sick. I hate it. Then one day they take me to clinic. Clinic right there, near my apartment in secret facility. Say they do simple procedure. I yell at doctor, but she not care. Only assistant tell me what happening when doctor out of room. They remove lots of eggs. Not so simple, but I have no choice."

"My god! That's so barbaric!"

"Yes, they want to start with good, athletic embryo. They take my eggs. Then they fertilize them with . . ."

Ting became too overcome with emotion to continue.

"I'll tell her, Ting," Ebba said, patting her on the knee. "They took Ting's eggs and fertilized them with Peng's sperm. We don't know how many embryos they made. We do know there are other top female athletes whose eggs they also harvested. Most of the women participated willingly, others tried to resist. Some of their eggs were fertilized with Peng's sperm, some with the sperm of other athletes. Swimmers, speed skaters, and more.

"After Ting's eggs were fertilized, they were frozen. Three times, they took one of her fertilized eggs and did whatever they do to edit the genes, then forcibly implanted it into her. These children are hers in every way. She loves them very much. She doesn't want her other embryos edited or used in any way. More than anything, she wants to get Mingyu back and expose the whole operation."

Ting stopped crying and began to speak. "Wang Shu one of first they edit. They do it only to see if they can successfully edit a gene. At the time they still work to optimize hemoglobin gene but want to be ready to put gene into human embryo right away when they finish. So, they decide edit eye color gene. Make blue eyes. Very simple, very easy to see if it work. As you can see, it work very well. When Wang Shu born, he a girl. Everyone surprised. No one explain anything to me. I very worried. I read what I can. Now I understand. What you call collateral damage. The testosterone receptor gene destroyed. I wonder if other damage to Wang Shu I not know about."

"I understand your concern. From what I can tell, Wang Shu is perfectly healthy right now."

"Right now, yes. But what about later? I read maybe the treatment can result in cancer. Things very bad with some of other children."

"Other children? What other children?"

"I live with other women they get eggs from. Some, they have babies die before they born. Others very damaged. One have no arms. One have bad heart. Die soon. Very sad."

"Oh, my god," I yelled. "That's exactly why the world agrees this sort of thing shouldn't be done on humans. We know there are errors with gene editing. We need to figure out how to make it more accurate before using it on humans. And then, agree on what it can be used for ethically. Increasing athletic ability, I can assure you, will not be an approved criterion."

"The Chinese government think is okay. If they make twenty deformed or sick people to get one super athlete, they satisfied."

"Who are these people? They are monsters."

"Yes. Peng and other members Communist Party. They cause suffering, but they not care."

"Why do they want to hurt Kang?"

"They not want anyone find out about project. If anyone test him, they will know. When I come here, I worry they kidnap him and bring him back to China. Now I see they think is easier to kill him. They have more like him in China, so not need him. Every year they make at least ten babies with special hemoglobin for better athletes. They also have project to make stronger muscles, called double muscling. Someday they make babies with both."

"Now what? What do you plan to do?" I asked.

"I must get Mingyu. I want proof about what they do and stop it. And I want best medical care for my children."

"Tell me about Mingyu. Is he healthy?"

"He get same special hemoglobin as Kang. When I leave China, Mingyu healthy. My brother, he know people who give him information. Last month he send me message, say Mingyu healthy. Now, I not know. With Kang, someone tell me they use technique call CRISPR/Cas9. With

Mingyu, they use another method, they say more accurate. Fewer accidents, but not know."

"Do you have a plan to get Mingyu out of China?"

"I no can go back. Too well-known. They arrest me right away. Same with Ebba. They know she help me here. I need someone else. Someone they not suspect."

"Like who? Do you have someone in mind?"

Ting looked down. "I hope you can find it in your heart to help me."

CHAPTER 11

Me? She wants me to help her? What could I possibly do? I'd never been to China. I didn't speak Chinese. I had a life in San Francisco, a job. I couldn't just leave. As much as I'd like to be, I'm not exactly a Bond girl or Superwoman. I don't run fast. I can't climb over a fence, and I can't bench press more than thirty pounds.

"I know is ask a lot," Ting said," but I have no one else. I need someone they not recognize, someone smart, understand the technology, and a good heart."

"I don't know," I said. "I have a job, an apartment, student loans." I stopped myself, aware these issues were minuscule compared to her problems.

"I have people to help. My brother, Lim, he is leader in secret anti-government organization. He speak English very well, much better than me, and will have people in Fengshou to help you. They have ways to communicate in secret."

"Why don't you apply for political asylum here? I'll pay for an attorney. You have a good case. After you tell them everything, I'm sure there'll be an investigation."

"I wish it that simple," Ting said. "There are three important Americans under arrest in China, in labor camps. If Chinese government can arrange it, they want to trade them for me and Kang. I not trust government here to believe my story and not send me back to China. Because I escape, China will send me to work camp. No one ever hear from me again. Kang, they send him back to train for Olympics. Hope he not get sick from gene editing damage when he older. I not know what they do with Wang Shu. They have no use for him. Maybe he stay here and be adopted. Maybe nobody want him."

"I would adopt her," Ebba said. "I love Wang Shu. But don't worry about that. You're not going to be sent back to China. I'll make sure of that."

"Thank you, Ebba," Ting said. "But you cannot perform miracles. That why I need Dr. Rosen to help."

I was starting to soften a bit. Should I consider doing such a mad thing? Daisy was already planning to go to China. Could I go with her? With prodding from me, maybe she'd help. She shares her parents' view of the Chinese government.

As young children growing up during the 1950s cultural revolution in the People's Republic of China, both her mom and dad were sent by their parents to live with relatives in Taiwan where the previous Chinese government had retreated from the Mao Zedong-led communists. In Taiwan, the children were told they would be reunited with their parents when the communists were overthrown. As everyone knows, that never happened. Mao Zedong stayed in power, Daisy's grandparents were unable to leave, and their families were never reunited. Her parents met in Taiwan when they were teenagers and later immigrated to the US. They never lost their hatred of the government of the People's Republic, a sentiment they passed on to their daughter.

How would I manage to go to China? There was my job. Could I get time off? Probably. Others could fill my shifts. What about money? I didn't have any vacation time saved up, so I wouldn't be paid for the days I'd miss. I hadn't managed to save much, between my high rent and student loans. Had I exhausted all sources? Daisy had savings. I knew I could borrow from her and work more shifts in the pediatric ICU to pay her back. They say nothing can ruin a friendship like borrowing money. Could our friendship hold up? I'd make sure it did. I would pay back every dime I borrowed.

Then there was Gabe. Every time I saw him at work, my resolve weakened a little. He was bad news. But the nurses didn't call him "Dr. Dreamy" for nothing. He continued to call, though less frequently, and there was a rumor he was seeing a newly hired pediatric cardiologist. No denying that hurt. Getting away from Gabe would be a good thing.

"What if I get caught?" I asked.

"Lim can make all arrangements. He do everything possible to make sure you not caught."

"But what if I am?"

Ting was quiet for a moment. "If you caught, then I offer me and Kang in exchange for your safe return. You have my word."

"Ting, are you sure you want to make that promise?" Ebba asked.

"Yes. Must try everything possible. If my plan fail, then it out of my hands. But must try."

"Let me think about this," I said. I couldn't believe I was entertaining this outrageous plan. It did have its appeal, getting out of my rut of work, sleep, work, sleep. I always found satisfaction helping people, although until now, I'd helped one person at a time. If I could put an end to the dangerous Chinese gene-editing program, I'd be helping countless people, yet unborn. It promised to be a hell of an adventure. And I'd get my mind away from Gabe. "If I were to do this, I'd want to go with my roommate. She's American. Chinese American. I'd have to tell her what I was up to. No way around it. Of course, I trust her completely. We've been best friends for a long time. She's like a sister to me."

"I cannot object if you insist," Ting replied.

"How are you supporting yourself now?" I asked Ting.

"My brother and his organization send me money, but they need as much money as possible for their cause."

"They want to send more," Ebba said, "but she won't take it. I've tried to help, too, but she refuses to take money from me. That's why she lives in this rat-infested dump. If the Chinese program is exposed and Ting is granted asylum, she will no longer live in fear for her children. The secret will be out, and the program will be closed down. She could get a good job as a translator, coach, or engineer."

"Engineer?" I asked.

"Yes, Ting has a degree in engineering. She did most of her schooling while she was training for the Olympics and finished college when she worked for the Olympic organization."

"What sort of work do you do?" I asked Ebba.

"I'm a buyer at Nordstrom. I make pretty good money, although it doesn't go a long way here in San Francisco. I do my best to limit our store's purchases from China."

After promising to get back to them in a day or two, I left the apartment and stepped outside into the dusk, under the gloomy cloud cover. The wind had picked up. Dried leaves, dirty napkins, plastic scraps, and cigarette butts swirled at my feet as the scent of someone smoking weed filled the air. Uber or walk? I decided to walk. I had a lot to think about.

CHAPTER 12

By the time I reached my apartment, it was almost dark. Daisy was in her room, working at her computer. I hadn't seen her much lately because she'd been spending most evenings with Brian.

"Home early," she yelled. "What gives?"

"You'll never guess," I answered. "I'm glad you're here. It seems like I haven't seen you for ages. I'm starting to think you might like Brian more than you like me."

"Never."

"You got some time? I want to pass an idea by you."

"Sounds intriguing. Anything to do with the dozen roses that arrived today? Sure hope not."

I looked on the kitchen table and saw Gabe's trademark dozen roses. I opened the accompanying envelope and read the card.

Miss you.
I've made reservations for us to stay in Carmel this weekend.

A few months ago, we'd had a lust-filled weekend in the quaint town of Carmel, less than a three-hour drive from San Francisco. I suppose he thought if we went to Carmel again, we'd have hot sex like before, as if nothing had happened. No apology. He was expecting me to forget his unacceptable behavior. Won't take "no" for an answer. All the more reason to get out of Dodge. I texted him I wasn't going to Carmel. No explanation.

"Definitely not," I answered. "I've had quite a day and can use a drink. I'm pouring us each a glass of zinfandel. Don't make me drink alone. That would be pathetic."

"Be right there." I heard Daisy scoot her chair away from her desk, followed by the sound of her slippers sliding over the rug. "Okay, don't keep me waiting," she said, sitting across from me at the kitchen table and lifting her wine glass. "What do you want to talk about?"

I moved the roses from the table to the kitchen counter. "How would you like company on your trip to China?"

Daisy lit up like a kid going to Disneyland. "I'd absolutely love it! Are you really thinking of coming with me? You'd better not be teasing me."

"I'm not teasing. It won't exactly be all play time for me, though. There are some things I'll need to do over there."

"Like what? What could you possibly have to do in the People's Republic?"

"Don't laugh, but I've been asked to go on a secret mission."

Despite my admonishment, Daisy laughed. "So now you're Nancy Drew? This sounds like a joke."

"It's no joke. It has to do with a brother and sister who are patients of mine."

Daisy stopped laughing. "You sound serious."

"I am. I'm at a crossroads here. The mom escaped China where she's something like a political enemy. She brought two of her children here with her. She has another child, four months old now, but she wasn't able to bring him. If she goes back, she'll be arrested. She wants me to get her son."

"Where is he?"

"He's being held in a government facility in Sichuan province."

"Why can't she just ask someone to bring the boy to the US? I'm sure the government doesn't need him. It's not like they have a shortage of people."

"Well, they want to keep this one."

"Why do I have the feeling you're leaving out some important information?"

"Because I am."

"I'm not a goddamn mind reader. Tell me what's going on."

"Well, it started when I saw an adorable five-year-old Asian girl. With blue eyes."

"You mean a part-Asian girl."

"No. One hundred percent Asian."

"Contact lenses."

"No. She really has blue eyes."

"Bullshit."

"Listen. Do you remember hearing about CRISPR/Cas9? It's a scientific breakthrough. I've told you about it before, but you probably weren't listening."

"Doesn't ring a bell. But then again, I usually don't listen to you when you go on and on about your medical stuff. No offense."

"It's merely about the most important discovery this century."

"The century's pretty young."

"Gene editing. Does that ring a bell?"

"Oh, yeah. Gene editing. I've heard of that. Sure. I guess it's for medicine what the advances in AI are for the computing world."

"Well, they each have their downside, like maybe robots will take over the world. In gene editing, there is the moral question regarding whether or not the technology should be used to cure diseases or create 'better' or 'super' people. Most scientists are dead set against the super people idea. There's also a problem in that the technology right now hasn't been perfected. The process doesn't work as planned all the time. Genes other than the targeted ones can be changed by mistake, with disastrous effects."

"I didn't realize that. How does that happen?"

"You could call it coding errors. You know how DNA is comprised of a long molecular chain, called a backbone, on which four molecules, called bases, are attached? These bases are abbreviated A, G, C, and T. The order of these bases determines the composition of proteins the DNA codes for."

"It's coming back to me now. You said the magic word. *Code*. With computers, it's binary, just zeros and ones. With you guys, there's four possible molecules at each site, so it's quaternary. Now I remember. *A* stands for adenoids or something like that."

"Adenine, actually."

Daisy laughed. "It's all the same to me."

"Don't be such a smartass. I'm sure you understand that like with computer code, in dealing with DNA you need to get the code exactly right or your program won't work properly."

"Sure. I get that."

"DNA is usually double-stranded, with the strands twisted around each other. The bases join the two strands together, always hooking up in the same way—G with C, and A with T. If the strands are separated, a single strand can be a template to make a mate, or complementary strand. The complementary strand is made by adding one base at a time to match up with the base on the template strand. That's how DNA replicates itself."

"Now you've made me have an unpleasant flashback to my high school biology class. I just saw Mr. Cramer with his bolo tie and pencil-thin mustache standing before the class, droning on about all that stuff. I swear, he was the most boring teacher I ever had. Perhaps with a more inspiring biology teacher, I'd have wanted to go into medicine, like you."

"We were in the same class, if you remember. I learned a lot from Mr. Cramer. Despite his nerdy appearance, he had a sharp sense of humor. I loved that class."

"Then I guess it was me, not him. Anyway, go on with your spellbinding tutorial."

"Getting back to gene editing, you need to know exactly which base in the target gene you want to edit, and you need to know exactly what the twenty bases around the site are."

"Okay, like finding a bit of computer code."

"Yes, exactly. Next, you have to synthesize a so-called guide RNA, a length of RNA that's complementary to the DNA in that area."

"I forget. What's RNA?"

"Geez, you computer geeks are so lame. That would be like me asking 'What's the difference between a hard drive and a memory stick.'"

"I've met people who don't know the difference. Doctors, mostly," Daisy said, smiling.

"Touché. Well, RNA is similar to DNA, but it has a slightly different backbone, and is usually single-stranded. It can be made with DNA as a template, using the same pairing up of bases, although instead of using the base T, RNA uses the base U."

"U instead of T. Got it. Fascinating stuff." Daisy exaggerated a yawn.

"I know you coders have the attention span of a three-year-old for anything that's not binary, so I'll try to make this simple. With current technology, making the guide RNA can be done pretty easily. Then, before it can be used to edit a gene, it needs to be incorporated into this giant, monster-size RNA molecule called CRISPR, which, I'm sure you already guessed, stands for clustered regularly interspaced short palindromic repeats."

"Naturally. Love the name. Whoever thought of it—I wonder what they named their kids."

"In case you can't tell, I'm ignoring all your snarky, immature comments. Pay attention or no video games for a week."

"You're so mean," Daisy said, with an exaggerated frown. "I'd like to see how long you'd listen if I started lecturing you on NAND gates."

"That's boring. What I'm talking about is interesting." Despite Daisy rolling her eyes, I continued. "Once the guide RNA joins up with CRISPR, it directs the CRISPR complex to the DNA segment containing the base you want to change. Then a protein called Cas9, with the help of the complex, cuts through both strands of the DNA at the designated spot. After that, one of two things can happen. The cell's natural repair mechanisms can rejoin the ends of the DNA at the cut site, often introducing a different base, or mutation, which will deactivate the gene.

"Or," I continued, "a small segment of DNA with a desired alternative DNA sequence can be introduced. The cell then incorporates that DNA segment at the cut area and, voila, the gene is edited, making a new and improved gene with the alternative DNA sequence." I was sure that was how Kang's DNA was edited; scientists had created a novel DNA sequence to replace a small part of his hemoglobin gene, thereby changing the characteristics of his hemoglobin.

"So, what's the problem? How can these mistakes you mentioned happen? The technique sounds straightforward."

"I'm impressed. You must have been listening to me."

"I had no choice after your ultimatum."

"Since you asked, let me explain. Biologic systems aren't as exacting as computer code. Whenever you depend on a series of complicated chemical reactions such as in gene editing, they don't always go according to plan. There is a bit of randomness at the molecular level, which can introduce errors. Also, if the DNA sequence you want to change happens to occur someplace else in the huge genome, CRISPR will edit that area, too, possibly resulting in disaster. Like if you write a story and want to change the name of the main character, Bill. You have your word processor change every 'Bill' in your document to 'Tom.' But your story gets messed up when 'billions' is changed to 'Tomions' and 'bills to pay' turns into 'Toms to pay.'"

"I see how that could be a mess. The old unintended consequences problem. Are you suggesting that this girl's blue eyes are the result of gene editing?"

"I'm sure of it. But that's only the tip of the iceberg. The Chinese government continues to conduct experiments on human embryos. Actually, it's gone beyond the experimental stage. They are designing humans to be super athletes. The brother of this blue-eyed girl has designer hemoglobin to give him superhuman stamina. Their goal is to dominate the Olympics once these kids are older."

"They're already using this technology?"

"Yes. It's very secret. Sounds ridiculous, but if I hadn't examined these two kids myself, I wouldn't believe it. Someone almost ran over the child with the souped-up hemoglobin. I took care of him in the hospital. The mother is desperate. She's convinced someone working for the Chinese government tried to kill him so no one will find out about their project."

"Sounds far-fetched," Daisy said. "But I don't know about my judgment right now. I've already had a whole glass of wine."

"Believe me. This child has abnormal hemoglobin that hasn't been described before, hemoglobin with the ability to deliver more oxygen to tissue, theoretically giving him incredible stamina so he can run super-fast and longer than otherwise. An Asian man with a knife, intent on killing him, came into the pediatric ICU using the badge of an employee, an employee who was later found dead. What do you have to say about that?"

"I'd say the plot definitely thickens."

I described my long visit with Ting and Ebba, Ting's reluctance to ask for asylum, and her desire to rescue the infant she left behind."

"What can you do?" Daisy asked after I'd finished.

"I want to help her. Go to China, photograph the whole operation, expose it to the world, and get her son."

"All that without being sent to a work camp for twenty years?"

"She says she has people over there to help. If I get in trouble, she'll turn herself in to get me released."

"That's a tall order. Sounds dangerous."

"I want to help this woman and her family. And frankly, I think I can use a big change in my life right now."

"I suppose you'd want me to help."

"Would love it."

"I was a Girl Scout for a while, but never did get my espionage badge. I'm sure I would have worked on it, though, if it were available."

"Does that mean you'll do it?"

"How 'bout I meet your new friend?"

CHAPTER 13

After getting Ting's permission, I walked with Daisy to Ting's small apartment, taking a circuitous route as instructed. I checked several times to assure myself we weren't being followed. Once we reached the front steps, I rang the buzzer. I recognized Ebba's voice over the intercom, asking who was there. After identifying myself, she buzzed us in.

We climbed the stairs and walked down the dark hallway in silence to apartment 218. Ebba was waiting for us inside, the door ajar. She smiled and invited us in. I forgot to watch my step and almost tripped over a plastic police car missing two wheels. Wang Shu was on the living room floor, playing with a doll missing an arm while Kang ran in circles making the noise of an airplane dropping bombs every few seconds. The scene reminded me of the usual clinic waiting room pandemonium.

Ting, who was putting groceries away in the kitchen, joined us in the living room, bringing with her two folding chairs from the kitchen table. She spoke to the children in Chinese, and they left the room while Ebba brought in two more folding chairs. After we were seated, I made introductions. Ting told Daisy everything she had revealed to me previously. Like before, she broke down in tears several times, and Ebba comforted her.

"I'm leaving for China in six weeks," Daisy said after Ting had finished.

"November?"

"That's right. Not the best weather, but it works well with my job. Is that enough time to get everything ready?" she asked.

"It will have to be," Ebba said. Then she turned to me. "You'd have to arrange time off from your job, get your plane ticket, and a visa."

"I can do all that. If I can't get the time off, I'll quit. Can't force me to work."

"I'm planning to be there for only two weeks," Daisy added.

"Plenty of time," Ting said. "You can see Great Wall, Forbidden City, and terra cotta soldiers in Xi'an. See places first, then go Fengshou and leave fast after you get Mingyu."

"I'm also planning to visit some cousins," Daisy added.

"Cousins? You didn't tell me that," I said. "I didn't know you had cousins there."

"Neither did I. Not until a few days ago. Since you're almost always at work, I didn't have a chance to tell you. My mother just laid it on me. I told you how she was sent to Taiwan to live with an aunt when she was ten. She had an older sister who stayed with her parents in China. Her parents died about twenty years ago, but she kept in touch with her sister until a few years ago when she died. What I didn't know was that my mom kept in contact with her sister's children, my cousins. She insists I visit them. They both live near Beijing. Mom says they speak a fair amount of English, which is good since I don't speak Mandarin."

"You should still have enough time to get everything done, but you may not be able to do all the sightseeing you want," Ebba said.

"Maybe they can help with our mission," Daisy volunteered.

"No," Ebba warned, "you must not tell them anything. You don't know your cousins. I'm sorry, but they could be in the Party. Could ruin everything."

"Okay. I won't tell them."

"First thing, tomorrow, you go to consulate for visa," Ting said to me. "Tell them you go to China for vacation."

"Will I need to rent a car?" Daisy asked.

"You cannot rent car in China. Cannot use international driver's license there. Lots of trains and buses can take you places. Also, my brother, Lim, can help you get around." Ting said.

"I suggest you dye your hair black," Ebba said, turning to me. "That way, you won't attract instant attention if the police wind up searching for you. Even though your hair is curly, it will be better if it's black. And cut it short. Less obvious."

"I can make that happen," I said. I'd never dyed my hair before. Or worn it short. This would be a first for me, but it would pale compared to the other firsts I'd experience on this trip.

"I have several pens for you to bring," Ebba said, changing the subject and reaching for four small oblong boxes on a nearby shelf.

"Thanks, but I already have a few Bic pens I was going to bring," I said, confused by Ebba's strange offer.

"These pens have hidden cameras that use tiny memory cards. You can get forty-five minutes of recording on each one."

Ebba handed three boxes to Daisy, then three to me. Daisy opened one and said, "Looks like they record on micro SD cards. I'm familiar with these. It'll be easy for me to set them up." She looked my way. "The thought of you trying to do it by yourself makes me cringe. I still have nightmares about the time you tried to use my Apple watch."

"Speaking of watches, we'll also get you a couple of watches with hidden cameras," Ebba said, showing pictures from a catalog. "They can each record for an hour. I know, the man's watch is pretty clunky, but it looks like a regular sports watch. The pink one isn't bad looking. You'll have more control over getting close-ups with these watches than with the pens. You decide who gets which one."

"I get dibs on the pink one," Daisy said.

"I knew you'd want it," I said. "Given how much you love 'Hello Kitty.' Me, I prefer the sports watch. Goes more with my serious spy persona."

"I can put more spy cameras in jewelry," Ting said. "I have it ready before you leave."

"I feel like I'm in a James Bond movie," Daisy said.

"You can be the Bond girl," I joked, trying to hide the fact that, in addition to being excited, I was scared.

"Don't expect me to make you martinis," Daisy answered.

I sensed her concern although she, too, tried to make light of the situation.

"You reserve flight yet?" Ting asked Daisy.

"I have. I'm flying from SFO to Beijing, then I fly back from Shanghai."

"What about reservations for travel when you in China?" Ting asked.

"I haven't done that yet. I'm planning to join a tour either before or after I visit my cousins."

"Where do cousins live?" Ting asked.

"They're in a place near Beijing called Langfang."

Ebba typed into her cell phone. "How will you get there?"

"My cousins live near each other in apartments. They sent me instructions for taking a local bus. Looks complicated."

"Bus ride take at least four hours," Ting said. "How many day you visit them?"

"I'll spend one or two evenings. I'm bringing pictures of my parents, mostly my mom, to share with them. If we can't get through everything in one evening, I'll stay another day."

"I think it's best if you get through your pictures quickly," Ebba said. "Spend one night, maximum. Take DiDi—that's like our Uber—back to the hotel rather than the bus, if you want to spend a little extra time. That will only take about an hour, according to Google Maps. You can visit your cousins right after you do your sightseeing."

"And Mission Impossible the rest of the time," I added.

"Now must plan," Ting said. "I do WeChat with my brother later to make plan.

"WeChat? What's that?"

"Biggest Chinese app for instant message, payment, social media. Huge."

"Why haven't I heard of it?"

"Used mainly in China. Very popular there. But have censorship. And spying. Not popular here but useful for contact with someone in China."

"Aren't you worried the government will be able to keep track of you if you use it?"

"I use what you call burner phone. Never from home. Always someplace else. Lim and I, we have special code. If a message intercepted, is okay. We make careful plan. Will call you when I have plan."

"I'll wait for your call."

"One more thing," Ting said. "Do either of you speak a foreign language?"

"I understand a little Mandarin," Daisy said. "My parents still speak it sometimes. But I don't speak it or read it."

Ting looked at me. "I speak a little French." Ting looked unimpressed. "I also know American Sign Language. I'm fluent in that," I added, feeling foolish for even mentioning it.

CHAPTER 14

I recognized Ting's voice. "We get together soon, please?" The call came when I was home reading a journal at my desk and Daisy was playing Grand Theft Auto in the living room. "Friday evening, seven, at my place is okay?" she asked.

It had been five days since we'd visited Ting. The following day, I'd asked Daisy if she could commit to the mission.

"My parents will be so proud," she answered. "I can't tell you how much they hate the Chinese government. It broke the family apart. They've never gotten over it. Sure, it's different now from when they were sent away because of Mao. But the government is still full of corruption, and the people aren't free. The Communist Party has a strong arm."

"It could be risky. Very risky."

"So is riding BART." I'd taken that to mean she was in.

Now holding my cell phone, I stepped into the living room to ask Daisy if she could meet with Ting on Friday at seven. Without seeming to break her intense concentration on the game, she nodded in the affirmative.

"We'll be there," I said into the phone.

"Make sure no one follow."

I wondered if I'd be able to sleep between now and then.

*

Daisy and I left the apartment shortly after 6:00 p.m. Friday. It was cold and windy, so we both wore jackets. We took a circuitous route, checking behind us periodically, to make sure no one was following. We escalated our surveillance as we got close to Ting's apartment. When we arrived, Ebba was waiting for us outside and shepherded us in. We again followed her to Ting's apartment, where she repeated the specific pattern of door knocks. When Wang Shu opened the door, Ebba swooped her up, gave her a big hug, and twirled her around several times. The young girl laughed with pure joy.

Daisy and I entered the apartment and closed the door. It was dark, a lamp in the living room providing the only light. Kang was playing with a plastic car, making the sort of noise young boys typically make when mimicking the sound of an engine.

"Please, sit down," Ting said, motioning to the folding chairs in the living room. Still cold, neither Daisy nor I removed our jackets. I concluded Ting couldn't afford to heat her apartment, although she and her children appeared to be comfortable wearing only light sweaters.

"Me and Lim, we have plan," Ting said. "Is not without risk."

"We know," Daisy said, "but we still want to do this, if there's a good chance for success. Let's hear the plan."

"Daisy, what time your flight land in Beijing?"

"Around 3:30, the day after I leave."

"Dr. Rosen, you buy ticket to fly with Daisy. You fly to Beijing together with return tickets from Shanghai in fourteen days. Many people start in Beijing, leave from Shanghai, so won't catch attention. Also buy train ticket for overnight ride to Xi'an on day five, leave late in day. On first day, you land in afternoon and stay in hotel. Sleep. Day two, you go on tour of city together. See usual things. Tiananmen Square. Forbidden City."

"That's a lot to see in one day," Daisy said.

"Yes, not much time, but you can find tour to do all this. Day three take tour to Great Wall and Summer Palace."

"I was going to spend my first evening and the next full day after we arrive sleeping, to get over jet lag," Daisy said.

"No time for that. Not if you want sightsee, see cousin, and do this important work."

"Okay, we'll stay up after we land and go to bed early," I said. "I'm sure it'll be easier than pulling three eighteen-hour shifts in a row at the hospital."

"That's not something I'm used to doing," Daisy said.

"Don't worry," I said. "I'll get you out of bed if I have to pour coffee down your throat and play marching songs. Now, Ting, go on."

"Next day, after Great Wall, is day four. Daisy, you visit cousins. Take only enough for overnight stay. While Daisy see his cousins, Dr. Rosen, you meet my brother."

"Please, Ting, call me Erica. How will I get to your brother?"

"I will arrange with him. Will tell you where to meet before you leave."

"Do you have a picture so I can recognize him?"

"No picture. But he meet you in a place with Chinese people. For him, easy to find you. In case is problem, you have any special jewelry you can wear?"

"I'll wear my Winnie the Pooh earrings. The kids in the clinic love them."

Ting looked at me in horror. "No! You cannot show any Winnie the Pooh thing in China. Too much attention. When people show Winnie the Pooh, they mock Xi Jinping, China president. Many think he look like Winnie the Pooh."

"Sorry, I didn't know that. How about my pineapple earrings? Will that do?"

"Yes, that work. Lim bring new fake passports for you and Daisy. Must keep them very safe. Get passport holder on belt to wear under clothes. Never let passports get lost or stolen, especially the ones Lim give you. Must show passport in hotel when you check in. Show them real passport."

"How will he get passports with our pictures on them?" I asked.

"Ebba can take pictures and email them to contact. Lim take care of the rest."

I was nervous. And electrified. I was starting to feel like a real spy. Then I realized I didn't need my special earrings after all. "Since your brother will have my passport photo, he'll be able to identify me without my earrings," I said.

"Wear earrings," Ting said. "You know how Americans say we all look alike? You all look alike to us."

"Where will my fake passport be from?" I asked.

"Pakistan."

That surprised me. I'd never pictured myself pretending to be from a Muslim country. "Should I wear a hijab for the photo?"

"No. Wear plain white blouse. Hair back. No makeup. No glasses."

"Why Pakistan of all places?" I asked.

"We need to get you into the facility where the gene editing is done so you can document as much as possible. Access is highly restricted," Ebba said. "No way could you pass for an Asian. But Pakistani, yes. Dark hair and brown eyes. No problem. China has very good relations with Pakistan."

"I don't speak Urdu or any of the other languages they speak there."

"Is okay. Nobody speak that where you go," Ting said. "But English universal language. Everyone you meet in Fengshou speak English."

"But I don't have an accent."

"Is okay. People not notice accent so much in language they had to learn. They will only think you learn English very well."

"What will be my cover?"

"It will be easier if you let me answer all your questions," Ebba said. "Ting already explained it all to me, and she can correct me if I make a mistake. Erica, you'll be a doctor from Aga Khan Medical School in Karachi. You'll be there to learn about gene editing in hopes of setting up a collaboration with Chinese leaders in the field. Pakistan has an unusually high rate of genetic diseases, including deafness, because of marriages between relatives. You'll say you want to develop a program to correct the mutations that cause these diseases. That will be your official reason for the visit."

"Interesting," I commented. "I'll need to read up on these abnormalities in Pakistan."

"Yes and become familiar with the region. Also learn about Aga Khan."

"I guess I'll at least need to know where it is and what the weather is like."

"Yes, but you have plenty of time. After you've been at Fengshou for a while, ask about gene editing to help Pakistanis be stronger and more energetic. Say the government wants them to be more productive. See if you can get them to talk about gene editing to make better athletes."

"Will do."

"Lim is in contact with a woman who works in reception. She'll do her best to look after you. I'll get her name for you before you leave. There are a few members of his organization who are trying to get jobs there. If successful, they will help you, too."

"What about me? Where will I be from?" Daisy asked.

"You'll be from Xinjiang, a territory in northwest China."

"But I don't speak Mandarin."

"No problem," Ebba said. "Most people there don't speak Mandarin. You'll speak Uyghur."

"I've never heard of that."

"I'm not surprised. Few people outside the region speak Uyghur. You'll be from the city of Kashgar. Most of the people there are Muslim, of Turkish descent, but there is a sizable Chinese Han population there, too. You will claim to speak only Uyghur and English, so like Erica, you will communicate with the staff in English. It is highly doubtful anyone there will speak Uyghur."

"What if they do?"

"The best thing you could do at that point is pretend to be ill and leave immediately to get medical care. We'd have to postpone your part of the mission. But it's extremely unlikely."

"What will be my part of the mission?"

"You will smuggle Mingyu out."

Daisy looked taken aback. "Me? Really?"

"I know it sounds risky," Ebba said. "You can always back out, but I can assure you Lim is very good about organizing operations. Please, wait to hear his plan before you decide. Meanwhile, prepare yourself. You'll need to do some reading about Kashgar and the Xinjiang territory.

There's been a lot of political unrest there. Someone may ask you about it."

"What's my cover going to be?"

"The administration will be informed that the government wants to build a second gene editing facility in Xinjiang. You will visit Fengshou to study how they house and take care of their pregnant women, young children, and babies. While you are touring the housing units, you will have access to Mingyu. The details of getting him out will be planned between now and then."

"How will I talk to Daisy while I'm there?" I asked.

"You won't. You will both need to work independently. You can't risk any sort of communication with each other while you're there."

"How will we meet up afterward and get Mingyu to the US?" I asked.

"Lim is working on that too. There are members of his organization all over the country, but sometimes communication is slow. These people may need to buy a new burner phone, or wait to be alone so they can make a call or send a text. China has many people. It's very crowded. Lots of the people Lim works with live with family. Sometimes parents, grandparents, nieces, and nephews live together in a small house. Some live in small apartments and share a room with other people. It can be hard to communicate privately."

"I guess we'll have to wait and see what the plan is," I said. "I hope it's a good one.'

"It will be," Ebba assured me.

*

All my colleagues agreed to work extra shifts to cover my absence for two weeks in November. One day shortly after the clinic closed, I asked Gabe for the two weeks off to visit China. I was unsure how he would react, as he'd been quite spiteful since I'd broken up with him.

"It would set a bad example if I gave you so much time off," he said. "It would look like favoritism."

"Favoritism?" I asked, aghast. "But we're not together anymore."

"Not everyone in the department knows that."

"Are you kidding? Everyone knows." My words were met with silence. "Look, I'm not asking for a paid vacation. Just time off, without pay."

"For a trip to China? Sorry, but that doesn't cut it. You either come to work every day you're scheduled and act like you love your job, or you resign."

I was prepared for that. Never one to make rash decisions, I had decided in advance what I would do if given this ultimatum.

"Then I quit. I'll work until the end of October. After that, I'm done."

It wouldn't be easy to fill my position on such short notice, but I was sure Gabe wouldn't back down. His face turned red as he clenched his jaw and his right hand formed a fist. Fearing he'd become violent, I turned on my heels and left. I felt free. No regrets. Sure, I wasn't in the best shape financially, but I'd be able to find work in almost any city I chose to live. I'd worry about that in mid-November when I returned. Hopefully.

CHAPTER 15

A week after our meeting with Ting, Daisy and I went to Nordstrom at the Westfield San Francisco Center, a large indoor shopping mall in the heart of the downtown shopping area. Waiting for Ebba in the bridal department, we both admired the wedding gowns on display. Two days earlier, I had gone to a beauty salon in my neighborhood and had my hair cut short and dyed black.

"Several of these dresses are less than a thousand dollars," Daisy marveled.

"I didn't know you could get a decent wedding dress for so little. Maybe I can afford to get married someday."

"Which one's your favorite?" Daisy asked.

I looked around at all the dresses on mannequins. "That one over there," I said, pointing to a fitted dress with off-the-shoulder sleeves, adorned with lace and beads. The mermaid skirt had a train, precisely the perfect length.

"I don't know how you do it," Daisy said, checking the price tag. "It's over seven grand. Probably the most expensive dress here."

"Guess I can't afford to get married after all," I said. "Oh, well."

A middle-aged saleswoman meandered over. "Can I help you young ladies?"

"Oh, thank you," I said. "We're here to—"

Our conversation was interrupted by a familiar voice. "Thanks for coming." Ebba, dressed in a smart business suit, was carrying a stack of papers.

Before either of us had a chance to respond, the saleswoman said, "Ebba, if it isn't my favorite buyer. I see you've brought a stack of orders for me to go over."

"Yes," Ebba said. "Please take a look at them while I show these ladies something in the back."

Ebba escorted us to a large dressing room and took her iPhone from a skirt pocket. "The walls and lighting here will be perfect for taking passport photos. This won't take much time. But first, we should try to disguise you a little. Let's make your eyebrows a little thicker." She removed an eyebrow pencil from a jacket pocket and thickened our eyebrows. Stepping back to admire her work, she said, "Now that's more like it. Who wants to go first?"

I volunteered. Ebba positioned me in front of one of the white walls, pushed a few wayward hairs of mine into position, and took several shots. After repeating the procedure with Daisy, she examined the images on her phone and declared success.

"I'll send these off later today. Should be no problem for Lim to have the passports ready on time. Oh, before I forget, take these." She took two pair of glasses from the same pocket that held the eyebrow pencil, one with square black frames which she gave to Daisy, the other with oval silver metal frames for me. "These are fake — no prescription. You can't wear glasses for your passport photo, but bring them with you to China and put them on when you visit Fengshou."

The three of us left the dressing room together. Ebba made her way to the saleswoman going over the papers at an elegant writing desk while Daisy and I headed toward the escalator.

"Frankly, the suspense is killing me," I confessed. "I'm dying to know. Is this going to work?"

"I sure hope so. If it doesn't, we could be in some serious deep shit."

Later in the day, my mother called to tell me about a new neighbor, a young man, who was stealing things from her apartment.

"Are you sure?" I asked. My mother lived in a fairly upscale building and had never complained of significant issues with her neighbors.

"Come here and see for yourself," she said. "My favorite sweater, the blue one, is gone. And the scarf you bought me for my birthday. Gone."

My mother wasn't one to misplace things, but I found it hard to believe a neighbor had broken into her place to steal things, especially things of such little value. Her speech was slurred, something I'd noticed before, but it was more pronounced now. I could no longer ignore it. "Mom, have you been drinking?"

"What kind of question is that? Of course not."

"Your speech doesn't sound normal."

"Well, I'm more than a little upset now. After all, I'm not safe here, not with a neighbor stealing my stuff."

"How do you know your neighbor took your things?"

"There's no other explanation. I called the police and told them about him, but they won't do anything."

"I suppose they're too busy with more serious crimes."

"I think my neighbor is bribing the cops."

This sounded preposterous, but then again, my mother wasn't one to imagine things. "Tell you what, Mom. I'll visit you and talk to your neighbor. But it'll have to wait until I get back from my trip."

"Trip? You didn't tell me you're going on a trip."

"I know. It's kind of sudden. I'm leaving in a few weeks to go to China with my roommate."

"How exciting," she exclaimed. "I'm glad you're finally going to take time off and have some fun. I forgot you have a roommate. What's her name?"

"It's Daisy, Mom." Strange for my mom to forget. She'd known Daisy as long as me, over twenty years.

"Of course. You should have a wonderful time. I'm sure you have a lot of planning to do."

"Tons. And there's one more thing."

"Oh?"

"I'm leaving my job. I couldn't get the time off I wanted, so I up and quit." I cringed, anticipating her disapproval.

"Great idea. You've been working too hard."

I was surprised and grateful my mother took the news so calmly. Didn't even mention Gabe. That was a relief, not needing any more stress at the moment. After we said our goodbyes, I called a woman I'd known for years who lived near my mom, one of her best friends. I asked about the new neighbor, and if she'd detected any change in my mother's speech lately. Instead of confirming that the new neighbor was a shady character, the friend said she'd been planning to call me soon, then filled my ear about my mom's recent odd behavior.

She was forgetting things and leaving items in places she'd been, while blaming others for stealing from her and moving her things around. Two days earlier, the police had brought her home when she'd gotten lost after walking to the neighborhood grocery store. Her speech was slurred sometimes, and she suspected my mom had started drinking. She'd looked but hadn't found any hidden bottles of wine or other alcohol in Mom's apartment. My heart sank. I didn't have time to deal with this now, of all times. Could my mother be a closet alcoholic? Did she have a brain tumor? At fifty-three years old, she was awfully young to be developing Alzheimer's disease. I hoped there was a less ominous explanation, perhaps an adverse reaction to medication, or a vitamin deficiency. I'd look into that when I got back. For now, I called Adult Protective Services and arranged to have someone look in on her daily until I returned.

That night, Daisy and I went over our checklist of things to do. I had already purchased my tickets to be on the same flights as Daisy to and from China, and we'd both booked the train from Beijing to Xi'an. We had scheduled tours of Beijing and the Great Wall through Tours by Locals on the web. Our reservations for four-star hotels in Beijing and Xi'an had been confirmed. We'd also reserved rooms in Chongqing, Yanang, and Shanghai, choosing the most expensive hotels on the web, since we had no intention of staying in those places. Each of us had a passport from an earlier time. My hair was now shorter and darker than it was in my passport photo, but I still had the same face and didn't expect to run into difficulty. It wasn't unusual for women to change their hairstyles and color.

Daisy had her visa, and I'd be picking mine up from the consulate tomorrow. We had secure passport holders and electric outlet adapters we'd bought on Amazon. Between us, we'd gotten over two thousand dollars' worth of renminbi, Chinese currency, from our banks to avoid leaving a trail with our credit cards in case we were later hunted by the Ministry of State Security.

A small box in our apartment was filled with our spy apparatus. We had the pens and the watches with cameras Ebba had ordered for us. Although illegal to own in the US, Ting had procured two cell phone jammers, small black box-like contraptions with four antennae of different lengths protruding. In addition, Ting had crafted a tight-fitting cuff bracelet with an artful design for each of us. At the center of both bracelets were three tiny cameras, each of which could record one hour of video when activated by pressing a colored faux gem near the lens. Photographs could be taken by pushing on a fake pearl.

We practiced for hours in Ting's apartment until we got the knack of aiming the cameras and taking videos and photos. After every try, we practically held our breaths as Ting removed the micro SD cards from the bracelets, uploaded their contents to her computer, and checked what we had captured. Although we were aiming at text in books, our first images were of the floor, walls, ceilings, and, occasionally, shoes. When we were finally successful in recording what we wanted repeatedly, I sensed relief, similar to the day I learned I'd passed my boards in pediatric critical care.

We packed lightly so we could move quickly between locations. Living in San Francisco, we had plenty of clothes for cold weather. With the addition of a heavy scarf and a pair of gloves for each of us, we were covered.

I spent all my spare time reading about Pakistan, in particular Karachi, the city where I would claim to be from. I looked over the list of professors in the department I would pretend to work in. After trying to learn a few words of Urdu, I gave it up. I doubted my pronunciation was even close to what a native speaker would say. Daisy and I spent countless hours quizzing each other about our respective new points of origin.

My last day of work, four days before we were to leave, the staff threw me a surprise party in the break room, complete with cake and ice cream. Gabe failed to show. It was difficult to answer the countless inquiries into why I was quitting my job to go on a two-week trip to China in November when the weather was cold and rainy. I explained I was worn out, tired, and wanted to take advantage of the opportunity to travel with my roommate. I tried to sound convincing, but considering the reception my explanation received, I probably wasn't. Martha's eyes were red from crying. I hugged her and told her she'd be a tremendous asset to whoever replaced me, and that I hoped we'd work together again in the future. Talking to her was doubly tough. I wanted to tell her I was actually going on a secret mission to rescue a child and hopefully save humanity from dangerous genetic experimentation. However, I maintained my wall of secrecy, telling myself many spies in the past undoubtedly suffered the same frustration.

The next day, Daisy and I discussed whether to let our two pathetic houseplants die or have someone water them a few times while we were gone. An idea popped into my head. I don't know why I hadn't thought of it earlier.

"Let's have Ting and her kids stay here during our trip," I suggested.

"Good idea. Should have thought of it before. It's a hell of a lot nicer here than the dump she's in now."

"Exactly. It's safe, and she can even take care of the philodendron and the ficus."

It would be hard to convince Ting to stay in our apartment. I'd have to do it in person. An hour later, I walked to her building and followed someone in. At her apartment door, I delivered the secret knock I'd seen Ebba perform, and Ting opened the door. She was surprised I was there, but waved me inside.

"I'm sorry I didn't think of this sooner," I said. "Daisy and I want you to stay in our apartment while we're gone."

"No, no. Cannot do that," Ting said, looking down.

"Please," I said. "We need someone to be there to water our plants. I know it sounds silly, but they have special meaning for me. If you don't stay in our place, we can't go."

Ting looked horrified at the prospect of Daisy and me pulling out at this late date. Before she could respond, I handed her an extra copy of keys to our apartment and mailbox. "Here. You need to do this so we can rescue Mingyu. You need a passcode to get in the building, and it's monitored by security cameras, so you'll be safe. We would be honored if you would stay there."

"Okay, then I accept."

"Thanks," I said. "Come over with your children the day before we leave. We have a washing machine in the apartment, so you won't need a lot of clothes." I gave Ting our address and the passcode to enter the building before I left.

The next day, Daisy and I went on a shopping spree, buying toys and clothes for the kids. We bought groceries in Chinatown where I deferred all purchasing decisions to Daisy. Both of us looked forward to seeing the reaction of Ting and her children to their new circumstances. I wondered if Daisy was thinking the same thing I was. Would we let them move back to their dingy apartment in the Tenderloin after we returned, or ask them to stay with us? I'd discuss it with Daisy later, after we were home from our trip and safe on American soil again.

CHAPTER 16

The afternoon before our flight to Beijing, Ting arrived with Kang and Wang Shu, everyone dressed in heavy coats with the hoods hiding their hair and much of their faces. She carried two suitcases.

"This so nice," she said, crossing the threshold and scanning the living room, kitchen, and dining area. "So big, so beautiful."

"We have a little surprise for your kids," I said, lifting a sheet draped over the glass and metal console table near the entryway, revealing a pile of toys.

The children squealed as they ran for the toys and began opening boxes, emptying their contents. Ting yelled something at them in Chinese and they stopped, suddenly quiet, their heads down.

"We want to spoil your kids a little bit," I said. "Do you know what that means?"

"I think so," Ting answered.

"Then let them play with the toys we bought for them. We've had a lot of stress planning for the trip. Now let us have a little fun watching your kids play."

"Okay," Ting said. She spoke to her children, and they laughed and began playing, singing, laughing, and making noises.

I showed Ting around the apartment and instructed her how to buzz in someone at the front door and operate the thermostat, oven, dishwasher, clothes washer, and dryer.

"What about plants? Don't forget to tell how I care for plants."

I'd almost forgotten about watering our plants, the reason she had agreed to stay at our apartment in the first place. Fortunately, they weren't quite dead yet. I showed her where we kept the watering can and explained the plants should be watered twice a week.

"Simple," Ting remarked.

I called my mom before going to sleep. She told me a woman had been visiting her every day to chat, but the woman had stolen her favorite red lipstick. I assumed the woman was from Adult Protective Service. Mom didn't remember I was going to China but wished me a good trip. Her speech was more slurred than I'd remembered it. I hardly slept that night.

Daisy and I said our goodbyes to Ting, Wang Shu, and Kang in the morning. Wang Shu was giving a bottle to her baby doll, and Kang was making airplane noises as he guided his fighter jet through the air. Suitcases in tow, we headed to the nearest BART station and took the SFO-bound train to catch our twelve-hour flight to Beijing. We'd planned to buy breakfast at the airport, but my stomach was so tense I couldn't eat. From the way Daisy looked, she felt the same. We went straight to the United gate and hardly spoke while we waited to get on our plane. In boarding group four, we barely had enough room to stow our carry-ons. We dared not check any luggage and risk the possibility someone might rifle through our things and discover our spy paraphernalia.

Daisy and I got settled in our seats and the plane took off almost on time. We were able to eat part of our meals when lunch was served several hours later. I dozed off while watching a movie I'd downloaded from Netflix onto my iPad and awoke to the sound of the captain telling us about the weather in Beijing. Cold and drizzling. We'd be arriving in a half hour, at 2:15 p.m. China Standard Time. I wiped the drool from my face, hoping no one had seen it, and gently prodded Daisy who was still sleeping.

"We're landing soon," I told her.

She lay still for a moment before responding. "I guess it's too late to back out. I had a doozy of a dream."

"Yeah, me too," I confided. "For a moment I was relieved to wake up. Then I remembered what we're here for."

"Getting cold feet?"

"No way. But I am a bit nervous."

Deplaning was slow. It seemed to take forever to go through customs. An expressionless agent performed a cursory search of my suitcase and carry-on, causing my heart to race and every muscle in my body to stiffen, but I was able to remain cool as ice on the outside. Thoughts of being found out and arrested raced around in my head, but I went through without incident.

I watched when Daisy was engaged in a similar drill. Every second seemed like a minute. I'm sure I didn't breathe at all while I watched the agent rummage around in her things, finally exhaling as he closed her bags and motioned for her to exit. When she joined me, we hurried out of the area, then collapsed into the first chairs we saw.

"Talk about tense," I said.

"No kidding. I thought I was going to have a stroke when the guy was going through everything. The pens, the bracelets, the watch. You sure we should do this?"

"Everything seems so much more real now that we're here. But yes, we've got to. I don't want to back out now."

"Ditto. Let's get to our hotel, shower, and have a glass of wine."

"You got it. Maybe some food too."

"And then sleep. We have a big day of sightseeing tomorrow."

We found the queue for taxis and waited nearly twenty minutes under the gray sky before reaching the front of the line. When we were in a cab, Daisy handed the driver a piece of paper with the name and address of our hotel, The Peninsula, in both English and Chinese, the latter written by Ting. The driver nodded, said something in Chinese, depressed the lever on top of the meter, and took off. Overtired, nervous, and a little hungry, I was glued to the window, observing hordes of black-haired people in cars, on bikes, and on foot going about their business. Our progress was often stop and go, and there were several times I was sure we were going to strike another car, run over a pedestrian, smash into a double-parked truck, or be hit by a bus. At least it got my mind off the peril we would soon face. We passed by tall buildings, many under construction with giant cranes nearby. Businesses with signs in Chinese, many also with English signage, stretched as far as I could see in every direction. Street signs bore Chinese characters above English lettering, the latter spelling the street names in Pinyin, the English transliteration. When we arrived at our hotel, an elegant building white on the bottom, red on the top, I noticed "The Peninsula" written in large white letters above the gold-framed door. Several feet above were six Chinese characters against a red background, saying I-have-no-idea what.

Our driver unloaded our bags, and we paid our bill in renminbi. The fare was in the range I had expected. We were off to a good start after having been warned to be on the lookout for scam artists trying to rip us off on our ride from the airport. I took a moment to look around, noticing the gray-brown haze enveloping the city, obscuring the view of buildings down the street. Somewhere during our taxi ride, the gray skies of the airport had become thick with the toxins and particulate matter Beijing is famous for. Stories of Beijing's legion air pollution are not an exaggeration. A sizable minority of pedestrians wore masks over their nose and mouth, presumably attempting to ward off the ill-effects of the city around them.

The hotel staff was youthful and friendly. A young man grabbed our bags and escorted us to the front desk. Despite their eagerness to help, the staff without exception spoke English poorly, making communication difficult. One of the men behind the registration desk turned to Daisy and spoke to her in Chinese, only to realize she had no clue what he was saying. Resuming the transaction in English, we completed the registration process. We showed our passports, got our room keys, and were escorted to our room, a double with two queen beds. It was luxurious, modern, and spacious with a desk, large flat screen TV, Nespresso coffeemaker, and well-appointed bathroom.

The bellhop explained the room features to us, but I barely understood anything he said. As his pitiful English was far better than my Mandarin, I felt hypocritical complaining to Daisy. I complained anyway.

We plugged in our phones and iPads. No need for our power adapters, since the hotel sockets accommodated western devices. Feeling hungry, we ordered room service before taking turns showering. By the time lunch came, Daisy was asleep. I signed for the food, took one bite of the turkey club sandwich—we'd decided to start eating local foods the next day—and fell asleep.

The sound of people talking loudly in the hall outside our room woke me. I was groggy and disoriented from my dream in which I was trying to order lab tests in the computer at work but couldn't enter the information no matter what I tried. It was daylight outside. I'd changed my watch to Chinese Standard Time and determined it was seven-thirty in the morning. We were to meet our guide in an hour. I shook Daisy awake and made two cups of Nespresso dark roast. We hurriedly dressed and ate some energy bars I'd brought from home. With our spy equipment and excess cash safely locked in the room safe, we were ready for the day.

In the lobby, we found our tour guide, a young man in his mid-twenties, and a twenty-something newlywed American couple who hailed from Alabama. Our guide spoke English well and, he told us, had lived in California for a year after college before returning to his homeland. We learned the new groom accompanying us was a NASCAR driver, a well-known one according to him and his heavily made-up wife. I didn't know whether it was true, having absolutely no interest in the so-called sport.

As we drove through the wild streets of Beijing, our NASCAR professional spoke obsessively about the cars and the drivers he saw, constantly reminding us the motorists in Beijing showed terrible technique, which explained why there were no Chinese NASCAR drivers. I wondered if the real reason was the Chinese were simply too smart to drive around in circles all day.

We visited Tiananmen Square, the Forbidden City, and the Hutong area comprised of ancient homes on small alleyways dating back to the Yuan Dynasty 700 years ago. While the happy young couple with us snickered at the pathetic lives of the people living in the Hutong, I found it a very interesting piece of preserved history. We visited a family in residence there who spoke proudly of their good fortune to live in such a charming, historic area.

After we returned to the hotel, we said our goodbyes to the others and went to our room.

"I felt a lot more at home with the Chinese people we met today than with that couple," Daisy said.

"Makes you wonder why they even came here," I responded.

"Wanted cool pictures for their Facebook page."

CHAPTER 17

I'd always wanted to see the Great Wall. This wasn't the way I had planned it in my mind for years, under a cloud of uncertainty about a clandestine mission. But I was determined to make the best of it. A van arrived at 9:00 a.m. to take Daisy and me along with two other American couples to the Great Wall at Mitianyu. One couple was from Portland, the other, Denver. Fortunately, neither had the bluster of the pair from the day before. Our guide spoke English well and was very knowledgeable about Beijing, lecturing us while he drove. The traffic was formidable, but once we were a distance from the city it was lighter, like a weekend driving around San Francisco.

In planning for the trip, I discovered you can't see all of the Great Wall. It's four thousand miles long, not counting the parts comprised of trenches and natural obstacles such as rivers and mountains. There are several popular places to view a section of it, and we were going to the most visited one, located in a mountainous area an hour and a half drive from our hotel. Our guide parked the van amidst the numerous cars, vans, and busses already in the large parking lot. We all got out of the vehicle and stretched our legs. As we were marshaled through the parking area, the smell of food from nearby restaurants made me hungry, until that feeling was squelched by cigarette smoke wafting through the air. We reached a nondescript low-lying building appearing to be approximately fifty years old. It was the modern-day portal we needed to pass through before experiencing the remains of the Ming Dynasty which, our tour leader told us, began around 1400 BC.

There it was, up a series of steps. Constructed of gray-tan stones and bricks, the vast wall undulated over steep hills, forming a giant serpent-like stripe which stood out sharply from the surrounding greenery. Once we ascended the steps and stood on the wall structure, our guide gave us a lecture on the length, height, and breadth of this national treasure. Not merely a wall, it was a raised walkway, wide enough for ten people—or five horses—to walk abreast, each section connected by guard towers. This part of the wall had been restored in the early two thousands, the formidable structure it once was now rebuilt from the pile of stones that had been all that remained after battling the elements for over two thousand years. The walkways were crowded with tourists, most of whom appeared to be Asian, although I noticed a good number of Caucasians and a smattering of black people. As I looked around in amazement, our tour leader described what it must have been like for the soldiers, commoners, and criminals who built it. The construction required the delivery of massive amounts of brick, stone, and wood. Countless workers labored to erect the wall, some of whom fell in and were left in place, incorporated into the wall itself for eternity.

Following the talk, Daisy and I wandered away from the entry point. It didn't take long to venture past the crowds, to a sparsely populated area where the rebuilt area of the wall abruptly ended, continuing as decayed remnants made of stone piles, the natural condition of the original wall in modern times. I tried to imagine workers bringing these very stones here and arranging them into the fortress thousands of years ago. Daisy and I stood silently, scanning the ruins of this ancient structure which wended its way over the rough terrain seemingly forever, surrounded by the peaceful forest. For a moment, I forgot about the task before us.

We returned to our group and enjoyed lunch at—believe it or not—a Chinese restaurant. Our next stop was the Summer Palace, a complex of ancient buildings around a picturesque manmade lake. We walked through several of the buildings where our guide provided us with historical information on their construction and the people who had stood in the very halls we were currently occupying. We ended our visit with a stroll through the Imperial Garden and a ferry ride across the lake with its many bridges, including the 17-Arch Bridge adorned with over five hundred carved lions, connecting the shore with an island.

Eight hours after we began, Daisy and I were delivered back to our hotel. We should have been exhausted, but instead were invigorated by what lay ahead. Tomorrow, Daisy would take a bus to visit her cousins and spend the night. I would meet Lim and begin planning the rest of the operation in earnest.

Daisy filled a small backpack with a change of underwear, toiletries, and pictures of her parents. Although she wanted to talk to her long-lost relatives about her exciting quest, she promised not to mention a thing about it to them.

I placed my pineapple earrings on the nightstand by my bed and fidgeted with them. Although I'd never been diagnosed with obsessive compulsive disorder, I now wondered if I suffered from it after all, as I checked that the earrings were still there several times during the night. They were my only assurance I would meet up with Lim, after all. I didn't sleep well. Neither, I discovered over breakfast the next morning, had Daisy.

I walked with her to the bus stop, arriving barely in time to hear the squeal of brakes announcing her transportation had arrived. I wished her well, and Daisy pushed her way through the crowd of commuters. She looked back at me nervously before boarding. I returned to our hotel and waited. It was two hours before I was due to meet Lim. I opened the safe to be sure our spy gear was still there. To my relief, the hair I had carefully placed between the watches lay undisturbed.

Wearing khaki pants, a light blue T-shirt, black sweater, and pineapple earrings, I left the hotel for the outdoor market where I was to finally connect with Lim. It's good I left plenty early, because I got lost three times. Although the local people tried to be helpful, in the end, the language barrier was too great, and I was left to negotiate the confusing array of streets with my cell phone. At last, I reached the correct market, which I confirmed by matching the Chinese writing on a red sign with the characters Ting had written down for me in San Francisco. Looking at my phone I smiled, seeing I was five minutes early. I found the fish stall with green lettering matching Ting's transcription, wiped the sweat from my forehead, and waited. I wanted to blend in, but from the unapologetic stares, I surmised I was nothing if not conspicuous. This was confirmed when two children, around five and six years of age, stood three feet away and studied me intently. After a short time, their mother found them, yelled some words, and steered them away. As I watched them blend into the crowd, their backs toward me, I felt a gentle tap on my right shoulder. Turning my head, I saw a youthful Chinese man wearing sunglasses, a blue baseball cap, and a black jacket.

"Erica? Are you Erica?"

It took a moment before I could speak. "Yes, I'm Erica. Are you Lim?" Of course, he was Lim. He must have taken me for an idiot. Who else could he be?

"Yes, I'm Lim. Do you mind if we leave and go someplace where we can talk?"

"Sure, that's a good idea."

He grabbed my hand and led me several blocks—pulled me actually—through densely crowded, noisy streets filled with shoppers, schoolchildren, peddlers, businesspeople, and workmen, to what appeared to be a store. I saw only Chinese writing on the sign outside. Once inside, the sounds of jackhammers, honking cars, and city busses disappeared. The dim lighting was reminiscent of a bar, yet there were no tables or bar stools. I smelled a combination of popcorn and cigarette smoke. Two men stood behind a counter, surrounded by shelves with snacks of all kinds, a commercial refrigerator stocked with drinks, including wine and beer, a few feet away.

One of the men scanned a QR code Lim displayed on his phone, then spoke as he pointed down a hall.

"Would you like something to drink? Or eat?" Lim asked me.

"I had breakfast a little while ago, so I'm not hungry."

Lim spoke to the man and held his phone up again with a QR code for scanning before taking two bottles of water from the refrigerator and a box of crackers from a shelf.

I had no reason not to trust Lim, but the situation seemed strange. Was this a movie theater? A whorehouse? Should I run?

"What is this place?" I asked.

"Don't you have these places in America?"

"I don't know. I don't know what this place is."

"It's a KTV."

"What's that?"

"You don't have karaoke TV where you're from?"

"We do have karaoke in a few bars. But not in places like this."

"Follow me, and you'll find out why these places are so popular."

I followed Lim through a hallway lined by closed doors. When he came to a room with an open door, we walked inside. He turned on the light and shut the door. The room was small, with threadbare carpeting, a worn faux leather couch, and black plastic coffee table. A large flat screen TV and control panel were mounted on a wall, and three wireless microphones lay on the table. Electronic equipment and speakers were on the floor under the monitor. A group of scantily clad Asian women singing and dancing was on the screen, although the sound was off.

"This is a very cheap place," Lim said. "Good places are much nicer. Better furniture, and you can order food and drinks from your room. Everyone likes KTV. Chinese love to sing, and you can get a private space for very little money. China is so crowded, it's hard to find privacy. This is the best deal."

"Now I understand." Already it was clear that Lim's English was much better than his sister's.

"You want to pick a song?" Lim asked, pointing to the control panel.

"I don't really want to sing—"

Lim laughed. "We need to have music on while we talk. To make sure no one can listen."

"Sorry," I said. I felt my face turn red. "Of course." I walked to the control panel, a touch screen with songs listed in Chinese and English. There were many pages of songs to scroll through, and I chose "Rolling in the Deep" by Adele.

Once the music started, Lim adjusted the volume, not too loud to prevent us from talking, yet not so soft we could be easily heard if someone were listening.

"Okay," Lim said. "There's lots to talk about." He sat on the couch and removed his cap and sunglasses. I was looking at the most handsome Chinese man I'd ever seen. Correction. The most handsome man I'd ever seen. "Why don't you sit down?" he said, smiling. Wouldn't you know it. He had a magnificent smile, with perfect teeth.

"Of course." As I sat, I quickly looked—a simple gold ring encircled his left ring finger. *Shit. He's married.* Ting hadn't mentioned that, but why would she? I berated myself for even going there. This was a serious situation. Lim was fixated on rescuing his nephew and exposing the horrors going on at the secret facility, Fengshou. Our backgrounds were so different, anyway, ideas of a romantic relationship with Lim were ridiculous.

CHAPTER 18

"I'm sure my sister has told you about the terrible things happening in our country now. The experiments with gene editing."

"She did. I still find it hard to fathom, but her children—their unusual characteristics—well, they are certainly consistent with what she described."

"If you find it even a little difficult to believe after hearing what Ting said and seeing her children—even carefully examining them—then you can imagine what others would say if she went to the American authorities about this. We need absolute proof this is happening."

"That's where I come in, right?"

"Yes. When Ting first told me she had described the situation to an outsider, I was very upset. However, she convinced me you understand. You are a good person and know how terrible this is. Not just because the government will use this technique to dominate the Olympics, but how they are doing it is reprehensible. They enslave women, athletes like my sister, and force them to undergo painful medical procedures to harvest their eggs. Then they keep them captive until their babies are born. Many participate willingly, that's true. But others, like Ting, want no part in this."

"Ting described some of the horrible deformities that have taken place. It appears the dangers predicted have become a reality."

"Unfortunately, yes. Although it appears that Ting's children are healthy, others have not been so lucky."

"How can they proceed knowing this?"

"No conscience. Not all members of the Communist Party are horrible people. Many simply want to be assured of a job and a decent life. But some, especially those at the top, want more. Power and money. The higher they get in the party, the more ambitious they become. The suffering of the general population, people they consider insignificant, means nothing to them. I believe they delude themselves into thinking they are acting for the good of the masses."

"In the US, while the welfare of the general population is very important, protection of each person's rights is paramount."

"The Chinese government says that's a Western value, not Asian. The individual is not important. Asian culture is centered around society, not the individual. In reality, that's true for some Asian countries, like China and North Korea, but not others, like South Korea and Japan." Lim paused. "You know, I would go to Fengshou and expose everything myself if I could, but I would never get in. I'm too well known. I know it's just a question of time before I'm arrested. My apartment and computer are monitored. I have to keep buying burner phones, so they aren't able to bug them. Sometimes I'm followed."

I reflexively inhaled deeply.

"Don't worry. I've gotten good at spotting the people following me. And losing them when they do. I usually wear a hat and sunglasses when I go out so I'm not so recognizable. Nobody followed me today on the way to the market."

"What kind of proof do you need us to get when we visit the facility?"

"Pictures, video, recordings. Having you, an American, a trusted doctor, witness this and testify will be immensely helpful. Testing Kang and Mingyu, if he's rescued, will be further proof. Politicians might argue that the pictures and recordings are fake, digitally created. But they can't argue the children's DNA isn't extremely unusual. Even blue-eyed Wang Shu's DNA will be useful. Half of the children's DNA will match with my sister. Except in the messed-up genes."

"Testing the DNA after I return to the US should be fairly easy to arrange. That evidence will be convincing. If the facility is inspected by an international organization, the UN perhaps, the evidence will be overwhelming."

"We're hoping the facility will be destroyed. Either before it is inspected, or afterward, when pressure from the rest of the world makes it impossible to continue. Either way, the gene editing will stop."

"Forgive me for prying, but could you tell me why Ting left without Mingyu? She never told me."

"Still too painful for her to talk about." Lim looked tense as he took a swig of water. "Ting was held captive at Fengshou. She lived in an apartment with her children. It was nice there. The children were happy. They were allowed to play and run around in the training facility. But she desperately wanted to be free and didn't want to be forced to have another genetically engineered child.

"The people in charge had no interest in Wang Shu. She wasn't designed to be an athlete. They only intended to study her to determine the feasibility of gene editing in general, while they perfected the hemoglobin gene changes. These people, on the other hand, were very interested in Kang. Ting was a world-class runner, and so was his biological father, Peng Yang. He is the head of this whole operation—a monster with ambition to be a top Communist Party leader.

"At the age of three-and-a-half, children destined to be athletes in this program are removed from their mothers to begin training. Their days are long and hard. They get certain privileges, yet in many ways, are treated like animals, their only use being their athletic abilities, which are maximized by the training program. Ting decided she needed to leave with her children before Kang was taken from her."

"I can understand why she was determined to get Kang out even if it meant leaving Mingyu behind."

"She never intended to leave him behind. In China, lots of people in the government can be bribed. Much more than in your country. The government is trying to crack down on that, although not too hard. I bribed a woman in charge of watching over Ting. The plan was for her to pretend Ting hit her in the head with a brick. Then Ting would run away with her children, through a hole in the fence. I would be waiting at the bottom of a hill on a motorcycle and take them all away."

"What happened?"

"The woman double-crossed us. She told Ting where to take the children, to the top of a steep hill where they could go through a hole in the fence. She promised to hit herself with a brick and pretend to be knocked out. Unfortunately, when Ting and her kids got through the fence, Peng was waiting. He told Ting to go ahead and leave with Wang Shu, but he would keep Kang and Mingyu. Ting refused to leave without all her children. He grabbed Kang and Mingyu and pushed Ting and Wang Shu down the hill. He told her she was an enemy of the republic, and if she didn't leave, she and Wang Shu would be arrested. She tried to climb back up the hill holding onto Wang Shu, but kept sliding farther to the bottom. Finally, she gave up and ran down the hill where I was waiting on my motorcycle.

"Miraculously, when she was close to me, Kang kicked Peng hard, and broke free. Being a small boy, he slid and somersaulted down the hill. Peng went after him, but being much larger and carrying a baby, there was no catching up. Kang reached us shortly after Ting and Wang Shu were on the motorcycle. I grabbed him and took off. Like, you say, 'a bat out of hell.' Ting was devastated leaving Mingyu behind even though she had no choice. At least she had Kang, who she had almost lost. That helped."

As I listened, I was transfixed by this story of motherly love and desperation. "That's an amazing story. How did she leave the country?"

"Ting came to the United States on a cargo ship that left from Hong Kong. For a price, they'll take anyone to a port on their route. It took a month before she landed in Oakland, where Ebba met her and helped her get settled. No border crossing. No wall, nothing."

"Ting is lucky to have Ebba's help."

"Ebba and Ting go way back. Ebba was a Norwegian Olympian and won a bronze and a silver in track. In the eighties, I think. Later, she came to China to coach and took Ting under her wing. She was like a mother to her, since our parents couldn't come to see us.

"After my sister was kidnapped, I was allowed to visit her occasionally. People at the facility told me all about the wonderful new program Peng was overseeing. I was told to convince Ting to cooperate. Of course, I was horrified, as was Ting. Instead of trying to talk her into participating, together we tried to think of ways she could escape.

"Soon afterwards, I told Ebba everything. She was furious. When it was clear she couldn't exert any influence over the program, she left the country and settled in San Francisco. I continued to work on a plan to help Ting escape. As you can see, it took me over five years. During that time, I became more involved in anti-government activities. I'm constantly harassed and followed."

"Why haven't you been arrested?"

"The only reason, I believe, is because the government thinks that by following me, they will find other anti-government people. Or maybe Peng thinks that by leaving me free, Ting will forgive him and come back to him. I don't really know. I'm on borrowed time. They could choose to arrest me at any moment."

"From what you've told me today, I'm sure Ting will never want to be with Peng."

"Never in a million years. Now for the plan."

CHAPTER 19

"There are two separate goals," Lim began. "The first, getting Mingyu, will be up to Daisy. The second, getting scientific information and direct evidence of the gene-editing program, will be up to you."

"I imagine there is a lot of security around the site."

"You're right. Lots."

"How will we get in?"

"I am making arrangements with a woman I know, a party member who works here in Beijing. She coordinates all the visitations and thinks I work in construction. I got to know her after saving her life when she was attacked by a robber one evening."

"You're very brave."

"Not really," Lim chuckled. "The robber is a good friend of mine. We had it arranged ahead of time because I knew I would need this woman's help."

"So, you pretended to save her life, and now she does whatever you want?"

"It's not quite that easy," Lim said, smiling. "After bravely fending off my robber friend, I did her favors like get groceries, change light bulbs. Then, when the time was right, I did what a lot of people here in China do to get something done."

"What's that?"

"I bribed her. Said I was doing a favor for my brother, a low-level government worker who thought helping these people could help him in the future."

"That sounds risky. What if she refused the bribe?"

"Well, she didn't. Like I mentioned before, bribery in China is quite common. I never asked her to do anything until now, when I asked her to arrange passes and tours for two important visitors to the center. One will be Daisy. Using the name Daiyu Li, she will pretend to inspect the housing of the mothers and children. You will be the other. Your name will be Nasim Malik, and you'll be there to inspect the research and medical facility. I promised my communist friend none of these visitors will be any trouble. They only want to learn more than their colleagues so they can get the most prestigious positions in their respective areas. I told her that due to time constraints, I will accompany both to Xi'an together, so they should visit Fengshou on the same day. To avoid suspicion, they need to arrive separately in Chengdu, the closest city to the facility. From there, they can be picked up by car and driven to Fengshou. With the money this lady is getting, she'll be able to buy an iPhone for her son and new furniture for her apartment. She is quite happy."

"Can you afford that?"

"I can get what I need for what's important."

"Are you confident you can trust her?"

"I have bribed her to do several sensitive things in the past. I know this type. Money is the most important thing to her. I can count on her."

"What if she gets caught?"

"So far, she's been very clever at covering her tracks. She told me it should be no problem for her to get the passes I requested. She's already working on it."

"What if they find out what she did later?"

"If the two of you have completed your mission, it doesn't matter to me. If she's caught, she'll go to prison. That's the risk she's taking. Believe me, she's doing this only out of greed. She's done some terrible things in the past to get ahead, so I won't feel sorry for her."

"Tell me about Nasim Malik."

"She has a medical degree and a PhD in genetics. She's on the faculty at Aga Khan University in Karachi. While Daisy is busy rescuing Mingyu, you will be given a tour of the facility by doctors and scientists to help you start a gene-editing center in Pakistan. I wouldn't be surprised if Peng wants to meet you. He is proud of the program and enjoys bragging about being the director of the whole facility."

"He sounds like a creep."

"As you would say in America, that's an insult to creeps. They'll probably tell you about the more legitimate work they are doing, like trying to eliminate thalassemia and abnormal blood clotting conditions. While they may be reckless with their gene editing for these disorders, those goals are at least understandable. But gene editing to produce super athletes by introducing a new type of hemoglobin and increasing muscle mass are not noble goals. They are the goals of a cheater."

"Do you think they'll tell me about that?"

"I imagine they'll want to keep it a secret, even from a friendly colleague. Ask all the questions you can. See if you can get someone to talk about it. Take all the videos and photographs you can. I imagine they will say a lot in Chinese that will be interesting to review later. Also, pictures of signs leading into labs will be helpful. I'm not a scientist, so I can't tell you all the things you need to explore. But the more you can document how they procure the eggs, fertilize them, perform the gene editing, and implant the embryos, the better. Where the women give birth, where the newborns stay. Whatever you can find out."

"What's the physical layout of the facility like?"

"The grounds are huge, with a large medical building comprised of several wings. There they do all the research and gene editing, perform the medical procedures, and deliver the babies. The mothers and babies are kept there a week after birth and monitored closely before being discharged.

"The housing complex is also big with apartments for thirty-five women and their children. There is a dining hall where everyone eats, a school for young children, and an exercise area, including a gym. Facilities for older children are currently under construction."

"How far are the living facilities from the medical buildings?"

"A quarter of a mile. It's a hilly terrain, so people get around on small vehicles like your golf carts."

"I suppose we won't be allowed to walk around on our own."

"Right. Both of you will always be escorted"

"Once Daisy gets into the living quarters, how's she going to find Mingyu and get him out?"

"I have someone on my payroll working at the reception desk. Her name is Min. She will help each of you. She'll find out where Mingyu is and let Daisy know. Then it will be up to Daisy to direct her tour to where he is."

"As if getting to him isn't hard enough, how is she going to sneak him out of there?"

"I hope your friend has a strong back."

"What do you mean?"

"My colleagues and I have given this a lot of thought. The facility is surrounded by a tall chain-link fence with barbed wire on top. I don't think it would be safe for her to climb it carrying a baby."

"I don't think she could climb it even without a baby."

"In our plan, she will leave with the baby through the main gate, in a car."

"That would be desirable for sure. But how?"

"You can get almost anything on Alibaba. We ordered a fake belly for her."

"Fake belly? What's that?"

"It's a prosthetic, made of soft silicone. When you put it on it looks like you have a big belly. Like you're pregnant. Even I would look pregnant if I wore one."

"Oh," I laughed. "They use those in movies. You want her to pretend to be pregnant?" I still didn't understand.

"Yes. We ordered the biggest belly they have. Looks like nine months. We hollowed it out so when she puts it on, she can fit a doll inside. A doll the size of a five-month-old baby, the same age Mingyu is now."

"She's going to smuggle in a doll for Mingyu to play with?"

"No," Lim laughed. "When she finds Mingyu, she'll have to get rid of her escort."

"How?"

"She'll pretend to collect data to compare with normal children. It's what you call 'B.S.' She'll explain that she needs to do a few simple neurological tests on Mingyu and listen to his heart. Then she'll ask her escort to leave the room so she can have total quiet. The escort will probably be bored, and happy to leave. That's when Daisy will take the baby doll from her fake belly and exchange it for Mingyu."

I'm sure I looked startled. That seemed crazy. "She's going to put the real baby, Mingyu, under the fake belly?"

"Yes. And wrap the doll up so it looks like Mingyu, sleeping. She needs something to sedate Mingyu. You can advise us on that. He'll be heavy, so she will need to practice carrying around the extra weight. Mingyu may get a little hot, but not dangerously so, and he'll be able to breathe through ports I've put in the belly. Once he's in place, Daisy will tell her escort she is feeling ill and needs to be driven back to Chengdu right away. The drive will be less than an hour."

"That's much too long. She needs to get someplace within fifteen minutes, tops, where she can take the baby out."

"Okay. She can say she has a relative she wants to visit in the nearby countryside. We'll work on arranging that."

"Daisy'll need to practice wearing that thing and positioning the doll and baby underneath."

"I will bring her everything she needs when you two are in Xi'an. I have a friend there with a baby girl. She's a little bigger than Mingyu probably is. If Daisy can manage carrying her under the fake belly, she can manage Mingyu."

By the time Lim finished describing the plan, I believed it just might work. I was exhausted from the tension I'd felt, imagining Daisy and I negotiating all those steps. "That's quite a plan," I said.

"We'll go over everything in more detail in Xi'an. This will be our only chance to save Mingyu and expose the program. Other than possibly saving all of humanity from something awful, you should feel no pressure." Lim smiled.

"Right. No pressure at all."

CHAPTER 20

After our meeting, which lasted over four hours, Lim walked me back to the hotel. To within a few blocks, anyway. He told me his face was well known by the government, and although he wore a hat and sunglasses, he didn't want to push his luck and be identified with me. That would put the whole operation in danger. He told me not to say goodbye, but to keep walking when the top of my hotel came into view. He would see us next in Xi'an to deliver our fake passports and the baby bump. I planned to spend a quiet evening alone in my hotel room reviewing the plans, researching genetic diseases in China and Pakistan, and learning more about Karachi and the medical school I was supposed to be working at.

Around 8:00 p.m., I received a message on my WeChat app from 'Marty.' Ting had me enter that contact before I'd left. I knew it was Lim.

Marty: Sorry I left you to be bored in your room. Would you like to meet for dim sum?

I assumed his wife was out of town, or busy. Perhaps she was involved with other operations going on in the organization. Lim seemed like the kind of guy who would know a lot of people he could hang out with. Maybe he wanted to get to know me better, to be sure I was trustworthy, despite his sister's assurances. I would give him that opportunity.

Erica: If you have time, I wouldn't mind leaving my hotel to have some dim sum since Daisy isn't here.

Marty: Take DiDi or a cab to Wangfujing West Street and Old Beijing Folk Custom Street. I'll meet you there and take you the rest of the way.

Erica: I'll leave soon. Make that a half hour.

I checked myself in the mirror. I could have used advanced notice. I looked like shit. Not that it mattered. But still, I had my pride. After a quick shower, I dressed and ran a comb through my wet hair.

I grabbed my coat and purse, locked the door and went downstairs to hail a cab. Ebba had told me about DiDi, the Uber-like service popular in China, but now wasn't the time to download the app and figure out how it works. The ride to the intersection took fifteen minutes.

No sooner had the cab stopped than Lim appeared out of the darkness. "Glad you made it," he said. His hair, black, straight, and two to three inches long, was messed up just enough to be sexy. Despite his large, thick black glasses, which I assumed were fake, he looked quite handsome.

"Glad to be here," I said. "I was climbing the walls in my hotel room."

Lim looked confused. "Climbing walls? How . . .?"

I laughed. "That's an American expression. Climbing the walls. It means someone is very bored."

"You Americans. Full of surprises. You want to do Karaoke instead of going for dim sum?"

"I'd prefer dim sum. I'm not known for my singing abilities. I might be arrested for being an enemy of the people."

Lim laughed. Sense of humor. Too bad he's already taken. He saw me shivering in the cold despite wearing my coat. "Sorry, you must be cold. Maybe I can warm you up a bit."

He placed an arm around my shoulders and my heart, probably lungs, too, melted. I felt warm and safe. He was only being considerate, knowing I was cold. But it felt good. I wondered what his wife was like.

"There's a place I like to go for tea and dim sum not too far away."

"That sounds wonderful."

"It's not fancy. It's not even nice," he said apologetically. "But there won't be tourists, and it will be quiet. Only local people go there."

"I'd love that. I try to avoid places that cater to tourists. I want to see where the locals go."

Lim smiled and led the way down several darkened streets with few pedestrians. We wound up on a well-lit narrow street, and he led me into a small restaurant where most of the tables were empty. Much of the furniture was scratched and the paint on the walls was peeling in several places. He smiled, waved at the person wearing a dirty white apron standing near the back, and steered me to a table by a window. Once we were seated, Lim removed his jacket. His shirt was short-sleeved, revealing his muscular arms.

"That's the owner. I know him," Lim said. "I come here all the time. Sorry it's so shabby."

"I like this place,' I said, trying to sound sincere. "Honestly. It looks fine."

The owner came by and Lim spoke to him in Chinese. As he left the room through a set of swinging doors, Lim and I began to talk. I learned that Lim lived several miles away. He couldn't find work, being someone with a low social score. Having never heard of the social score, Lim explained the government's system for rating people's trustworthiness, based on information gleaned from various sources. Those not loyal to the Communist Party had low scores. Lim's unsatisfactory rating precluded him from many things, including getting credit, purchasing a plane ticket, and landing a job, although he was a skilled computer programmer. Not once did he mention his wife. He probably thought talking about her would bore me.

I told Lim how I loved being a pediatrician but had recently resigned my position so I could take this trip. I had no job to return to but was confident I could find another when I was ready.

Sometime during our conversation, the owner delivered tea and dim sum to our table. Lim poured tea, and we sipped while we spoke. I struggled to eat one of the dumplings without making a mess, but failed miserably. Lim smiled, and told me to poke through them, rather than try to grab the slippery things. That worked. I asked him what his plans were after we rescued his nephew. He became quiet, looking around to be sure no one was listening.

"I have been doing important work here, work I am dedicated to. But my family, my sister and two of her children, are in America. Soon, if all goes well, all of her children will be there. I haven't told you yet about how I plan to get Mingyu to her."

Despite all the planning, that detail had not been described. "I'm all ears," I said.

"Ears? You are only ears? I don't understand." Lim looked upset.

"Sorry, another American expression. It means 'I'm ready to listen.'"

"Good. I thought maybe you had a terrible disease," Lim said, then laughed. His expression turned serious, and he added, "I plan to take my nephew to his mother myself. On a cargo ship to Oakland, California."

"Are you planning to stay? Stay in the United States?"

"That is my wish. By the time we arrive in Oakland, you and Daisy will have turned the evidence over to your government. All of us—me, Ting, Wang Shu, Kang, and Mingyu—will apply for political asylum. I hope the government will accept our application. It all depends on the proof you and Daisy get."

My mission seemed all that much more critical. Not only was I responsible for potentially saving humanity, but I need to do whatever I could to make sure Lim and his family were granted asylum.

Until now, I hadn't thought much about how to handle the information we were going to gather. We would need to get it to the US government in such a way they would see how important it was. Perhaps it would be best to work through the FBI. Or would the CIA be better? My senator or congresswoman? I'd discuss it with Daisy. We needed to seem credible. Each step of our mission was important, and this last step was no less so.

After we left the restaurant, Lim walked me to a busy street and hailed a cab. He spoke to the driver in Chinese. "I'll see you in Xi'an," he said before he closed the cab door.

On the ride back to my hotel, I reflected on our conversation. He still hadn't mentioned his wife. Was he planning to take her to the US?

CHAPTER 21

Too wound up to sleep—I couldn't tell if I was nervous, excited, or what—I lay in bed imagining what success would look like. Mingyu would be reunited with his mother. The Chinese gene-editing program would be exposed. World opinion would be swift. The production of super athletes would stop, although it would be hard to verify. The Chinese government might blame rogue scientists for the whole thing, might even claim their experiments were for the good of humanity, but most likely their Olympic team would be banned, for how long I didn't know.

I'd read that WADA, the World Anti-Doping Agency initiated by the Olympics, was aware of the potential for gene editing being used to enhance athletic performance, but they were unprepared for what China was doing. They had discussed looking for changes in genes over time, in case an athlete underwent genetic modification after they started competing. In no way could this pick up embryonic stem cell gene editing in which the changes would be present before the first sample was taken. To detect embryonic gene editing, they'd need to set up a new level of testing to look for unusual genes or genetic differences between athletes and their biological parents. The real purpose of the Chinese program, Olympic domination, would no longer be tenable once such testing was in place. But that was a long way out.

Meanwhile, Ting, her children, Lim, and probably his wife would be granted asylum with permanent US residency, possibly citizenship, down the road. I would . . . I think that's when I fell asleep. When I woke, I needed to plan the rest of my day. Daisy was due to return that afternoon in time for us to catch the overnight train to Xi'an. I ordered breakfast in my room and began packing. Daisy had already packed her suitcase, arranging her clothes in such a way she could easily shove her small overnight bag into the larger suitcase. I needed to check out by noon to avoid an extra day's charge. Once my suitcase was zippered shut, I glanced at my watch. 11:15 a.m. I had another forty-five minutes to enjoy the quiet of my room and think.

I concentrated on remembering all the things I'd learned about Karachi, Aga Khan Medical School, and the gene editing questions I needed to ask. I wondered where Lim would be staying in Xi'an. With a buddy? On a park bench? Where did homeless people stay in China? I worried Lim might be picked up by the Chinese police if he were without a place to stay. I knew I was being irrational—he'd been around the block a few times and surely had street smarts.

At noon, I was in the hotel lobby settling our bill and checking our bags with the bellhop for holding until Daisy returned. I sat in a lobby chair and waited, reading about global warming on my Kindle. I didn't want to focus all my anxiety for the future only on gene editing. Lost in a description of the politics surrounding the best ways to approach atmospheric methane and carbon dioxide levels, I was jolted from my book by a familiar voice.

"If it isn't my favorite bookworm."

I looked up to see Daisy smiling at me. "Glad you made it back," I said. "I haven't spoken to a soul in hours. You'll have to tell me all about your trip."

"It was interesting."

"Not sure what that means."

"I think you have to bow down to me or something now. I found out I'm a direct descendant of the Ming dynasty."

"Really?"

"No. But feel free to bow down anyway."

"Not likely."

"These cousins of mine seem to hate each other. One, Changpu, is a member of the Communist Party. So is his wife. The other, Lan, I'd say is not a supporter of communism."

"That does sound interesting."

"It's a good thing I never mentioned anything about our mission. If I had, my commie cousin and his wife would probably have me thrown in prison."

"And sell your organs."

"That too."

"So why doesn't he have his sister arrested?"

"Good question. He probably suffers from a twinge of family loyalty. Anyway, it appears Lan is vocal about certain things but doesn't actually do anything subversive. Sometimes I couldn't understand everything they were saying. Their English isn't great. When they started going at it in Chinese, I was totally lost."

"Did you at least enjoy sharing family pictures with each other?"

"Yes, I could see how much their mother resembled my mom."

"Which cousin did you stay with last night?"

"Changpu, the commie. He has a much bigger apartment than his sister. There are real advantages to being a card-carrying Communist, I guess."

"Do you think they'll visit you? People here are allowed to go to the US now."

"Some are. I doubt if the commie is interested, but I'd bet Lan would like to. She probably wouldn't get the government to approve, though. I really like her. She never married, which considered a big embarrassment here, but she is happy being single. She's pretty and outgoing, so I'm sure she's single by choice. I'll bet a lot of men have been interested in her in the past. And now. She mentioned she's been seeing a man for several months. I picture her going through men like crazy, getting bored with them, then dumping them."

"Sounds like someone I know."

Daisy laughed. "That was the old me."

"Right. You've been with Brian all of four months now."

"Well, I'm not bored yet. Now tell me about your meeting with Ting's brother. You should have lots to tell me. Does he have everything worked out?"

"Almost, but there are still aspects that need to be fine-tuned. Tomorrow we have a tour of the terra cotta soldiers. Lim will come to our hotel afterwards so we can start going over the details. He also needs to bring us a few things. Like our passports, and your fake belly."

"My *what?*"

"You heard me. Your fake belly. You're going to pretend to be pregnant—very pregnant. You'll wear a large faux baby bump made of silicone. On the way in, you'll hide a baby doll under it, and on the way out, you'll hide the real baby."

"Holy shit. How am I going to do that?"

"That's what we'll talk about tomorrow. It's probably going to take some practice."

"Gee, I forgot to bring my maternity clothes with me."

"Hopefully Lim has that covered."

"Well, I look forward to meeting him tomorrow night."

I checked my watch. "Hey, we better get our bags and head out to the train station. I'll fill you in on everything once we're on the train."

We retrieved our bags from the bellhop, flagged a taxi, and made it to the station with time to spare. We boarded the sleeper car for the thirteen-hour trip to Xi'an. Plenty of time to talk about Lim and his plan, and get some sleep before we'd arrive at our destination.

CHAPTER 22

We arrived in Xi'an the next morning, fairly well rested. Daisy now knew as much as I did about Lim, our plans, and the reason Ting had arrived in the US without Mingyu. The first thing I noticed stepping out of the train terminal was the oppressive air pollution, even worse than in Beijing. The air was brown with toxins and microscopic bits of fly ash from coal-burning plants and other industries. Almost half the people were wearing protective masks to filter out airborne particles.

We hailed a cab and went to our hotel. Daisy registered for the room, and we took our luggage there. The living area was spacious, with a comfortable couch, two stuffed chairs, a table to eat at, a Nespresso maker, and a desk. The bedroom was equally roomy, with two queen beds. I unwrapped one of the round soaps in the bathroom, appreciating the perfumed scent, and washed my face. We ate an early lunch at a nearby hole-in-the-wall, and at 12:30 p.m. returned to the hotel lobby to meet our guide for the afternoon, a young man around thirty years old. He had a cough, probably from breathing in the foulest air on the planet day after day.

After picking up an American couple at another hotel, our escort drove us to the terra cotta army, a collection of thousands of life-size soldiers, hundreds of horses, and chariots, all made from clay in the latter part of the third century BC. Presumably buried to protect the tomb of emperor Qin Shi Huang, they are considered the eighth wonder of the world. Even at age thirteen, Qin saw the need to plan ahead, starting the construction of the warriors and mausoleum following several attempted assassinations. The project continued until he ultimately died at age forty-nine, probably from poisoning. Shows that if people keep trying to kill you, someone will eventually get the job done. I hoped we would succeed in our mission so people would stop trying to kill Kang.

The enormity of the exhibition was spellbinding and took my mind off our future challenge for several hours. When we were dropped off at our hotel around 4:30 p.m., the reality of the hard work ahead hit me. The fun part was over. Was I up to the task? Would I disappoint Lim and Ting? Would I wind up in a Chinese prison?

Daisy and I plugged in all our electronic devices. At 6:00 p.m. Lim sent me a WeChat message. He was waiting in the lobby, so I went down to greet him. At first, I didn't recognize him in his floppy hat and sunglasses. He was carrying two bags, the smaller one smelling of food. Chinese.

"Everything starts in forty hours. We have a lot to do to prepare," he said, "so I brought dinner."

"Nice," I said. "I'm sure Daisy will appreciate it."

On the elevator ride to our room, Lim told me that from now until we left, Daisy and I should stay inside the hotel. If anything out of the ordinary happened, such as getting hit by a car, or being witness to a street crime, our mission could be compromised. He'd get us food and whatever else we might need.

"What if something happens to you?" I asked.

"Don't worry about me. I know my way around much better than the two of you."

Once we reached my room, I introduced Daisy to Lim. We sat around the coffee table, Daisy on a stuffed chair, Lim and I sharing the couch. Lim removed his hat and sunglasses. When he ruffled his hair, now free from under the unattractive hat, I practically swooned. *Get a hold of yourself, girl. He's unavailable. Good thing, too. Being on the verge of a dangerous mission in a foreign country, is not the time and place to start something with a guy you need to rely on, you barely know, is from a different culture, and is probably a jerk. No matter how good looking he is.*

After minimal small talk, Lim began going over important details of the operation. "First, you must both travel to Chengdu, the city closest to Fengshou. It's almost seven hundred fifty kilometers from here. Once you leave this hotel the day after tomorrow, you won't be able to contact each other until after you've completed your mission and left the facility."

Daisy and I glanced at each other. "That's going to be pretty scary," I said.

"I know, but it's necessary. There can't be any indication that your visits are related." He turned to Daisy. "Daisy, you'll take the high-speed rail."

"How long will that take?" Daisy asked.

"Four-and-a-half-hours. Women aren't allowed on planes in late pregnancy, but the railroad won't be a problem. You'll arrive shortly before noon." Lim turned to me. "Erica, your trip will be shorter. You'll fly to Chengdu. That'll take approximately two hours, and you'll get there around 11:15 a.m., so you'll arrive before Daisy. You'll leave the facility after her, because your visit will take longer." Speaking to both of us, he continued. "You'll be picked up separately by drivers from the center. You both need to reserve flights from Chengdu to Shanghai for later that day, using your real names. Daisy, you should leave in the late afternoon, and Erica, you should leave around six that evening. That should give you both enough time to reach the airport after your visit to Fengshou. Arrange to fly home from Shanghai on the earliest flights possible after you land there. Now, before I go on, anyone hungry? We should eat before the food gets cold."

"No time like the present," I said. As Lim carried the food to the table with his back toward us, Daisy mouthed the word "gorgeous" to me and giggled.

"Something funny?" Lim asked, turning around.

"I think we're a little overtired," Daisy said. "Don't worry, we weren't laughing at you."

Over duck, noodle, and vegetable dishes I didn't recognize, Daisy and I described our overnight train ride and tour of the terra cotta army.

When we were done, we filled the trash can with the food cartons. I wiped the table clean, made three cups of Nespresso, and we got down to business.

Lim brought over his large bag and reached inside.

"Here are your fake passports. Keep them in a safe place, away from the real ones. You can't afford to get them mixed up. When you enter the facility, they will check your passport. Be sure to give them the fake one. Security is very tight." He turned to Daisy. "I already told Erica that one of the women who will register you at the reception desk, Min, is on our payroll. She will assure everything goes smoothly, and she'll let you know where Mingyu is located by slipping you a note."

"What if she doesn't?"

"She's depending on the money she'll get from me for her son's tuition. She won't back out."

"But what if—?"

"You Americans don't understand the importance of bribe money. We rely on it very much here. Don't worry, if Min doesn't give you Mingyu's location, you can ask your escort to see all the infants around five months of age. There won't be many. If they don't take you to Mingyu right away, think of a reason you need to see a different baby. Even if they don't tell you the infants' names, look for a one-centimeter brown birthmark on his lower right back. And here," he said, removing a picture from his wallet. "Here's a picture of Mingyu when he was three months old. Study it now. Give it back to me before you leave for the train. The day of your visit, some of the workers, especially the younger ones, will be a bit distracted. I scheduled your visit for November 10 on purpose. The next day is November 11, or 11/11, Singles Day."

"That doesn't sound like a very exciting day," I said. "Not that there's anything wrong with being single."

Lim laughed. "It's not really about being single anymore. Now it's the biggest shopping day in China. So many discounts. People go crazy, especially the younger ones. They're very interested in all the latest fashions and gadgets. Things they can't afford. On Singles Day, they can buy things for much less. I'm not sure they can afford what they buy even at a discount, but they buy it anyway."

"I've never heard of it before," I said.

"Now I understand," Daisy said. "My cousin, Lan, mentioned getting a piece of jewelry she likes on Singles Day. I thought she was telling me the jewelry was for single people, but it came out wrong because her English is so bad."

"Yes. Many people are very excited to shop on this one day. For days before, they look at all the cheap prices and make a list of what they want to buy. So, when 11/11 finally comes around, they are ready to shop. The day before is when everyone is very focused on searching for deals. It's a good day to visit the facility. If something is a little unusual, the clerks and guards will be more likely to ignore it."

"Every little bit helps," I said.

"One of the trickiest parts of the mission," Lim said, "will be getting Mingyu out." Lim pulled a tan rubbery item from his bag, a semi-rigid elongated dome shaped roughly like half an egg. Shoulder straps were attached at the narrow end, while bands on the sides had Velcro ends for connecting behind the back of the wearer. Daisy and I looked at the contraption, then at each other, and started to laugh.

"I have to wear *that*?" Daisy asked.

"Come on, Daisy. You can't back out now," I said. "You won't have to wear it for long. Not even close to nine months."

"I know, I know. It's just that seeing it is different than imagining it. This isn't what I thought I was signing up for a few months ago." She paused. "But I'm all in."

"Good," Lim said. "Here are maternity clothes to try on over it. You can try it on in the bedroom."

"Good idea," Daisy answered.

Lim and I talked about the layout of the facility as Daisy was trying on her prosthesis in the next room.

Several minutes later, Daisy re-entered the living room, announcing her arrival with a loud "Ta-Da!" She looked unmistakably pregnant in a white maternity blouse and black skirt. "How do I look?"

Lim and I both stared for a moment. "Looks like you're very knocked up," I said. "If I didn't know better, I'd say you have that glow." Daisy and I laughed.

"I don't understand your jokes," Lim said. "But it looks convincing. How does it feel? Can you walk around okay?"

Daisy commenced walking around the room, then skipping. "Seems fine," she said.

"Can't say I love your blouse," I said. "All those ruffles around the neck. It's not you. No offense, Lim, but I'm not sure about your taste in women's clothes. I do like the three buttons with the sparkly bling, though." I was talking about three buttons covered in rhinestones buried in the ruffles.

"I was thinking the same thing," Daisy said. "Buttons are pretty, but I'm not a ruffle person. Nevertheless, I'll wear this blouse for the cause."

"I'm glad you see the importance. Now put this under your belly," Lim said, pulling a life-size doll from his bag.

Daisy grabbed the doll, then disappeared into the bedroom for a few minutes. She returned, grinning. "Fits fine with room to spare."

"Great," Lim said. "The real test will be tomorrow. My friend will bring her six-month-old baby here. Then we can test the fake belly with a real baby."

"How did you get someone to agree to bring her baby to test this out?" I asked.

"She is someone in my organization. Someone I trust very much, who, like me, understands the evilness taking place in Fengshou and wants to see it stopped. I'm sure she'll be watching us closely to make sure no one hurts her baby. Now, Erica, I have to ask you about sedating Mingyu safely. What should we use?"

"Good question," I said. "I don't recommend sedating babies—"

"I understand," Lim interrupted. "But it's necessary. If he isn't sedated, Daisy will never get him out, and Ting won't ever see him again. He will be treated harshly. Forced to train all the time even if he hates it."

"Okay, I understand. I'd say your best bet is Versed. It takes at least fifteen minutes to kick in, though. Can you get it?"

"I know a nurse who will get me whatever I want from a local hospital if I can't buy it in a pharmacy."

"Someone you can bribe?" I asked.

"Yes. She is very greedy."

"How do you get all this money for bribes?"

"Our organization has ways of getting what we need."

"You steal it?" I asked. I understood the need for money to defy the government but wasn't comfortable working with a criminal, even if it was for a good cause.

"No stealing is involved," Lim said. "Now, I'd like to see your camera devices. It's important to get pictures and video. Without that, even if they do DNA testing on Ting's children, people won't be convinced that their strange DNA is a result of experiments done at Fengshou."

"I understand," I said. "People didn't believe stories of the Holocaust when people escaped and talked about it. Not until the Allies liberated the first concentration camps and people could see what was happening with their own eyes."

We showed Lim where all our devices were charging on the kitchenette counter.

"You can change back into your normal clothes now," Lim said to Daisy as he looked over the equipment.

Daisy withdrew to the bedroom for a short while. I had barely enough time to tell Lim we'd practiced with our recording devices for hours back home, before Daisy returned carrying her belly, maternity skirt, and blouse.

"Now, let me show you something on your ugly blouse," Lim said to Daisy.

Daisy placed the garment in Lim's outstretched arm. "See here," he said, pointing to the sparkly buttons, "these are add-ons."

"Well, they're an improvement," Daisy said. "But you didn't have to go to all that trouble to make the blouse look better."

I nodded in agreement.

"My apologies, but the buttons weren't added to make you more stylish," Lim explained. "Two of the three buttons are spy cameras."

Daisy and I started laughing at the same time.

"No way," Daisy said, leaning over to inspect the blouse.

"Didn't you notice a little extra weight here?" Lim asked.

"Now that you mention it, I did. But I figured it was from all the ruffles and the backing sewn in for them."

"That backing has the electronics for the cameras. Look closely at the two top buttons. Each has a small central hole. That's where the cameras are. Those cameras come standard with plain black buttons. I consulted with someone having more fashion sense than me. She made the ruffles to complement the buttons. Then she painted the buttons white and covered them with rhinestones."

"Impressive," I said.

"Sorry if I offended you," Daisy said. "This is nothing short of brilliant."

"Each of these cameras can record for forty-five minutes. So, between them, you have an extra hour and a half of recording time. I have chargers for them. You'll need to practice, but you'll be able to operate them by pressing them precisely the right way. The cameras vibrate when you turn them on and off."

"I have an idea," Daisy said. "I can say I'm having indigestion and press the buttons, the way pregnant women often press above their bellies."

"I love it!" I said.

"It's important to video everything, not only the facility from the outside and the living quarters where Mingyu is staying. Try to video other children and their pregnant mothers You have enough recording time on your devices to leave several cameras on at once to capture everything around you. Now, this may be difficult." Lim's voice grew quieter. "I've heard there is a building where they keep their mistakes. It will be important to document that, if possible."

"Mistakes? This is the first I've heard they keep them someplace," I blurted out. I had assumed most so-called mistakes died right away or stayed with their mothers if they survived.

"Ting knows of stillbirths and some children with minor birth defects. There are rumors of others who survived with severe defects. They keep them together in one place while they study them and perform experiments on them. They refer to them as unfortunate experimental failures. I believe sometime in the future they will murder them. But that, to my knowledge, hasn't happened."

I was horrified and was sure Daisy was, too, from her expression.

"We absolutely must succeed," I said.

"This program can't be allowed to go on," Daisy added. "I think we're all in agreement about that. But I'm afraid all this tension has worn me out. I need to go to sleep soon, or I'll be no good tomorrow."

"No good?" Lim asked. "But I'm sure you are always good. Today, tomorrow, the next day."

Daisy and I laughed. "Another crazy American expression," I explained. "It means she'll be very tired. Not her best for getting things done."

"I understand now," Lim said. He turned to me. "How about you? Can you go over some more plans with me tonight?"

"I'm not tired so I can stay up a little longer. We can go to the lounge downstairs. I don't want to bother Daisy. She needs to get her sleep. Without it, she'll be a cranky bitch tomorrow."

"Bitch. Isn't that a dog?" Lim asked innocently.

"It's also a derogatory word for women. But amongst friends, it's okay. She knows I'm kidding. She knows I love her."

CHAPTER 23

Lim put on his hat and fake glasses before we exited the room. There were two other couples in the dimly lit lounge when we arrived. We sat as far from them as possible and ordered a pot of tea.

"You know a lot about my family," Lim said, "but I don't know anything about yours. Do you live with your parents?"

"My father died, but my mother's still alive. She lives several hundred miles from me. In the US, grown children don't live with their parents if they can afford not to."

"That must be hard, living so far from your mother."

"We talk on the phone a lot. I've been worried about her lately, though. She's become very forgetful. I need to look into that when I get back."

"There's nothing more important than family. That's why Ting and her kids are so important to me."

I sensed in Lim a deep concern for his sister and her family, a devotion to doing whatever he could for her. "Do you have siblings?" he asked.

"I had a brother. I was very close to him. He had cerebral palsy and was deaf. A few years ago, he was run over and killed by a car, so it's just me and Mom now. I'm glad I have Daisy, too."

"I am very sad for you, losing your father and your brother, and having to worry about your mother." Lim's sincere tone impressed me. He seemed so capable and determined in his cause, yet had a soft, gentle side. Our waitress served our tea and poured each of us a cup. "What you and Daisy are doing is very special," he continued. "I want you to know how much Ting and I appreciate this."

"Your sister's story was so compelling, how could I not?"

"Easy. I don't think many people would do what you're doing."

"I must admit, I'll be glad when this is over."

"I can't blame you for being nervous. I've tried to make the plan as safe as possible, but there are no guarantees. Something unforeseeable is always possible. If you or Daisy are caught, Ting and I will do whatever we can to make sure you can return home. If we go to prison, it will have been worth it. At least we tried."

"What about your wife? What does she think about you being involved in something so dangerous?"

"My wife?" Lim looked confused.

Great acting. He almost had me fooled, trying to show me his deep concern for humanity and the feelings of others, but now I saw right through him. I was certain he'd never considered her wishes. Probably enjoyed acting like he was single so he could hit on women. Must have forgotten to remove his ring.

"Yes, your wife. She can't be happy you're spending so much time organizing this and risking so much."

Lim continued to look at me with a puzzled expression, then broke out in laughter.

"I don't see what's so funny," I said curtly. I regretted bringing up his downtrodden wife, not wanting anything to interfere with our good working relationship at this point.

"You must have noticed my ring. I wear it because, well, now don't think I'm conceited, but sometimes I have problems with women. For some reason, they seem to like me, and get in the way of my work. I wear the ring so they leave me alone. It usually works. But the truth is, I'm not married."

I was glad the room was dark so he couldn't appreciate the look of surprise and relief I was sure showed on my face. I fully understood how women would be drawn to him, and he wanted to avoid any awkwardness by wearing a ring. On the other hand, he could be a total slimeball, lying about his marital status. Thinking about it another second, I figured that was most likely. I glanced at my watch. "It's later than I realized. I think I should go back upstairs."

I thought I detected a look of disappointment on his face, but it was hard to tell, the lighting being suboptimal.

Lim walked into the elevator with me.

"Where are you staying?" I asked.

"I'm sleeping on the floor of my friend's apartment."

"That doesn't sound very comfortable."

Lim chuckled. "It's better than sleeping behind a dumpster. I've had to do that many times."

"Do you travel around much?"

"I usually have to meet with people in other cities at least once a month. I've gotten used to sleeping on people's floors and city streets, out of sight from the chengguan, the government people who remove the homeless."

"That sounds like a hard life. No wonder you want to move to America."

"It was a difficult decision. I want to continue helping in the struggle against our government. But, like I said, I want to be with Ting and her children, my only family. I hope to help my friends here from afar."

When we reached my floor, Lim said, "Let me walk you to your room."

A short walk from the elevator, we reached the door to my room and stopped. There was an uncomfortable silence as I fished my room key card from my purse. I opened the door and looked back at him as I walked inside. He looked as anxious as I felt as he said, "Goodnight."

CHAPTER 24

I didn't sleep well. Daisy gently shook me and placed a cup of Nespresso on my night table.

"It's eight-thirty in the morning. Time to get up. Lim said he'd be here at nine. Or is he hiding under your covers?"

"Funny."

"The guy's a real dog. Don't think I haven't noticed how he looks at you, and how you look at him. I don't have to remind you that he's married, even if he never mentions his wife. Remember our vow."

"I know. 'Never mess with a married man.'"

"I'm glad you haven't forgotten. I was beginning to wonder."

"Maybe he's not married."

"Is that willful blindness talking? I saw the ring, girl."

"He said he wears it so he doesn't have to beat women off with a stick."

"I thought I'd heard everything. I never pictured you for someone so naïve."

"We can talk about this later. Right now, we need to get dressed."

I showered and dressed quickly, then combed my hair and touched up my face. I resisted wearing my killer red lipstick—didn't want to appear too obvious. Didn't want to be beaten with a stick. I checked myself in the mirror and was satisfied I looked pretty hot, but not too obvious. Seconds later there was a knock on our door.

I opened the door after checking the peephole, and smiled at Lim standing in the hallway, wearing a different, equally unattractive hat and glasses. He smiled back. I could tell he was glad to see me. There was chemistry going on, and the reaction was going in two directions.

I invited Lim inside and shut the door. He greeted Daisy and got down to business. "My friend Nuwa will be here soon with her daughter, Qiang. Practicing with her baby is crucial to getting Mingyu out. I am very grateful she is letting us try this out with Qiang. While we're waiting, let me remind you to record as much as you can. Even if it doesn't seem important at the moment. Also, I want you both to know that we now have someone working in the Fengshou cafeteria who is on our payroll. If something comes up, she'll get a message to you."

"How will we recognize her?"

"You won't need to. She'll find you if necessary."

"Can we get breakfast before we start?" Daisy asked, seeming almost panicked at the thought of tackling the difficult task ahead without morning sustenance.

"Nuwa will bring food for breakfast from McDonald's. You Americans like that, don't you?"

"Lots of us do, although we don't like to admit it," Daisy said. "Right now, I think I'd eat anything. I don't know about Erica. I hope she can eat what Nuwa brings. She's Jewish."

"Jewish? I didn't know," Lim said, his face turning slightly pink. "You don't eat pork?" Lim asked, turning to me.

"Well, I try to limit the amount I eat. I'm not really religious, but it's a tradition with my people to stay away from pork." I wanted to kill Daisy for introducing awkwardness at this time. I saw right through her—she was trying to emphasize our different cultures, make Lim think I was peculiar, someone to avoid.

"No problem," Lim said. "I live near a place where they hold Jewish services and have dinners on Friday. Sometimes I eat there when I have very little food. They are very nice to me. All the Jews I have met are good people."

Good answer. Take that, Daisy. "What about you, Lim?" I asked. "Do you have a religion?"

"My parents considered themselves Taoists, but they were never very observant. I suppose I consider myself affiliated with Taoism, but like you, I'm not religious." Lim's phone vibrated, and he checked for a message. "Nuwa and Qiang are in the lobby. I'll get them."

I dreaded Lim leaving me alone with Daisy. I knew she would interrogate me about my thoughts regarding Lim, tell me she'd noticed him looking at me in a non-platonic way, and warn me that I needed to understand he was married despite his denial. That's exactly what happened.

I was relieved when Lim returned shortly with Nuwa who was pushing her daughter in a stroller, a bag containing breakfast hanging from the frame. Lim put the "Do Not Disturb" sign on the outside door handle as Nuwa spread a pink blanket on the floor. Then she lifted Qiang who was holding a rattle in her chubby fist and placed her on the blanket. While the infant attempted to slither around, moving barely an inch with great effort, Nuwa kept an eye on her. For the most part, Qiang was quiet while we wolfed down breakfast. Nuwa's English was limited, but she was friendly and eager to help with our project.

When we were finished, Lim picked up Qiang and kissed her on the cheek. He said a few words to Nuwa in Chinese, and they both laughed. "The last time I saw her, she was only one month old," he said, turning to me. Holding the baby in one arm, he used the other to place the fake belly on top of the coffee table, concave side up. Next, he gently placed Qiang on her back inside the cavity. When she bent her legs toward her pudgy middle, we all saw she easily fit inside the bowl-like apparatus. After watching Qiang lie comfortably in the fake belly and wiggle her legs for a few seconds, Nuwa picked her up and held her.

"Mingyu is more than a month younger than Qiang," Lim said, "so he should have plenty of room. But this is just the first step." He picked up the belly and pointed to two holes. "Note these ports on either side here. They're one-way valves, one to let fresh air in, the other to let exhaled air out. They're placed below the fullest part of the belly so when the blouse hangs down straight, the fabric won't block them. When the baby is inside, it is important not to obstruct the vents with your arms.

Now, Daisy, please put this back on with the doll inside, so we can figure out how you're going to make the switch."

Daisy went back into the bedroom. When she returned, she again looked like a pregnant woman in her last trimester.

Then the real work began. Daisy struggled to remove the doll from her faux pregnant belly by reaching under the bottom of the contraption, feeling around for the legs, and trying to pull it out from under the silicone dome. The size of the belly made the procedure difficult. Impossible, actually.

"You need to use Velcro opening," Nuwa said. "Open the back to take doll out. Then put baby in, close Velcro again. Hard to do. Must practice."

"When I first put it on, I pulled the belly up from below with the Velcro already attached," Daisy said.

"Much easier to put on that way with nothing inside," Nuwa said. "I try it at home before Lim pick it up yesterday. Cannot put things in and take things out without opening back. Sorry."

Daisy opened the belly in the back under her blouse and tried to reattach the strips of Velcro, swearing under her breath. Twenty minutes and two broken nails later, she had mastered opening and closing the Velcro smoothly.

"Now you must practice securing the real baby under that," Lim said.

Nuwa reached into her bag and produced a cloth papoose. She handed it to Daisy. "Put this on. Adjust straps to be right height, so baby's butt a little above bottom of belly. Legs can fold up in front."

Daisy looked at the papoose in her hand and hesitated.

"Let's go into the bedroom," I said. "I'll adjust the straps so they're the right length."

In the bedroom, Daisy removed her blouse and the belly, then put on the papoose. After adjusting the straps, I invited Nuwa to bring in Qiang. Nuwa gently placed her daughter in the papoose, and Qiang started to cry.

"She okay. She not like strangers," Nuwa said.

Nuwa helped Daisy suspend the fake belly from her shoulders, then carefully positioned it over her baby, making sure it didn't press on the precious cargo inside. Holding the belly against Daisy's abdomen, she told Daisy to attach the Velcro. Grunting twice, Daisy succeeded in reaching back and attaching the Velcro strips tightly together. "Now let's see if I can do this all by myself," Daisy said. She opened the Velcro attachments, pushed the belly hanging from the shoulder straps away from her body, removed Qiang from the papoose, and handed her to Nuwa. "Now, here goes."

"I will time it," Nuwa said. She took a stopwatch from her pocket. "Go," she said, pressing the start button.

Nuwa and I watched in silence as Daisy took Qiang, placed her in the papoose, then attempted to cover her with the fake belly, and attach the Velcro. After two failures, and a few outbursts of crying from Qiang, Daisy was successful. Looking at her after she'd put on her maternity blouse, I was sure no one would ever suspect there was a six-month-old infant under there.

"Excellent. Seven minutes," Nuwa said. "Next time will be faster."

I walked back to the living room, expecting Daisy and Nuwa to follow me, but they lagged behind. I heard them speaking in low tones. *Dammit, Daisy.* I was sure she was pumping Nuwa for information about Lim's marital status. A minute later, Daisy and Nuwa entered the living room. "Seven minutes," Nuwa shouted to Lim.

"Very nice," Lim said. "If I didn't hear Qiang in there, I'd think you were pregnant."

"That won't be a problem after a dose of Versed," I added.

"This is damn heavy," Daisy said. "I don't know how far I can walk with all this weight."

"But you've been training with weights for this," I said.

"Yes, but only a few days. Pregnant ladies, remember, work up to this. It ain't easy." She waddled back to the bedroom to remove Qiang from the belly. Returning, she handed the baby to Nuwa.

"I get you back brace," Nuwa said. After putting Qiang in her stroller, she disappeared with the baby before anyone could argue.

"There's a store that sells medicines and medical supplies not too far from here," Lim said. "She should be back soon. That's where I got this Versed." He pulled a small box from the back pocket of his pants.

"You need to tell me how to give this to Mingyu," Daisy said. "Let me see the box."

"Good luck," Lim said, handing it to her.

Daisy stared at the Versed packaging a few seconds before remarking, "I don't understand this at all. Might as well be written in Chinese."

Lim took the box from her.

"It would help if you told me what the concentration is, in English," I said.

Lim studied the writing on the packaging. "Looks like two milligrams per milliliter."

"Just like the US." Lim handed me the box and I opened it. "Great. There's a syringe for dispensing it."

Not knowing exactly how much Mingyu weighed, I wanted to err on the low side since the medicine can be dangerous without medical supervision. I opened the bottle and showed Daisy how to fill the syringe with the right amount of Versed syrup.

"Give him one point five milliliters," I instructed her. "Drip it inside his mouth, on his cheek, so he can't spit it out. It will take fifteen minutes to kick in. Maybe more. Here, you try measuring it."

Daisy took the syringe and bottle and measured out one and a half milliliters, then slowly dripped the medicine back in the bottle.

"We're not going to give Qiang the medicine," Lim said, "so you'll have to get it right on the first try. But you can give her an equivalent dose of milk for practice."

Nuwa returned with a back brace which Daisy tried on with the baby under the bump. "Much better," she said. She would have to remove it before opening the faux belly, then replace it after Mingyu was safely in place. She practiced this several times and found it to be fairly easy. Following that, Daisy removed the fake belly, took the baby out of the papoose, and practiced giving her 1.5 milliliters of milk Nuwa had in a bottle.

"I've written this all out for you, Daisy," Lim said. "Study this and remember every detail."

"I think I've got everything straight in my head already. They think I'm interested in how they house the children. I find out where Mingyu is from Min at the front desk. I tour the facility and take all the pictures and videos I can. I say I want to perform neurological tests and listen to the heart of a baby around five-months old after I've seen everything else. I get my escort to take me to Mingyu and check to be sure it's him. If it's not, I make up a reason why this baby isn't appropriate, like he looks too tired, not tired enough, too small, or too big. I tell her I need quiet, so she should wait outside. I give him one point five milliliters of Versed by syringe and slowly dispense it on the inside of his cheek. I take off the back brace, open the back of the belly, and take out the doll. I wait until Mingyu is sleepy, put him in the papoose I'm already wearing, and wrap the doll in Mingyu's blanket. Then I reattach the belly and back brace. When I'm done, I go outside, tell the escort I don't feel well, and must leave right away so I can lie down."

"Perfect," Lim said.

"Sure, if all goes well," Daisy said. "What if my escort comes into the room while I'm making the switch? What then?"

"Not likely. Fengshou recently hired a new childcare aid, who happens to be a member of our organization. She will be watching for you and will talk with your escort while you are alone with Mingyu. She won't leave until you come out and say it's time to go."

"How do you know you can trust her?"

"She is very motivated. Her father was murdered by the government in Tiananmen Square when she was five years old. She is a devoted member of our group, and I trust her completely. Min will arrange Mingyu's next feeding to be three hours later, so the switch won't be discovered until you're long gone. Tell your driver you are meeting a cousin from Chengdu near the Longchi National Forest Park to visit the Panda Breeding Research Center. I've arranged a reservation under your fake name at the Holiday Inn Express in Dujiangyan Ancient City. It's a fifteen or twenty-minute drive from the facility. That's the closest hotel I could find.

"Once you're in the car for the ride back, turn on your cell phone jamming device, in case they want to call your driver back for any reason. As an extra precaution, one of our members is now a gardener at Fengshou. He will be stationed near the front gate. After he sees each of you leave, he will move his truck to block the gate so if you are discovered more quickly than we anticipate, no one will be able to chase you until he drives his truck out of the way. He figures he can delay anyone going after you by ten minutes.

"Once you are in your room, remove Mingyu from the papoose and wait for me. It will only be a few minutes. I will be waiting outside the hotel, so I will see when you arrive."

"What about Erica? Will she be there?"

"She will not be done with her tour by then."

"What if Mingyu needs medical attention?"

"I doubt he will. But if he does, and you are still at the facility, have your escort get a Fengshou doctor. If you have already left, call this pediatrician." Lim handed Daisy a small piece of paper.

"Okay. Once I'm in the hotel room, Mingyu is safe, then what?"

"In three hours, someone will discover Mingyu is missing. You will be the prime suspect, and they will be looking for you, starting at the hotel where you were dropped off. We will need to leave right away for the airport.

"I will ship your luggage back to the US, except for the overnight backpack you take to Fengshou. Remember, they will be looking for Daiyu Li. They may have figured out you are not pregnant, but you will be wearing different clothes, no glasses. You will be hard to recognize. Have you ever ridden on a motorcycle?"

"Sure, when I was young, carefree, and wild."

"I will borrow a motorcycle to take you to the Chengdu airport." Lim turned to me. "Unless something happens during your tour, Erica, you will not arouse suspicion. To be safe, turn on your cell phone jammer, too, when you leave. Have your driver take you directly to Chengdu airport. I will be there helping Daisy get on her flight to Shanghai. After I am sure she is safely on her way, I will see you off on your later flight."

Turning to both of us, he said, "By the time the government figures out who you both really are, you should be safely back in the US, or at least on your way. But if either of you gets arrested before you leave the country, ask to speak to someone at the American Embassy and phone me right away. I will get you home safely. I can secure money for bribes. If that doesn't work, I am prepared to confess to a terrible crime. As a last resort, Ting will offer herself and Kang in return for your release. Assuming you make it back to San Francisco without incident, please update Ting. Tell her I have Mingyu and should get him to her as we planned."

It was four in the afternoon, and we had our plan. Nuwa wished us luck and left with her baby. Daisy and I reserved our flights to Shanghai and back to San Francisco. There was nothing more left to do but wait. And fidget. And get nervous. After asking us what we'd like for dinner, Lim ordered our next meal on his phone.

"Dinner will be here in fifteen minutes," he said. "I don't want to risk anyone seeing our room, so I'll pick it up in the lobby."

"Let me pay for it," I said, aware of how frugally Lim lived. I figured I could afford the cost of dinner much more easily than he.

"Already paid for," he said. "It is simple here. Everyone orders and pays for meals with their phones. We have an excellent delivery system. Very fast. Do not worry about the cost. Like I told you, I have ways of getting what I need."

Soon, Lim received a text that our food was downstairs. While he went to retrieve it, I turned to Daisy. "I guess that damn male pride is at work in China, too. I wish he could admit he can't afford to feed us."

"I could have told you that male chauvinism is alive and well all around the world. Don't worry, though. I don't think it's a big problem with him. From what I can see, he's very considerate and respectful of you."

"I'm surprised to hear you defend him."

"Don't be mad, but I checked with Nuwa."

As if I didn't know.

"She assured me that Lim is, indeed, single. Broke up with his last girlfriend six months ago because she complained too much about his work. Has worn a wedding ring ever since. She spoke very highly of him."

"I forgive you. However, the situation here doesn't exactly allow us to explore our compatibility. Especially with his background being so different from mine."

Lim returned with our dinners. The food looked and smelled good. I didn't have much appetite but managed to finish my meal and expressed my appreciation to Lim for treating us to dinner.

After dinner, Lim left and Daisy and I went to bed. I wanted a good night's sleep so I'd be sharp the next day, but spent another restless night in bed. I must have fallen asleep because I remember the alarm clock waking me at 7:30 a.m.

We had a lot to do that morning. I dressed in a brown skirt and white blouse, Daisy in the maternity gear. After we took turns fixing each other's brows with the eyebrow pencil, we put on our fake glasses and placed our real passports in secure holders under our clothes, our counterfeit passports in our purses. Daisy packed her suitcase, leaving out a few clothes to put in her backpack. Lim came with breakfast from McDonald's at 8:15 a.m. but neither of us felt like eating.

Daisy left first to catch the high-speed rail train to Chengdu. I gave her a long hug before she exited the hotel room, laughing nervously when I jammed up against her false belly. Despite Lim's assurance, I didn't know if or when I would see her again. I wished her luck and hugged her again.

"I think I should call my mom now," I told Lim. "This will be the last time I'll be able to talk to her before returning home."

"You're a good daughter," Lim said. "I'm sure your mother appreciates that, even if her mind isn't what it used to be."

I picked up my cell phone and called. It was afternoon there, one day earlier. She had forgotten about my trip to China and complained that she'd started to read several books, but didn't like any of them. I worried that she simply couldn't understand what she was reading. The lady from Adult Protective Services was still visiting her, but Mom was convinced she'd stolen a pair of socks. After saying I hoped to see her soon, I disconnected the call.

"I can tell you are upset," Lim said. "Will you be okay?"

"Lately, all my conversations with my mom have been disturbing, but I don't have time to dwell on that now."

"You will be able to see her soon. Then you can arrange for her to have the best care." Lim put a comforting arm on my shoulder.

"Thanks," I said. "Now I need to get all my stuff together for my big day."

A half hour later, it was time for me to leave for the airport. I would be on my own now. Ever since I was a little kid and realized the first grade wasn't the scary place I'd built it up to be in my mind, I haven't been afraid of things. I never got nervous before tests in high school, college, or medical school. But I was scared now. So sick to my stomach, I went to the bathroom, thinking I was going to throw up. Eventually, the feeling passed.

I emerged from the bathroom to say goodbye to Lim. He kissed me on the lips. It was quick, but definitely a kiss. Stoic to the end, I noticed a small tear form in his eye as I left.

"I know you will do well, and I will see you soon," he said.

"I hope so," I answered.

"The next time I see you, I will have my nephew. It will not be long."

CHAPTER 25

Other than the thoughts and worries churning in my mind, the trip to the airport and flight to Chengdu were uneventful. When I left the baggage area in Chengdu, my luggage in tow, a young man with a sign reading "Dr. Nasim Malik" was waiting for me. It felt strange going by a different name, but Daisy and I had practiced answering to our new appellations.

I walked up to the bearer of the sign who was preoccupied, studying his iPhone. I remembered what Lim had told me about Singles Day being the next day.

"Hello, I'm Dr. Malik," I said. I felt like a fraud, but he didn't seem to notice. Instead, he looked up, quickly touched his phone screen a few times and slipped it into his back pocket.

"Follow me. I take suitcase."

I walked by the young man's side as he dragged my bag toward a parking area. His English was barely passable, and he didn't appear to want to talk, so I didn't press it. When we got to the vehicle, a gray minivan with Chinese writing on the side, I asked how long the drive to the Great Harvest facility was.

"Little more than hour. Unless bad traffic." He opened the door to the back seat, I got in, and he closed the door. I watched him put my suitcase in the back, then take his place behind the wheel. He made a phone call, said a few words in Chinese, and we were off.

We drove for at least forty-five minutes through heavy traffic, dodging buses, bicycles, pedestrians, and other cars. The city went on forever, the sidewalks full of people. We passed through areas with tall, modern buildings, many with signs I recognized including Intel, Microsoft, Nokia, Citigroup, and JP Morgan, then neighborhoods with older, dilapidated high-rises having storefronts lining the sidewalks, most with signage in Chinese only. This was a huge city. I couldn't believe I'd never heard of this place before the trip. After a while, the buildings got smaller, and the streets less crowded. We eventually made our way to a rural area with winding roads and hills covered in lush greenery. It had been over ninety minutes by the time we came to a stop before a tall wood fence with a security gate. A small sign in Chinese identified the site. I assumed we were at Fengshou. My stomach tightened.

The driver pressed a button mounted near the van rearview mirror, and the gate slid open. A guard wearing a Red Army uniform standing in a small building to our left nodded and waved us in. We drove uphill a short way before a large compound comprised of approximately ten buildings came into view. A fence surrounded the complex as far as I could see, undulating over hills and reminding me of the Great Wall I'd seen several days earlier.

We rode past several small buildings before parking in a circular driveway in front of a large, two-story modern building of concrete and smoky glass. "You here," the driver said. He exited the car and popped the rear hatch to remove my suitcase as I got out of the vehicle. I looked around and imagined Daisy riding in the back of a similar minivan. I felt so alone. A small group of janitors apparently on break stood near the edge of the driveway, smoking while looking intently at their cell phones. A young woman, another janitor judging from her apparel, was sitting on a rock retaining wall apart from the rest, reading an e-book.

The driver escorted me through a set of formidable double doors into the building's sleekly modern, spacious lobby. Two women, each wearing a uniform consisting of a white blouse and navy jacket, stood behind a long counter. The driver spoke to the older one briefly. I only understood the words "Nasim Malik." He turned and left, leaving my suitcase in front of the counter. The woman he'd spoken to motioned me to her while the younger one appeared engaged with her cell phone.

"Welcome Dr. Nasim Malik," the older woman said. I noted her nametag which, in addition to a Chinese character, read "Min." My stomach relaxed.

"Please, can I see passport?" Min asked officiously. She looked at me knowingly and said almost inaudibly, "Welcome. I treat you like anyone else. Others check my work."

I handed Min the Pakistani passport in my purse. My pulse quickened upon realizing she likely needed to check for an entrance stamp. She first carefully studied my picture, then me, looking up and down several times. She walked over to her colleague who seemed irritated at being interrupted from her important shopping activities and showed her my passport photo while saying something in Chinese. My heart rate remained elevated, as I stayed in high alert. The second woman looked at me, then back to the picture several times. Finally, she nodded and handed my passport back to Min. I realized the two were having difficulty matching my Caucasian features to those in the photograph. Min returned to her station and began thumbing through the pages. To my relief, she found a China entry stamp, and smiled. Fortunately, Lim and his team had taken care of that.

"I hold your passport while you here," she said. "I also need cell phone. No picture or recording allowed."

I handed over my cell phone, which she placed in a cubbyhole behind her along with my passport.

"Now I must see in purse."

Once the woman had rifled through my purse and handed it back to me, she wrote my name on a badge and inserted it into a badge holder on a lanyard which I put around my neck. She walked around the edge of her desk to collect my suitcase and dragged it behind the counter.

"Luggage stay here," she explained. "I call director now. He show you around." She lowered her voice before continuing. "Must tell you something." She looked around, then at her colleague who was focused on her phone. "Look for—" Just then, two guards approached Min from behind. Each seized one of her arms, almost lifting her off her feet. Min's eye's opened wide, as she began to tremble. An older woman walked over and yelled at her as the guards took her away.

The young woman who had been seated next to Min put down her cell phone, folded her hands, and spoke in English for the first time. "Your tour will begin soon." She must have noticed my look of shock, and added, "Don't worry about her. She is incompetent. Must get fired."

I knew it was more than that. Someone had discovered her bribe. I wondered if she would tell all to the authorities right away, and if the others undercover had been discovered. One thing was certain—she wouldn't be there to give Daisy Mingyu's location when she arrived in a half hour. My hands were shaking as I wiped the sweat off my forehead with a tissue I found in my purse, hoping my nervousness went unnoticed. I breathed in and out slowly to calm myself. A few minutes later, a handsome, thirtyish, fit-looking Asian man wearing a dark suit came through a doorway and greeted me. He smiled coldly as he held out his hand and said in pretty good English," Welcome, Doctor. I am Yang Peng, the director."

Although in Chinese fashion he stated his surname first, I recognized the name instantly as the man behind the operation. The biological father of Ting's children, and many of the children designed here. A monster.

"I was told you are visiting us from Aga Khan Medical School in Karachi."

"That's right."

"How is the weather there now? Is it cold like it is here?"

"Oh, no. Still hot. Should cool down next month." I wasn't sure if he was really interested in the weather in Karachi, or was testing me. I had been studying many facts about Karachi and had it covered.

"I understand your government is interested in setting up a human embryonic stem cell gene-editing program."

"That's right. We have a population with a lot of consanguinity."

"Excuse me, what is 'consanguinity?'"

"We have a lot of tribes, groups of people who stay together and inter-marry. Many people have parents who are related. Because of that, we have a lot of birth defects, especially deafness. We want to explore ways to eliminate much of the deafness."

"Have you identified the genetic mutation involved?"

"Unfortunately, there are many different mutations. We have already characterized hundreds. That makes the problem extremely difficult. To have an impact, we need a program where we can determine the genetic abnormality involved in each family with hearing loss, and then synthesize a segment of normal DNA to replace the abnormal one."

"Your application is different than ours, but the general methodology will be similar, I believe. I am not a scientist, but I understand what the scientists here do. In this building, we do everything from egg harvesting, fertilization, and gene editing, to implantation of the developing embryos. Prenatal care and maternity services are in another building. I will take you first to the area where we harvest eggs and do the implantation."

I walked with Peng down a long well-lit hallway, with people in white coats walking quickly, passing us in both directions. I activated the first of my three bracelet cameras, holding my arm to film the hallway and catch signs on doors. We turned right and walked a short distance until we came to an office with an opaque window. Peng knocked, and I followed him inside. He introduced me to a middle-aged woman with short, graying hair, and explained that she was the medical doctor in charge of harvesting eggs and implanting embryos.

"What we do here is no different than what is done in a conventional in vitro fertilization lab," the doctor said, speaking nearly perfect English.

Except in a conventional lab, your patients would be there willingly.

"I will show you the area where we treat the women," the doctor continued.

I walked with her and Peng to a door with Chinese characters on a nearby placard. We entered a small reception area behind which was a hallway leading to a series of empty, squeaky-clean examination rooms, the doors open. In each room was a computer, an exam table with stirrups, and a small table on wheels with medical supplies and equipment. I removed a notebook and pen from my purse and began taking notes as my bracelet recorded everything I could see.

"We harvest eggs here when they are ready. With five exam rooms, we can do up to five patients at a time. Usually, we do two or three two days a week. We anticipate a higher patient volume in the future. After the patient has been treated with follicle-stimulating hormone and luteinizing hormone, we do ultrasounds to see when the eggs are ready. When they are ready, we give an injection of human chorionic gonadotrophin and harvest the eggs thirty-six hours later."

"This looks pretty standard," I said, remembering the photos of in vitro fertilization labs I'd seen on the internet before leaving for China.

The doctor next showed me a small room with two stainless steel counters, a refrigerator, sink, and shelves containing small boxes, labeled in Chinese. She opened the refrigerator to show me racks of tubes containing pink liquid. "This is the special medium we use to hold the eggs we harvest. We warm it in the water bath over there," she said pointing to a metal box partly filled with water, set on one of the worktops. "We have a special formula that works better than the media other labs use. We use different proportions of some of the amino acids and add human serum."

"Human serum?" I asked. "Aren't you afraid of transmitting diseases? And variation from batch to batch?"

"We have a good source. Very dependable. Doesn't change."

I wondered where they got "safe" human serum. Perhaps a group of prisoners they kept disease-free. The use of human serum was highly unusual.

"Do you do this procedure yourself?" the doctor asked me.

"No, I'm involved in the gene editing. I don't do egg harvesting or embryo implantation. Others take care of that."

"Our procedure here is probably similar to what is done at your facility. We sedate the patients with midazolam and propofol. Then we harvest the eggs through the vaginal wall under ultrasound guidance. We try to get at least twenty at a time. Since our patients are young and healthy and we have optimized our procedure, our success rate is very high. We get a successful pregnancy seventy-five percent of the time."

"Very impressive," I said, aware that forty percent success was considered good. I moved my braceleted arm around to capture the entire room. "Do all of your patients have a genetic disease?"

The doctor began to answer, but Peng spoke up loudly, drowning out her voice. "Patients come here because they have had babies with severe forms of thalassemia who have died. They want to be sure their next baby is healthy. We do gene editing only on those who are at great risk of having the most severe forms of thalassemia. We replace the abnormal parts of the genes with normal sequences of DNA."

The doctor looked like she wanted to speak but was afraid to.

"I'll take you to where we do the editing," Peng said.

Finally, after all this time preparing, I was about to see the lifeblood of the operation.

CHAPTER 26

I thanked the doctor before Peng led me around the corner to a small antechamber where we donned disposable masks, caps, surgical gowns, and booties. "We keep the room very clean," Peng explained. We entered a large lab filled with activity. Men and women suited up similarly to us were busy at various tasks, including pipetting, weighing chemicals, and carrying test tubes. Some were studying Petri dishes through lenses on large microscopes, most of which were inside sterile hoods which lined two walls of the lab. Almost all microscopes were connected to monitor screens I estimated to be twenty inches, displaying what the operator was seeing through the eyepieces.

Ten white incubators, each roughly the size of a kitchen oven, were stacked in one corner of the room. On top of several rows of black lab benches were centrifuges, water baths, racks of sterile test tubes, disposable pipettes, and other supplies. Mounted around the ceiling were at least ten cameras aimed in varying directions. They must have covered every square inch of the lab. Peng called one of the men over to us. An elderly short, wiry man with gray hair and thick wire rim glasses, he appeared somber and humorless.

Peng introduced him as the director of the embryology department. "He oversees the egg preparation, fertilization, incubation, removal of cells for testing, and embryo freezing. The actual editing is done back there and is overseen by another group," Peng said, pointing to a smaller room in the back of the lab.

I shook hands with the older, bespectacled man, who failed to crack even a hint of a smile. I wondered if Min had divulged my true identity, and I was about to be arrested. The man interrupted my thoughts by asking me what I wanted to see. I decided to keep up the pretense of being a Pakistani doctor as long as I could.

"Everything," I said. "We want to expand our service to include embryonic stem cell gene editing. Right now, our hospital performs only standard in vitro fertilization. I'd like to see how you edit the embryonic stem cells so we can start a similar program. From what I've been told, your success rate is remarkably high."

The embryology director's English was easy to understand. "Yes, we have very good success rate. I optimize the media we use for egg and sperm preparation in addition to embryo incubation."

"Can you walk me through the steps from processing the harvested eggs to acquiring fertilized, edited embryos ready for implantation?"

"We can start over here," he said, walking toward one of the sterile hoods. I followed, pad and paper at the ready. Peng wasn't far behind.

We stood by a young female technician who was manipulating pink fluid in a Petri dish set on a microscope stage. On the monitor, we watched cells being sucked into a pipette and expelled repeatedly. I was glad I had more than one recording device. I used my bracelet camera to capture the motions of the technician and my pen to record the images on the monitor.

"Most hoods, incubators, and water baths at thirty-seven degrees Centigrade. Best to keep cells healthy that way. Technician, he cleaning up eggs we harvest this morning," the elderly man explained. "All the cellular material and fluid around them need to be washed away. The sperm have already been concentrated in gradient and washed with our special medium. The washed sperm keep warm in water bath there." He pointed to a nearby lab bench as he spoke. "Once eggs are ready, we drop sperm around each one and incubate them in one of our carbon dioxide incubators overnight."

"Of course," I said, remembering that the medium used requires the presence of high carbon dioxide levels in the surrounding air to maintain the proper pH.

"By tomorrow, almost all of eggs will be fertilized, but will not yet have divided into two cells. We check under microscope for presence of two pronuclei, one from the mother, other from the father, to confirm fertilization."

"Then what do you do?"

"Once egg fertilized, someone from Gene Team does gene editing. That done in little room Mr. Yang Peng showed you."

The elderly man and I followed Peng into the smaller room. Inside were two sterile hoods, each with a microscope and attached video screen. A man around forty-five years of age wearing a mask, cap, and disposable gloves was focused on a petri dish atop the microscope stage under one of the hoods.

"You lucky," the embryology director said as we crowded into the room. "Dr. Song, the Gene Team director, is doing a gene edit right now."

I positioned the bracelet and pen to record Dr. Song and the images on the monitor, respectively.

"If you look at the screen here, you can see what Dr. Song is doing," the embryology director said. "The big cell there is, as you must know, the egg. We know it was fertilized because you can see the pronuclei, the two subtle round bodies, inside."

"Oh, yes. I think I see them," I said, straining to see circular structures in the egg. Dr. Song remained silent while he used the computer mouse under the sterile hood to maneuver an arrow on the monitor to the two pronuclei.

"That's what I thought," I lied. Actually, I'd picked out one of the two. I in no way considered myself an expert, much less a person of competence, in this area.

Dr. Song said something in Chinese and continued his manipulations.

"Dr. Song needs quiet so he can concentrate," Peng said.

"He is about to introduce our versions of CRISPR and Cas9 into the cell, to start the editing process," the embryology director whispered.

I wondered what he meant by "our versions" while we watched the screen in silence. With a steady hand, Dr. Song slowly pushed a micropipette tip through the membrane of the egg. Then he squirted the contents of the pipette directly into the cell interior. Nothing visibly changed, but I knew the molecular workforce introduced into the egg, too small to see, was beginning to do its job. Dr. Song withdrew the micropipette from the cell and exhaled. He put the Petri dish lid in place and turned to us.

In English difficult to understand, he explained. "I just introduce our Super CRISPR, or SCRISPR, with guide RNA and modified endonuclease we call Cas9b, into egg. Now, wait."

"What gene are you editing there?" I asked.

Dr. Song ignored my question and abruptly left the room with the Petri dish. Through the doorway, I saw him place the dish containing the microscopic atrocity into an incubator.

"We have several genes we are actively editing currently," the embryology director answered, seeming to look at Peng for approval. "We also have other genes we are working on."

"What genes are you currently editing?"

Looking at Peng nervously, the older man answered, "We have done four hemoglobin gene edits in embryos of couples with previous child born with thalassemia major. We have also edited genes of three embryos where the mother is hemophilia A carrier." His body language told me he was lying. He knew better than to divulge what they were really doing with their gene editing, even to someone they deemed friendly to their government.

"How do you know, for sure, the embryo you edit would have been affected?" I asked.

"We only know, given that one or both parents are carriers, embryo is at significant risk for bad mutation, so we edit gene proactively. We are working on method where we can wait until fertilized egg has divided into two cells and then analyze one of the cells to determine if it contain mutation. If no mutation, we will let remaining cell develop normally. If it have mutation, we will edit remaining cell. Unfortunately, using current technology, second cell does not develop normally. We do experiments now to find conditions for second cell to develop okay."

"Interesting," I said. "Couples must come here from all over the country to have the procedure done. I imagine you have a long waiting list."

The embryology director looked increasingly uneasy. He was not a good liar. "Yes, most definitely. There is long waiting list. They come from all over."

"The women stay here while they get hormone injections before harvesting the eggs?" I asked.

The embryology director looked at Peng, who answered himself. "Yes, they stay here. We have housing for them in another area of the facility."

"How long do they stay here?"

"For the duration of their pregnancy, so we can monitor them."

Dr. Song returned to the room with another Petri dish which he placed on the microscope stage. The three men spoke quietly amongst themselves in Chinese. The embryology director turned to me and explained. "Now Dr. Song has embryo that underwent gene edit six days ago. Embryo has been developing in incubator, so is now at blastocyst stage. Once he put in focus, you will see it on monitor. He will remove some cells and send for DNA sequencing. The whole genome will be sequenced. The remainder of the embryo is frozen while we wait for results. The frozen embryo can be implanted any time if the DNA okay. If the DNA not okay, the embryo is destroyed."

"How long does it take to analyze the DNA?"

"A few days. First, it is sequenced, then it is compared to normal."

"Where is that done?"

"Our Next Gen Sequencing lab is upstairs."

While we were talking I saw the blastocyst, a fluid-filled spherical arrangement of cells with an ovoid cell cluster focally attached, come into focus. To me, it looked like a ping-pong ball with a large wad of gum inside stuck to the wall. I remembered enough embryology to know that the cells in the cluster, the gum wad, would potentially develop into a baby, while those around the perimeter, the ping-pong ball, were destined to develop into the placenta, if implanted. I watched Dr. Song remove a clump of cells from the perimeter and place them in a labeled test tube containing pink medium. The blastocyst, barely large enough to be seen with the naked eye, resealed itself after the cells were removed. Dr. Song pressed a button inside the hood and waited. A young man entered the room and took the test tube.

"He is going to deliver the cells to our DNA sequencing lab. Dr. Song will now freeze the blastocyst."

I checked the time and switched my recording to bracelet number two as Dr. Song took the Petri dish containing the blastocyst to the other sterile hood.

"This hood is at room temperature," the embryology director explained. Then he described the steps Dr. Song took in preparing the specimen for freezing as he did them. First, the petri dish containing the blastocyst was placed on the microscope stage. A brief laser blast caused the liquid inside the blastocyst to leak out, and the ping-pong ball-like structure collapsed. The caved in blastocyst was subsequently aspirated into a pipette and washed in small quantities of special medium before being transferred to a long, thin tube, and plunged into liquid nitrogen. Once frozen, it was transferred to a nearby liquid nitrogen tank on wheels, the size of a large keg of beer. Dr. Song pressed the button again, and the same young man appeared. This time he took the liquid nitrogen tank and wheeled it to another small room, where numerous other tanks were stored.

"Now you've seen the process," Peng said proudly. "Dr. Song has many more embryos to process today, all from the same egg harvest. After we get the DNA results, we will discard the bad embryos. Usually, about seventy percent are good."

"I hope you're going to show me where you do the DNA sequencing," I said.

"We can go there next," the embryology director said. He and Peng escorted me through the hallway. I wondered if I was about to be led to an interrogation room, but to my relief, we went to a lab around the corner. Inside, the elder man pointed to six white and black box-like machines the size of refrigerators in the middle of the room. Each had an attached monitor displaying data.

"These are the workhorses of the lab. Our Next Gen sequencers. Any one of them can sequence entire human genome in less than four days. Twelve at a time."

"Impressive how fast these machines work," I said. "We have an older version in our laboratory. Takes a week. Even that's remarkable considering it took almost fifteen years and around three billion dollars for the first human genome to be sequenced." I was sure I sounded fairly knowledgeable, which was no small feat considering I hadn't known any of this until I began preparing for the trip.

We stood and watched a few seconds as the machines quietly carried out their task of determining the order of A's, T's, G's, and C's in the DNA threads they were tasked to decode.

Peng took me to the back of the lab where technicians wearing lab coats and gloves were lined up in front of a long bench on which sat small centrifuges, test tube racks, vortex mixers, heat blocks, precision repeat pipettes, and pipette tips. A desktop machine the size of a footlocker sat near one end. Through the clear cover, I saw a robotic arm with disposable pipette tips aspirate small amounts of fluid from vials and deliver them into a white microtiter plate, a plastic block the size of an iPad Mini, with twenty-four wells arranged in four rows.

"This is where the DNA is processed before it goes on the sequencing machines," Peng said. "We automate whatever we can to save time. We have a standardized process for extracting and cleaning up the DNA, cutting it into manageable sizes for the sequencers to handle, and getting rid of the pieces that are too long or too short."

I'd read about this process, whereby long DNA strands are broken into fragments several hundred base pairs long. The order of A, T, G, and C from all the fragments is subsequently analyzed by a computer to find overlapping segments, enabling the exact sequence of the entire DNA strand to be determined. "I would love to have a copy of your written procedure to compare to our own," I said. "I see one of your technicians at the other end of the bench is loading samples to be put in one of your DNA sequencers."

We walked to the edge of the bench where we observed the technician load samples onto a glass device approximately three inches long and one-inch wide. Peng spoke to him quietly while he finished. Afterward, we followed him to one of the large machines where he placed the glass apparatus holding the samples inside a small opening. Then he entered data into the computer's touch screen.

"This looks a lot like a machine I saw in the US, made by an American company," I said.

Peng and the embryology director chuckled. "There is a reason it looks like that machine," Peng said. "But it was made here. The company that made it is in Chengdu. They can sell you some of these machines for much less than the Americans, if your university is interested."

I understood this to mean they had purchased an American machine, dissected it, and made a knock-off, or had directly stolen the manufacturing plans—another bonus I had caught on camera.

"I'm sure our lab director will want to pursue that," I said. "Once our operation is up and running, I anticipate we'll need at least ten of these machines."

I felt a hand grab my shoulder. My heart raced as I turned around, expecting to see a guard about to arrest me, but instead faced a young man wearing a lab coat. "Dr. Malik," he said in broken English. "I Dr. Lee Mike. I understand you from Aga Khan Medical School."

"That's right." I smiled, trying to hide my angst, wondering why this man had approached me.

"You must know Dr. Afzal Kashani, from the medical genetics department."

Shit. I've been found out. Was this a test? I'd studied the names of everyone in the genetics department but didn't recognize that one. Was the website not up to date? Was Kashani a new faculty member? I'm sure I had the deer-in-the-headlights look, while I tried to think.

"I'm sorry, but I don't think I know him," I answered.

"How can that be? He's been there over ten years and has hundreds of publications."

I felt my face turn red. I needed to stall for time so I could think. "Does he go by another name?"

Peng stared at me intently, as in my head I frantically went through the list of faculty members I'd memorized. I imagined his next words to be "The jig is up."

"Dr. Lee yelled out to another colleague walking by. "Hey, Delun, what was the name of that professor we met on the faculty of Aga Khan Medical School when we attended the conference in Chicago last year? Wasn't it Afzal Kashani?"

"That was his name," the colleague said. "But he wasn't from Aga Khan. He was from Khyber Medical University."

"Oh, I forgot," Dr. Lee said. "My mistake. Or as they say in Chicago, my bad." He laughed and walked away.

I sensed the tension in the room dissipate, but I was still on edge.

CHAPTER 27

"I will introduce you to Dr. Pan next," Peng said. "Dr. Pan is largely responsible for our success, along with Dr. Deng, who you will meet later. Together, they succeeded in creating SCRISPR and Cas9b, mentioned by Dr. Song, vastly improving our editing capabilities compared to the standard CRISPR and Cas9 used elsewhere. With their modifications, our error rate is much lower. By checking the entire sequenced genome, we can prevent implantation of almost all embryos with gene editing errors."

"That technology is, of course, of great interest to us," I said, noticing the skillful insertion of the word "almost" into his boastful description of their program's safety.

"Dr. Pan is an expert in computerized modeling of macromolecules. His lab designs novel proteins predicted to have the attributes we want. These proteins can be made overnight in our synthesis lab and tested for the desired properties. If the protein functions like predicted, we can determine the DNA sequence we need to insert into the embryo's DNA to produce the improved protein. We can manufacture whatever DNA sequence we need in two days or less."

"I'm looking forward to learning how you design proteins using computer modeling. It's a particular interest of mine. We have no real expertise in that area at any of our universities, yet it is such an important field. It will become even more important as genetic engineering becomes more developed. I want to become our country's leader in that field."

I followed Peng to another wing of the building where he led me upstairs to a lab with rows of computers, the screens constantly changing. People were sitting in front of scattered computers, entering data.

Peng shouted something in Chinese, which I believe included the name "Pan." A middle-aged man with thinning hair came from the back of the room. "This is Dr. Pan," Peng said, before speaking to the man in Chinese.

"This where we run models of protein molecules," Dr. Pan explained in heavily accented English. "When I asked to modify protein, I decide which amino acids most likely to accomplish the goal. Then we model how changes affect protein configuration in three dimensions. We choose best configuration."

"Where can I find the program you use?" I asked.

"Cannot find. Only here," Dr. Pan answered.

"Perhaps we can work out a cooperative arrangement," Peng said. "If you need protein modeling, Dr. Pan could do the work here. Then you could determine the changes in DNA required to change the protein and synthesize the DNA in your lab. This is something that can be set up by our governments."

"Governments?" I asked.

"Our program is very costly. It is paid for by our government. Our leadership is willing to share our expertise with others, for the sake of humanity, but might want something in return," Peng answered.

"Like what?"

"I do not get involved in such negotiations. Trade practices, military bases, UN votes, those are the things our government is interested in."

It was time to switch cameras on my bracelet. I pressed the appropriate fake gem to activate the next camera and began to sweep my arm for optimal video capture. As I prepared to say something about all the remarkable equipment, Dr. Pan interrupted. He was staring at my bracelet. My heart pounded.

"Excuse me, please, but can I see your bracelet?" he asked.

Damn. He saw me press the gem. He knows. I looked around, thinking my best chance might be to run. As if I could escape.

Dr. Pan reached for my arm and bent over. "May I?" he asked, bringing the bracelet close to his eyes without waiting for my permission.

He wasn't holding my arm tightly, but I was sure his grip would instantly tighten if I tried to bolt for the door.

"Is there something wrong?" I asked, my voice shaky.

"No. But I notice your bracelet. Very pretty. My wife have a birthday next month, and I think she like a bracelet like this. Where you get?"

"A street market in Karachi." He looked disappointed. Now was an opportunity to build up my credibility. "I've bought other things from the artist who made this. I'm sure I can find her and ask her to make another one. I could send it to you."

"Thank you, thank you." He wrote his address on a piece of paper and handed it to me. "How much it cost? I pay you now."

"Bracelets like this are inexpensive. I would like to send it to you as a gift."

The man bowed. "Thank you."

"We cannot waste any more time here," Peng said, "so I will take you to see Dr. Deng."

Peng exited the room and I followed, capturing images of the signs on the labs we passed. He stopped before an office with an open door. Inside, a woman with her gray hair pulled into a bun was bent over some papers. She and Peng spoke to each other back and forth several times before introductions were made. I finally had an audience with Dr. Deng. She offered me a seat across from her desk. Peng took the other seat.

I smiled as I moved my pen into position to record this scientist, so important to the program. "I understand you have made unique modifications to the gene-editing process used in most labs."

"That is correct." Dr. Deng spoke English without an accent. "Our SCRISPR molecule accommodates pairing with a DNA strand twenty-four bases long, rather than the usual twenty. This dramatically reduces the number of errors. There are fewer errors in mismatching, and there is a reduced chance of having a site in another gene, one not targeted, that has the same sequence."

"Very clever," I said.

"That is not all. We have modified the DNA cutting protein, Cas9, to remove the unwanted DNA base pair rather than just make a cut. This greatly increases the efficiency of the repair."

"Very impressive," I said. That was not an empty compliment. What Dr. Deng was describing was truly brilliant and potentially game changing. "Have you done any work with deafness?" I asked, feeling obligated to ask about the condition I claimed our facility was eager to prevent.

"No, we have not worked on that."

"What about hemoglobin disorders?" I asked. "I understand you haven't made much progress working with thalassemia."

"We began working on that fairly recently."

"I'm surprised. I assumed that was one of the first diseases you started with, since it is a leading genetic disease in your country." I was pushing it, wanting to see Dr. Deng squirm, which she did. A proud woman, I could tell it was killing her not to be able to tell me that they had recently finished designing a revolutionary hemoglobin, and that thalassemia was only a secondary concern.

"Things are more complicated than you think," Dr. Deng said tersely.

"Have you considered editing genes that don't affect people's health?" I asked.

"Like what? Why would we want to change a gene that doesn't improve health?"

"Some people, people with a lot of money in my country, are interested in editing genes to improve their children."

"Improve? What do you mean by that?"

"Change eye color or shape of the ear. Stronger, smarter, more athletic. Things like that."

"That is not allowed," Dr. Deng said. "International agreement." Then her pride took over. "But if we know the gene responsible, we can do that. I am sure."

"Have you ever done anything like that before?" I asked innocently.

"I would never confirm such a thing if we—"

"We would never do such a thing without international support," Peng interrupted, giving Dr. Deng an admonishing look. "If international opinion changes, we could perhaps work with you on such projects. We've bothered Dr. Deng enough. I see it is after one-thirty already. Can I interest you in lunch, Dr. Malik?"

"I would like that very much." I doubted I would see or hear much of importance during lunch, so on the way I turned my bracelet camera off.

CHAPTER 28

Peng escorted me downstairs to a cafeteria serving dim sum, noodles, fish, chicken, bok choy, broccoli, snow peas, and many vegetables I didn't recognize. Looking around for the woman Lim said was part of his organization, I spotted workers bussing trays, dishing up food, and cleaning the floor, but no one made eye contact with me. I worried that Min might have given me up, or had identified the cafeteria worker. After placing several dishes on my tray, I followed Peng into the dining area. My hands were shaking so much, the plates on my tray were rattling. There was no cashier, so I assumed the food was free. The dining area was large, with round and rectangular tables scattered throughout the space. The room was half-full with workers, some in white coats, others in street clothes or uniforms, eating and conversing. Peng led me to a round table near a window, and we sat down.

I didn't see Min, but the other receptionist was seated nearby, accompanied by another young woman dressed similarly. Both were obsessed with their cell phones, ignoring each other while scrolling through the small screens in their hands. At another table, the janitors I'd seen earlier were eating and drinking tea, focused on their cell phones. Curious, I looked around for the lone janitor I'd noticed upon my arrival earlier. I spotted her sitting alone, eating a plate of noodles and reading an e-book, fifteen feet away.

"This is a very nice cafeteria," I said. "I'm sure the people who work here appreciate it." I began eating. Fortunately, I was well versed in the use of chopsticks because no western cutlery was available.

"Yes. Since there is no town nearby, it is necessary. I hope you are learning a lot from your visit here."

"This visit has been very helpful. I'm quite impressed with your facility. Oh, look, I just noticed this," I said, spotting a fortune cookie on my tray.

Peng did not appear amused. "Last year one of our cooks made fortune cookies and gave them to foreigners. She thought it was funny, giving them a silly American invention. Needless to say, I fired her. When I find out who did this today, I will fire her, too."

"Oh, please don't do that. I'm sure whoever did this meant no harm."

"Workers here must take their jobs seriously. No time for joking around. After lunch, I will take you to our synthesis lab, the last stop—"

As Peng spoke, I spotted an officious-looking young woman with black glasses and short hair, dressed in a black skirt and matching blazer, scanning the room. She quickly fixated on Peng and walked toward us. Placing her hand firmly on his right shoulder, she interrupted Peng mid-sentence. He looked irritated, but gave her his full attention while she spoke to him rapidly in Chinese. There were several hurried exchanges. Peng looked disturbed.

"You must excuse me," he said turning toward me. "I must attend to something right away. My apologies."

He wiped his mouth with a paper napkin and looked around the room, spotting the receptionist and her companion. After throwing his napkin on the table, he walked over to them and quietly spoke. He then escorted them to my table. "These ladies will keep you company while I am away. Please, take your time and finish your lunch. I will return if I can."

The two young women appeared much more interested in shopping on their cell phones than talking to me. I took the opportunity to grab Peng's discarded napkin by the edge and place it in my purse. Then I took a few chopsticks-full of fish in silence, essentially ignored by my tablemates. I picked up my fortune cookie and opened it. The message inside read:

You will have good luck if you look for signer

The message was hand-written. It occurred to me that someone had gone to a lot of trouble to get this message to me, but I didn't understand it. What sign was I supposed to look for?

My thoughts were interrupted by a strange sound—a loud laugh, a bellow, or strange animal noise. I turned toward the noise and noticed several people looking at the lone janitor still reading, oblivious to the few comments I heard that appeared to be directed at her. It hit me like a train: the woman was deaf. She had read something amusing, and, like many deaf people, her expression was louder and coarser than that of hearing people, not mitigated by social norms. Now it made sense. She was deaf and probably didn't speak, so her colleagues ignored her. Min had said "look for" before she was taken away, and the fortune cookie message told me to "look for signer." Could it be both messages were meant to tell me to look for someone who can sign?

I interrupted my babysitters and asked, "The woman over there. Is she deaf?"

"Yes," said the receptionist I'd seen earlier. "She a deaf-mute. Do not let her bother you. She not hurt anyone. Everyone ignore her. She do her work okay, I am told."

My heart broke for this marginalized woman. She obviously could communicate—she was reading a book, after all. "Can I speak to her?" I asked innocently.

"She cannot talk. She dumb. And stupid." The receptionist laughed at her own joke.

I didn't crack a smile. "I'd like to try. I am interested in deafness and want to learn about how it is handled in your country."

"You not supposed to talk to anyone but us," the young woman said, annoyed.

"Can I sit with her, then? You said she doesn't talk."

The receptionist said something in Chinese to her colleague, who looked up from her important cell phone shopping and shrugged. After they exchanged a few more words, the receptionist turned back to me. "Okay. But I must to go with you."

I walked to the deaf woman's table, my chaperone next to me. When my shadow covered the janitor's e-book, she looked up and screeched, a surprised expression on her face. She stared at me and my handler, her eyes darting back and forth between us.

I sat down and signed "Hello," simultaneously saying "Hello," speaking out loud as sign language translators often do.

The deaf woman looked at me strangely and signed back, "Hello."

I casually lay a recording pen on the table, camera aimed at the janitor, to capture a video of the silent conversation with my new acquaintance. My chaperone sat next to me and became lost in her cell phone.

"Do you know American sign language?" I signed, while saying, "Do you know American sign language?"

A bigger smile, I never saw. She signed, "I studied it in Shenzhen. I learned English there too. I hope to move to America one day. The book I'm reading is in English."

She showed me her e-book, *The Grapes of Wrath*. I figured this woman was not stupid.

She signed, "My name is Chang Wen. What is your name?"

I couldn't bear telling her a lie. "My given name is Erica," I signed while saying "Dr. Nasim Malik." From her excitement in signing with me, I figured she didn't communicate with anyone else there, a conclusion borne out by what she revealed next. She was extremely lonely because no one there knew sign language, and none of her colleagues tried to communicate with her.

I signed to her that I wondered what it was like working there and was very interested in the research being conducted, but said out loud, "I would be interested in knowing how you became deaf." My chaperone remained glued to her cellphone, looking up at me now and then.

Wen explained that she had taken the job because it is hard for deaf people to find employment in China, and the pay was more than she could make elsewhere. It turned out to be a nightmare job, though. She had a small apartment in the facility but wasn't allowed off the grounds. She had been able to visit her ill mother once, but since losing her mother, hadn't received permission to leave the premises. Mailing letters was not allowed. She felt more like a prisoner than an employee, receiving her daily work schedule in writing. Because of her limited ability to communicate, she was given tasks others complained about doing.

I asked Wen if there was anything else disturbing about the facility while saying, "I am sure you're grateful to the government for the education they gave you." It was difficult signing while saying something completely different.

"Plenty," she signed. She informed me that while some of the women living in the housing for mothers and mothers-to-be were prisoners, most were free to come and go. She was aware of a number of stillbirths, many of which had obvious physical abnormalities. It was her job to dispose of them in a furnace behind the hospital. She was also asked to dispose of babies with birth defects who died after they were born. There was a building that housed fifteen children ranging from ages two to five, who suffered from various debilitating medical conditions. She suspected there was some sort of dark experimentation going on but had no proof. I continued to interrupt her now and then, signing "Please continue" while saying things such as, "I understand why you would welcome a cure for deafness, even a risky one," and "I see you were fortunate to get this job."

Since Wen had cleaned floors and emptied trash in all areas of the facility, I asked her what she knew about the research projects being conducted, while asking out loud, "What were the most valuable parts of your training?" She gave no details, but had seen labs labeled *special hemoglobin, hemophilia, glycogen, fast-twitch muscle,* and *double muscle.* She had to spell out many of these words, there being no sign for them. Currently, little was going on in the special hemoglobin or double muscle labs, so she figured the research there was near completion.

She had seen a large freezer with four side-by-side glass doors, each door assigned to several labs. Curious, she had opened the doors and seen numerous trays of small tubes labeled with numbers. She suspected they contained DNA samples since papers laying around on bench tops and discarded in the trash were mostly about DNA sequencing and synthesizing.

I thanked her for the information and asked for her WeChat address while saying, "Thank you very much." Throughout our twelve-minute conversation, I learned a lot about the secrets of Fengshou in full view of my unsuspecting chaperone.

I retrieved my pen, returned to my original seat, still accompanied by the young woman who had witnessed my entire conversation, and finished my lunch. It was another fifteen minutes before Peng returned with the officious-looking woman I had seen earlier. His face was flushed, and he was sweating. Two guards ran past the cafeteria window. It struck me. They had discovered Mingyu was gone. We hadn't expected them to notice until at least an hour after I had left the facility. My pulse quickened upon realizing the significance of the situation. Had Daisy found Mingyu? Had she and the baby gotten to the hotel where Lim was waiting? Had they left the hotel without being discovered? Were they in imminent danger? Was Daisy in custody? The suspense, the uncertainty, was killing me, but I needed to appear unfazed. My throat was dry, and it was difficult for me to talk, but I managed.

"Is everything okay?" I asked innocently, my stomach tied in knots.

"A problem has come up which I must attend to," Peng answered. He introduced me to the woman standing next to him, the assistant director, and left hurriedly.

The assistant director sat next to me. "I understand you want to see the lab where we make proteins and DNA segments to order."

"Yes, that's right."

"I will take you now. We cannot waste time."

I activated the camera on my bracelet as I followed her. She walked quickly up the staircase I'd come down to reach the cafeteria. On the second floor, we entered a large lab with rows of machines.

"To the right are the DNA synthesizers, to the left, the protein synthesizers," the assistant director said.

I watched a technician in a white coat enter information on the touch screen attached to a DNA synthesizers. The machine, the size of a double oven on its side, displayed a complex array of robotic arms, vials, tubing running every which way, and pressure gauges. Set on a lab bench, hissing sounds from the release of pressure emanated from somewhere in its depths. An older woman approached us, and the assistant director introduced her to me as the head technician in the lab. In poor English, the technician gave me a rudimentary explanation of the main parts of the instrument and held up a microtiter plate. "Each DNA we make go in one of these wells. Take two day," she explained.

The woman directed me to one of three identical machines on the other side of the room, a metal box-like structure somewhat smaller than the DNA synthesizer and looking quite different. She pointed to the vessels hanging from the bottoms of shelves on the upper part of the machine. "These hold amino acids." Counting the containers, I concluded they separately held the twenty amino acids which are the building blocks of proteins. Tubing from these receptacles fed into a round device approximately the size and shape of a salad spinner. "We grow protein here," she said, pointing to the round apparatus. "It microwave. Make reactions faster. Each protein molecule attach to resin. Add one amino acid at a time. Can make protein in few hours."

I had a lot of questions about how exactly these complex machines worked. They were obviously automated, and this lab had a lot of experience operating them and getting the desired results.

"Very impressive," I said, making a grand sweep with my braceleted arm.

The assistant director received a call on her cell phone and proceeded to stare at me as she listened to the person on the other end. When she disconnected, she walked over to me, a cold look on her face. "We must go now," she said. "You have seen everything."

I was being rushed away. Not every question of mine had been answered, but I felt I had captured everything I needed on video. Once the conversations I had recorded were translated into English, there would likely be even more evidence of the nefarious goings on there.

Walking back to the reception desk, I was reminded of the precarious situation Daisy, Lim, and Mingyu might be in. I collected my things and thanked my escort. There was not a hint of expression on anyone's face. I hadn't a clue what was happening. I looked for Min, but she was nowhere to be seen.

My driver appeared, loaded my suitcase into the back of the van, and we were on our way to the Chengdu Shuangliu International Airport. As we approached the gate, a gardener walked toward a truck parked on the left. I found the cell phone jammer in my purse and turned it on as the gardener's truck started to move behind us, blocking the gate exit behind us. I was relieved to be leaving Fengshou, but my heart was pounding, my mind was racing, and every one of my muscles was tense during the hour and fifteen-minute ride. I exited the van at the curb nearest China East Airlines and collected my suitcase. When my driver was no longer in sight, I turned off the jammer, whipped out my cell phone, and sent a message to Lim on WeChat. "Where are you?"

CHAPTER 29

The airport terminal was large, the inside spacious with a high curved ceiling. Rather than welcoming, it looked more like the inside of an airplane hangar. People rushed by while I tried to get oriented. I had a ticket for a China East Airlines flight to Shanghai, but the plane didn't leave for over three and a half hours. Daisy's flight to Shanghai was scheduled to depart in a little less than two. As I scanned the vast space, my phone vibrated.

A message I was sure was from Lim provided great relief.

Unknown: Go to sitting area past the bathrooms to the left of the China East Airlines counter.

I would soon find out if Lim had Mingyu, and if Daisy had arrived. I walked past the bathrooms, toward an area with rows of seats, most of which were occupied. I carefully scanned the crowd. Two old Asian women talking. A Caucasian couple with two kids running around in front of them. An empty seat. An old Asian man wearing thick black glasses, holding a baby. Two teenage Asian girls studying their cell phones. Stop. The old Asian man was looking at me. Smiling. On closer inspection, he wasn't old at all. It was the gray hair that fooled me: a wig or flour or whatever. I was elated as I sat next to Lim and laid my eyes on Mingyu for the first time. I could barely see his face, but he looked peaceful sleeping in Lim's arms.

"It is about time you decided to show up," Lim joked, speaking quietly while staring straight ahead.

"I can't tell you how worried I've been. Can I hold the baby? What about Daisy?" My speech was pressured. I tried not to look at him, but it was too difficult; I'd been waiting so long to find out what had happened.

"Do not look at me, and do not turn around. Daisy is two rows behind us. She is fine. There is a coffee bar close by. I am going there now. Wait thirty seconds and follow me. Daisy will follow you. Get something to drink, walk to the back, and sit at a table. We can talk there. Then you can hold Mingyu."

Lim picked up the baby and started walking. I couldn't wait the full thirty seconds, so after a long fifteen seconds, I got up and went in the same direction. I managed to suppress my need to turn around and see if Daisy was behind me.

At the coffee bar, I ordered a small coffee. My hand was shaking uncontrollably, causing me to spill some of the cream I was adding. I awkwardly soaked up the mess with paper napkins, trying to act nonchalant while my stomach felt like a clenched fist. I looked up to see Daisy ordering at the counter. I headed for the back of the room and saw Lim, already seated, smiling. He was stirring his tea. I imagined him saying, "Bond, James Bond," and laughed to myself as I sat next to him. I picked up Mingyu who looked at me for a few seconds before grabbing at various parts of my face. He was adorable.

"You okay?" Lim asked.

I was so choked up I could hardly speak. "I'm fine. Just tense. Tenser than I've ever been, I think."

Daisy came over and sat across from us.

"I've been so worried about you," I blurted out. A gush of tears followed my words. That wasn't like me, but I wasn't in control.

"It's okay," Daisy said, patting my hand. "See, I'm here. We're all here."

"It's miraculous," I said. "During lunch, the director was suddenly pulled away and I saw guards running. I was so afraid they'd caught you."

"What time was that?" Lim asked.

"Around two."

"I left at one-thirty," Daisy said. "Looks like they found out what I'd done a half hour after I left."

"At least you were already gone by that time. I'd hate to think what would have happened if you hadn't gotten away," I said.

"We have less time than we planned for. We should get you on an earlier plane, if possible," Lim said, turning to Daisy. "They're looking for you. Or Daiyu Li, to be more exact. It may not take long to figure out that's a phony name."

"I did notice cameras all over the place at Fengshou, so they've got pictures of me, for sure. But since then I've lost my glasses and thick eyebrows," Daisy said.

"Do not be overconfident. Once they have your real name, your passport picture will be at every airport. The government has very sophisticated facial recognition software. If they consider you a top priority, they will use it to find you."

"What should I do?"

"We need to change your flight right away."

"First, you've got to take a minute to tell me what you saw," I said. "I'm dying to know."

"It's quite a facility. They have lots of apartments for the moms and the kids. My guide was a young woman. She paid much more attention to her phone than to me. She even showed me a pair of cowboy boots she was excited about. Eighty percent off. I didn't have the heart to tell her they were hideous."

"So, they bought your pregnancy?"

"Absolutely. Asked me if it was a girl or a boy, stuff like that. I tried to be consistent. I think I told everyone it was a boy. Or a girl. Can't remember now. My guide was rather open with me since I was supposedly going to set up a similar facility in east China. She even told me that a few of the women, although they have strong bodies, have weak minds, and don't understand the greatness of what the program is achieving. Those women are imprisoned for the good of society. Most of the women, however, support the program. They're allowed to do whatever they want, within reason.

"All get free room and board. The apartments are nice. Those who are willing participants get flat-screen TVs, computers with internet, and cell phones. There are regular van trips to nearby places they can sign up for. Oh, and I saw a little girl running around, about the same age as Wang Shu. And guess what color her eyes were?"

"Blue?"

"How'd you guess? My guide told me she was one of the first edited babies. Like Ting said, they wanted to edit eye color before moving on to more important things. So, they chose changing eye color because it's so easy to see."

"Makes sense," I said. "If you're a psychopath."

"I found out they're currently trying to make many types of super athletes including runners, skaters, weightlifters, swimmers, and gymnasts, so they have multiple male donors. I saw the house where one of the men lives. He donates sperm for the future swimmers. He was on a two-week trip to Europe, so I didn't see him. The house was over-the-top luxurious. My guide said the men have to be treated like emperors because they're so important. It took all my willpower not to wring her neck. The men do practically nothing, just jerk off into a cup now and then, while the women do all the heavy lifting."

"Nothing surprising there," I said. "Anything else?"

"Things were looking normal until she took me to the building they call—get this—the Building of Disappointment. That's where they keep their mistakes, their disappointments. It was horrible."

"Did she say what will happen to these children?"

"No. She told me these kids serve to remind the scientists how important it is to be very careful. They also study them. She didn't elaborate on that. I imagine they'll murder them once they are of no more use." Daisy stopped and took a deep breath. "I couldn't wait to get out of there."

"Did she talk about what genes they're currently editing?" I asked.

"They have forty-five kids now, ranging from newborn to four, with specially designed hemoglobin to increase oxygen consumption. They call it 'athletic hemoglobin.' They have a bunch of super muscular kids too. They lack something called myostatin. Without myostatin, muscles grow much larger than normal. Those kids are expected to become gymnasts, weightlifters, and stars in things like javelin throwing and jumping. Five newborns have both athletic hemoglobin and lack myostatin. So far, according to my escort, those kids are doing okay, but they're still young, so they observe them closely. They're starting to work on increasing the number of fast-twitch muscles, which I'm told makes people run faster, but they haven't gotten too far with that yet. She said there are other exciting things they're working on she doesn't even know about."

"Did you get this on video?" I asked.

"Only everything."

"Did you have a hard time finding Mingyu?"

"Min wasn't there, so I had to wing it. I asked to see children five months old. Mingyu was the second baby my guide took me to. He looked just like his picture. I told my escort I needed privacy to test him. She was looking for things to buy on her phone, so she was happy to leave me alone with him. I confirmed it was Mingyu by finding his mole. The switch proceeded as planned. I had a little difficulty getting him to drink the medicine. I spilled some, but he drank most of it. I took the doll out and put Mingyu in the papoose. He was pretty heavy, but once I got him situated and secured the brace, I could manage. I wrapped the doll up well. You'd have to get very close to see it was a doll. Then I waddled out, saw my guide speaking to another woman, said I felt sick and needed a ride to the hotel to meet my cousin. Just like we planned.

"I was almost starting to relax. Everything was going smoothly. That is, until on my way back to the reception desk, my guide told me they were starting a new procedure today, and all the infants were going to get vitamins starting in fifteen minutes. I nearly peed my pants. I practically held my breath until I'd gotten my stuff at the desk and was in the van leaving the gate. I was glad I had that jammer and doubly glad about the gardener. I saw him pull up behind us and block the gate as we left."

"You must have been so worried on the ride to the hotel."

"No kidding. By the time I got there, I was exhausted from the tension. I can't tell you how relieved I was when I got to my room. On top of everything else, my back was killing me. I took off that belly and got Mingyu out of the papoose. He was already kicking before I got to the room. The clerk at the front desk saw one of those kicks. He looked pretty freaked out, so I commented about how this one kicks so much more than my other kids did."

I laughed, imagining the clerk thinking Daisy's baby was demon-possessed.

"Lim came up right away. He changed Mingyu's diaper while I washed my face to get rid of those ugly eyebrows. I left my glasses and the belly under the bed and changed my clothes. We were out the door in five minutes, with Lim carrying the baby in the papoose. Mingyu cried a little, then fell asleep. We got on the motorcycle Lim had borrowed and came here. It was quite a ride—me, him, and the baby. But here we are."

"They are hot on Daiyu's trail by now. We need to get Daisy an earlier flight to Shanghai. The sooner she gets out of the country, the better," Lim said to me.

Daisy's cell phone signaled a new message. "Strange," she said, after reading the text. "It's my cousin, Changpu."

"Which one's that?" I asked.

"The Communist. He said he wants to give me something that belonged to my mom's mother. He wants to know where I am."

"That sounds like what you call fishy," Lim said. "Do not answer."

"But my mother will kill me if I don't get it. She would absolutely love to have something to remember her mother by."

"Why did he not give it to you when you were visiting?"

"He forgot. Or only now realized how important it would be to my mother."

"It is probably a trap."

Daisy's phone registered another message. "OMG," she exclaimed as she read the message. "This is from my other cousin, Lan. She says Changpu has seen the photo of a woman who kidnapped a child near Chengdu, and there is a massive search for her. Changpu thinks the picture looks like *me*. Lan says she is sure he is mistaken and doesn't know how he could think that, but wants me to know he is informing the authorities that I am the kidnapper. She says I should be very careful."

Daisy looked up, a stunned expression on her face.

"Your cousin Lan is smart," Lim said. "She wants to warn you, but knowing her message may be intercepted, is making it look like she is not helping anyone who she thinks is guilty, so she cannot be blamed. Turn your phone off. You need to leave immediately." He thought for a moment. "Let us see if we can get you on a plane to Seoul. No visa needed. Once you're there, they cannot touch you. You can arrange a flight home from there."

We hurried to the China Eastern Airlines counter to change Daisy's ticket, hoping it might take Changpu some time to convince his superiors she was the kidnapper and get the word out.

CHAPTER 30

An East China Airlines plane with seats available was leaving for Seoul in less than an hour. Lim thought the better of it. If the government was looking for Daisy and discovered she was on a Chinese plane, they could require the plane to turn around. Things would be different on an airline not under the thumb of the Chinese government.

We didn't waste time trying to return Daisy's ticket. Instead, we rushed to catch a shuttle to terminal one. There, we ran to the ticketing counter of Asiana Airlines, a South Korean company. We discussed the options and came up with the best solution. Daisy reserved one of the few remaining seats on a flight leaving in forty-five minutes—a middle seat, but she didn't complain. Then she arranged a connecting flight on American Airlines to San Francisco. The wait in Seoul would be long, and the woman at the counter pointed out to us several times that flying to Seoul was not the best way to route the trip, but we insisted. She mumbled something to herself and made the reservation.

Next, we discussed who should carry the information we had recorded. If they caught either of us, everything Daisy or I carried would be confiscated. We agreed the chances of me being arrested were less, so Daisy handed me the memory cards from her recording devices. I removed mine and place all the memory cards in the change compartment of my wallet. Lim dumped the devices themselves in a Men's restroom trash can. We had little time to say goodbye. I gave Daisy a long hug, thanked her, and wished her well before she got in line for security.

We watched Daisy inch forward in line. After she finally disappeared behind a wall, I asked Lim what the woman at the counter had mumbled.

He smiled. "Stupid, crazy Americans. Can't reason with them."

Lim told me he planned to stay in China with Mingyu for a few days to take care of loose ends that had come up before making his way to Hong Kong to catch a cargo ship to the US. I was a bundle of nerves. I wouldn't know for sure if Daisy was safe when my plane boarded in a few hours. Not hearing anything was no guarantee that Chinese police hadn't stormed her plane before takeoff and dragged her off. I asked Lim to wait with me.

"Of course," he replied. "I won't leave the airport until I'm sure you're safely on you way back home. You didn't think I'd desert you, did you?"

"I wasn't sure. I know you're busy—"

"We've been under a lot of stress, focused on your visit to Fengshou and rescuing Mingyu. Now we can relax a little. I don't need to get busy with other matters right away."

"I don't think I'll relax until I'm on American soil."

"I feel the same. Once I get to America with Mingyu—if I get there—I'm hoping to get to know you better. When there's less pressure. Maybe we could get a head start on that right now."

"That would be nice."

Mingyu was getting cranky, his crying attracting annoyed looks from people around us. Lim had only three diapers left. I took Mingyu into the restroom, changed his diaper, and fed him bits of tofu Lim had been carrying around. We went to a bar for a drink to celebrate our near completion of the mission. Not wanting to let our guard down, we ordered a pot of tea instead of a celebratory alcoholic drink. I talked about my childhood, my job, and living in San Francisco. He told me about growing up on his parents' farm, joining the Olympic Team, and the disappointments that followed. Perhaps it was wishful thinking, but I sensed we were growing close. I felt comfortable and safe with him. After two hours had passed, Lim's expression suddenly changed to one of shock. He grabbed my arm and pointed behind me. I turned to see Daisy's face on a TV monitor. The sound was muted.

"That was fast," Lim said. "I think they will be able to connect you to this quickly." Lim fiddled with his phone. "I am going to listen to the TV through my phone so I can hear what they say." He held the phone up to his ear, then nodded. "Got it." Lim focused on the TV monitor behind me as he listened on his phone, his wrinkled brow conveying his uneasiness. He began to translate as he listened. "The true identity of this American agent is Daisy Wong. She has been identified by an exemplary and courageous Chinese citizen and Communist Party member. We are uncertain why she chose to kidnap an infant who is a Chinese citizen, or where the baby is. We believe she has fled the country like a coward, and that she has left the baby with her accomplice. Anyone who knows the whereabouts of the child or the accomplice should contact the authorities immediately. The child's parents are very worried."

"I'm so glad you insisted Daisy take the Korean airline."

"Me, too. The Chinese government might try to convince authorities at the Seoul airport to question her, but it shouldn't go any further than that. Now let us get you a new ticket before they have your real name. You need to get on an earlier flight."

"But I take off in only a few hours."

"Every minute counts. Chinese police are not stupid. People get in trouble when they underestimate them. They will find out the name of the person who stayed in hotels with Daisy, if they do not have it already. They will question everyone at the facility the day Mingyu was taken. They will go over all the videos from surveillance cameras. Once they have your passport photo, they will learn it was you who pretended to be Dr. Malik."

I reflected on my conversation with Wen. Even if the video wasn't clear enough to interpret, they might think it odd I carried on a long *tête-à-tête* in sign language.

I began to gather my things, when Lim reached across the table and grabbed my arm again. "Wait! Look!" He pointed to the TV. Any doubt I had about the capability of the Chinese government evaporated that instant. A picture of me taken from a camera at the facility was on the monitor, looking back at me. I was now wanted by the police. If I'd been worried before, I was terrified now. The idea of twenty years of hard labor didn't sit well with me.

CHAPTER 31

We were out one of the airport doors in minutes. I wasn't sure whether Lim had paid for our tea, but that was the least of my concerns now. Leaving the borrowed motorcycle at the airport, Lim and I caught a cab to an inexpensive hotel Lim was familiar with in a rather sleazy part of town. As we entered, he asked if it would be okay to share a room there, promising he'd sleep on the floor. I agreed. I'd feel safer with him in the same room. I offered to pay for the room, but he refused.

The hotel lobby was drab with two worn mismatched armchairs occupied by persons who appeared to be biding their time. The clerk behind the desk was smoking despite the no smoking sign displayed in universal signage. Lim spoke to the clerk and showed a fake ID. Once he had obtained the key, we walked up the two flights of stairs to a small, dreary room with a bed, a single chair, a dresser with an old-style cathode-ray tube TV on top, and a sink. The bathroom was down the hall.

Lim must have seen the look of horror on my face. "I should have found a nicer hotel. I'm used to staying in hotels like this, but you've probably never stayed in such a place before."

"You're right, I've never stayed in such a room. But it's okay. You're on a budget." I wasn't being honest. I would have paid for a nicer room, but due to his pitiful male pride, we were staying in a dump because that's all he could afford.

Lim, who was carrying Mingyu in the papoose, laid his nephew face up on the bed. "Before we decide what our next step is, I think I should get more diapers and food for Mingyu."

"Don't forget to buy formula," I reminded him. "Extra clothes and a small toy for him to play with would also be nice."

I watched Mingyu kick his feet and struggle to roll over. With a little help from me, he landed on his stomach and tried his best to crawl, managing to scoot himself forward a half-inch. He seemed normal for his age developmentally. And happy. I hoped no mistakes had been made in his gene editing, mistakes that would show up later.

Lim returned with diapers, formula, two bottles, soft foods, an infant-sized outfit, and a plastic ring with colorful key shapes attached for Mingyu to play with.

"You clearly don't know how to shop for children," I admonished him. "The outfit you got him is pink, covered with ballerinas. It's for a girl."

"That's not a mistake. The police will be looking for a baby boy."

"Of course. I should have known."

"From now on, let's call him by a girl's name." He deliberated for a moment. "Xia, let's call him Xia."

"Okay, Xia it is. Maybe we could watch TV for a few minutes to see if there's any new information about the kidnapping."

Lim turned on the TV and switched channels, looking for news. With no information forthcoming, he left the TV on a news channel. Since it was in Chinese, I didn't know what they were talking about.

"Do you think Daisy's safe now?" I asked.

"Probably. If they'd caught her, it would be announced on the TV. Unless they think that keeping it a secret will help catch you. She's probably halfway to Seoul. We won't know with certainty for another three hours. I think we should make our plans based on the assumption Daisy will arrive safely in the US."

"I'll send a text giving her a heads up so she'll see it when she lands," I said.

"Do not say anything outright in your message," Lim warned. "In case they are able to take her phone."

I sent her a text.

Everything is fine here. Don't be alarmed, but police are looking for someone who looks like you in connection with an infant kidnapping. For some reason, they have your name by mistake. Police might want to question you when you land, but since you'll be in South Korea, it won't take long to clear this up. Have a good trip.

"After we know she is safe, we can make plans for your escape," Lim said.

We spent the next few hours dividing our time between playing with Mingyu and watching TV. A ping from my phone announced a text from Daisy.

Landed. Thanks for your message. Will deplane soon.

I hadn't realized how tense I'd been until I became aware of my muscles relaxing upon the news Daisy had landed safely. Now my brain needed time to recalibrate, much like directions on a GPS map after you miss a turn. I wasn't free to leave the country, not with China's sophisticated recognition software looking for me at every public place, especially airports. They had my face, and probably my name.

Lim seemed deep in thought. We might have sat in silence for an hour if Mingyu hadn't cried out, announcing the need for a diaper change. Lim was the first to react. He put a fresh diaper on his nephew and washed his hands. Drying them with a towel, he said, "I need to find a way to get you out of China."

"You and Mingyu, too."

"Our escape is already worked out. Do not be mad at me, but I am partly happy you could not leave right away." Those words were the only bright spot in the middle of this disaster. "I think we have a lot in common."

"There's a lot about us that's different, too."

"Like what?"

176

"Only our language, our cultures."

"Not as different as you may think. I speak English pretty well, or so I am told."

"True. But you were raised in a communist country, with different customs. Different everything."

"Look around. China is quite modern, in case you have not noticed. In some ways, we are more advanced than you are in the US. Digitally speaking, that is."

"Oh, and you surpass us in human embryonic genetic engineering, too."

"That is not fair. You know I am against that. And I share what our government calls Western values. That is why I want to leave this place, especially now that I have no family here."

"You're right. I don't know why I said that."

"You know what the biggest problem is for couples when one is western, the other Asian?" He waited a moment for me to answer. When I didn't, he answered his own question. "It is the parents."

I felt remorse for starting this line of conversation, since he had no parents.

He took a seat next to me where I'd been sitting on the bed and kissed me. Not just a quick peck. A real kiss. We might have done more had Mingyu not started cooing. We both laughed. "I think he approves," Lim said. He picked up his nephew and swung him around gently, while Mingyu giggled.

After a few minutes of play, I received a text from Daisy informing me that following brief questioning by the South Korean police, she was released and was now waiting for her United flight to San Francisco.

"I am glad she is safe," Lim said. "Now for our plan. You had better keep your phone off. We can share my burner phone. I am sure they are looking for me too. After all, they know I tried to help Ting get Mingyu out of Fengshou before."

"I feel like we're a modern-day Bonnie and Clyde," I said. "Only with a baby."

"Who are Bonnie and Clyde?"

"They were a criminal couple in the US almost a hundred years ago. There was a popular film about them, in the sixties, I believe. Made them into a very sexy couple."

"Sounds like us. What happened? Did they get caught?"

"It didn't end well for them. We'll have to be smarter."

"First, I have to figure out the best way for you to escape the country. Planes are out. Driving would not make any sense. The countries bordering China are a great distance away, and the roads to reach them are terrible. It is doubtful you could get to any of the borders without being caught. That leaves escape by water."

"I'll go on the cargo ship with you and Mingyu."

"It is a very long trip. Besides, I only arranged for me and Mingyu. Since you are a US citizen, you can take a boat to someplace close, then fly to the US. There is South Korea, the Philippines, and Taiwan. Taiwan is the closest. Less than two days by boat from Hong Kong. I will arrange for you to leave from Hong Kong, since that is where Mingyu and I are leaving from. It should not be hard to get you on a cargo ship to Taiwan from there. We will just have to spend a little more time together." He smiled and kissed me again, causing me to forget about the troubles ahead for a brief moment.

"How will we get to Hong Kong?"

"Train. Then we have to cross the border into Hong Kong. I have already made plans for me and Mingyu to be smuggled in. It will be easy for you to accompany us. But there is something else I want to do first."

"Something else?"

"I am sorry, but there is someplace I need to go before I leave. It is very important to me."

I wondered what could be so damn important he would postpone leaving when the police were hunting for us.

Lim looked sorrowful as he continued. "I doubt I will ever come back to China after I leave. I want to see my parents' graves."

I sat in stunned silence. This would delay us by days. It might take a long time to locate the burial site. I didn't even know where his parents had lived. China's a big country. But I understood.

"Where is your hometown?" I asked.

"It is a tiny town, near the Yangtze River. The area is beautiful. Since neither of us can fly now, we will take a train to Wuhan, then travel by motorcycle."

"So, I'll get to see the Yangtze River after all," I said, happy I wouldn't have to explain to anyone why I'd gone all the way to China and hadn't seen the famous river—if I ever made it back to San Francisco, that is. "Wuhan—that's where that big pandemic started, the one with the coronavirus."

"It is, but my parents died years before that. I will give you a private tour of Wuhan. It is a very nice city. But first, let us get out of this dump and find a decent place to spend the night. We can take a train first thing in the morning."

We left the hotel, Lim a bespectacled gray-haired man carrying his granddaughter, wearing a backpack, and pulling a suitcase behind. I wore sunglasses despite the overcast skies. We purchased more clothes for Mingyu, then found a beauty supply store where I bought a stocking cap and a wig with long, straight black hair, which I secured to the top of my head with double-sided tape. Bright pink lipstick and purple eyeshadow gave me a new look. With brown eyeliner, I gave Mingyu, aka Xia, a prominent mole on his right cheek.

Lim took a picture of me showing off my new look. "We can use this to get you a family visit residence permit for the train. They are much easier to get than fake passports, and they do not check IDs very carefully at train stations. We can pick it up tomorrow on our way."

"And Mingyu?"

"He does not need one. Not for a train."

We walked for a half hour before we found a decent hotel. I asked Lim if I could pay for it, but he refused to let me. I'd have to work on his macho pride when there was more time. Other than that, he was perfect.

After Lim had registered and we were safely in our room, I fed Mingyu. We explored the area for something to eat, settling on a noodle restaurant. I noticed I was the only Caucasian in the place. The food was fair at best, but it was warm and salty, something I found comforting. We went back to our room and watched the news. Sure enough, my name—my real American name—was splashed across the screen, below my picture. An instant later, Lim's picture and name were displayed.

"What are they saying?" I asked.

"Nothing surprising. I am an enemy of the people, and you are a treacherous American criminal. Anyone knowing where we are needs to notify the police."

"Shit."

"Don't worry. You will be okay here so long as you do not go out. I need to leave for a few hours, though," Lim said.

"You've got to be kidding,"

"No, I am not joking."

"A sarcastic American expression. I don't want you to leave now, especially with the Chinese police searching for us, so I pretended I thought you were making a joke."

"Unfortunately, I need to do something, and I assumed you would prefer to stay here, where it is safe."

"I don't feel safe here alone. Are you going to visit your secret wife? Is that why you don't want me to come along?"

Lim laughed. "No, it is not my secret wife. It is my secret factory."

"Factory?" That's the first time I'd heard of it. "What kind of factory do you own?"

"It is a Bitcoin mining factory. I set it up to finance our organization. It pays for everything we do. And this expensive hotel room. It makes quite a lot of money, actually. So, you see, there is no reason for you to pay for any of this."

I smiled, realizing he didn't have macho male pride after all. He was perfect. "Bitcoin mining? They come out of the ground?"

Lim laughed. "No, they are made by computers. Are you curious?"

"Absolutely."

"Then I will show you."

"I can come?"

"Yes, but it is a forty-five-minute ride from here. You sure you want to?" Lim applied gray hair color from a spray can and put on his sunglasses while he spoke.

"I'm sure."

"Bring all the memory cards from the spy devices. Keep your wig on and make sure your head is down so the cameras do not catch you."

Lim put Mingyu in the papoose, and the three of us got on a yellow and black motorcycle he rented down the street. I kept my face buried in his back as much as possible while riding out of town. After leaving the city behind, we rode through the rural countryside for what seemed like over a half hour, before coming upon a series of warehouse-like buildings. It was dark outside, but I could see fairly well, thanks to the bright lights.

"We are here," Lim announced.

"This doesn't look like much," I remarked. I got off the motorcycle, my legs stiff from the ride. "Why is this out here in the middle of nowhere?"

"Cheap electricity. Free, actually. The government, in its wisdom, set up a power plant here, but there is almost no one to use it so they do not charge for it. Bitcoin mining takes an incredible amount of electricity, so I set this up near an almost infinite source of power, compliments of our government. Not an original idea of mine. Other Bitcoin mining operations are near large sources of cheap or free power."

"Who knew?" I remarked.

"People in the Bitcoin business."

I laughed. "'Who knew' is another American expression, meaning either, 'I didn't know that,' or 'many people know this.'"

"Who knew?" Lim countered, seeming to enjoy using American idioms as soon as he learned them.

He led me inside one of the buildings. Row upon row of metal shelves contained stacks of computers interconnected by a tangle of variably colored wires. Small green light-emitting diodes burned continuously. I saw a worker obscured by rows of computers, appear to fiddle with some wiring in the distance. The loud whirring of cooling fans made it hard to talk in the large, windowless room.

"These computers process over a trillion calculations per second."

"My god, what are they calculating?"

"I will take you upstairs where it is quieter, and we can talk more easily."

I followed Lim up a flight of stairs to a room with five small tables surrounded by chairs. "We can sit here, in the eating room."

Lim and I sat at one of the tables and let Mingyu lie face up atop some clean paper towels he found and laid on the carpet. "This factory makes a lot of money," Lim explained. "We have over twenty employees here, and we pay them well. They oversee the operation twenty-four-seven. All those computers you saw downstairs basically keep the Bitcoin mining operation going. It takes immense computational capacity to record all the Bitcoin transactions worldwide and chain them together in what is called a blockchain. By providing the computational power, we are rewarded with new Bitcoin. We started off much smaller but have grown as we have made money. As more Bitcoin is produced, more computational capability is required. We recently upgraded much of our hardware to keep up."

"How do you use all the Bitcoin you have?"

"Some businesses accept Bitcoin directly, but many do not, so we convert a portion of our Bitcoin to currency using cryptocurrency exchanges. Its value is volatile, so I do my exchanges when the Bitcoin price increases."

"I never understood how this works. Still not sure that I do."

Lim smiled. "It confuses a lot of people. Something has come up, and I thought it would be easier for me to handle it in person than over the phone. Want to see what I call the War Room?"

I smiled and nodded. Lim put Mingyu back in the papoose, and I followed him to a large room with ten young men and women sitting at tables, each engaged with a laptop computer. Lim pulled up an empty chair and sat near one of the men. The two of them became involved in an animated conversation, in Chinese, of course. I think Lim may have forgotten I was there and that Mingyu was sleeping in the papoose he was wearing. After a half hour, Mingyu began to stir and Lim appeared to reenter our world. He looked up at me. "I think he his diaper is dirty," he said.

"Want to give him to me?" I asked.

"No, we are done here." He said a few more words to the man he'd been speaking with and led me to a small room with several computers. He took my memory cards and went from one computer to the next, inserting them in the appropriate ports. "From here, I can upload all the files to a Dropbox account I have in the cloud, registered to a fictitious person in Canada. I figured since I needed to come here anyway, it would be a good idea to have backup copies of everything you and Daisy recorded. I will send Daisy instructions for downloading this when we get back to the hotel so she can get a head start and begin to organize it all once she reaches San Francisco." After he'd changed Mingyu's diapers and the data had been copied to the cloud, we were on our way. It was late by the time we returned to our hotel room.

Mingyu fell asleep on a blanket we doubled up and placed on the floor. Lim sat at the desk and spent fifteen minutes sending Daisy instructions for downloading the information he'd uploaded to the cloud. I was organizing the clothes in my suitcase when Lim came over to me. "I think it is time," he said

"Time for what?"

"Time to get to know each other."

He kissed me lightly on the lips. Not sure what to do, not knowing how things were done in this culture so different from my own, I grabbed his hand. Lim held me and kissed me deeply. I felt like a schoolgirl experiencing her first kiss.

Lim smiled and turned off the overhead light. With only the dim illumination of the nightlight in the bathroom, he removed his shirt to reveal his still-chiseled Olympic physique, then led me to the bed and had his way with me. Or, to be more accurate, we had our way with each other. And yes, they do it the same in Communist countries.

I didn't get much sleep. I was no good the next morning.

Mingyu was the first to wake. I lay in bed, thinking about Lim. He was really into me the night before. Literally and figuratively. But would the same hold in the light of day? I'm sure I wasn't looking my best. When I turned around, Lim was still in bed, propped up on one elbow. The sunlight through the window hit him just so, casting shadows accentuating his perfectly etched features and the sculpted muscles of his arms and chest. A ripped Ken doll. From the waist up, that is. The similarity was striking due to Lim's almost total lack of chest hair. Nice.

"See," he said. "I think we are compatible."

"No argument from me."

"I would like to explore that some more, but I am afraid it'll have to wait. We need to get going."

"Do you feel guilty?" I asked.

"About what?"

"You didn't sleep on the floor last night like you promised."

Lim smiled. "Technically, that promise was only for the first hotel we checked into. I never promised to sleep on the floor here."

We dressed, packed, returned the rented motorcycle, and hailed a cab. Lim gave the driver directions in Chinese, and twenty minutes later, after the usual dodging of pedestrians, bicycles, and cars, we arrived at a high-rise apartment building. Lim paid the driver and we entered the building with me carrying Mingyu. I was glad this building had an elevator. We were headed to the eleventh floor.

When we reached the apartment door of Lim's contact, the baby was grabbing my face and my wig. Luckily, he didn't pull it off, but it made me aware that I needed to keep him away from that mop. I should have gotten a shorter wig.

Lim greeted the middle-aged man who answered the door and introduced me. We walked into the upscale apartment, past the modern kitchen, and into a spacious living room with modern furnishings. In broken English, the man invited us to sit on the couch, spoke a few words to Lim in Chinese, then disappeared down a hallway.

"It is not quite ready," Lim explained.

I heard loud voices from another room, two men arguing.

"The comrades seem to be disagreeing," Lim said, grinning.

"They're members of the party?" I asked, surprised. What they were doing was in flagrant violation of the rules of their government.

"Not at all. They are criminals. But they are also comrades. That is what we call gay men."

I laughed. "I didn't know."

"We have our expressions, too."

Several minutes later, the middle-aged man reappeared, a flustered look on his face. He again spoke to Lim in Chinese as he handed him an envelope. Lim reached in, pulled out an official-looking card, and held it up. He smiled and said something to the man, who returned the smile. Lim took out his cell phone, brought up a QR code which the man scanned, and we left.

"Do not lose this," Lim said, handing me the card. "It is your family visit residence permit. In case you were wondering, the comrades got into an argument over whether you look more like Kim Kardashian or Angelina Jolie."

"Goes to show," I said. "We all look alike."

"Not to me." We caught another cab and Lim directed the driver to the train station. We arrived thirty minutes later. The terminal, a large glass and steel building, was confusing, with hordes of people coming and going. Fortunately, Lim knew where to buy our tickets and catch the train. Going through the security check with my luggage, the officer took only a cursory glance at my card and waved me through. There was nothing to do for the next eighteen hours until we would arrive in Wuhan the following morning.

CHAPTER 32

I don't know when I fell asleep, but Lim gently nudged my shoulder after we arrived in Wuhan. Feeling confused by my dream of swimming to the US while evading sharks, giant squids, and fire-breathing Chinese dragons, I freshened my lipstick and wiped my sunglasses clean. Lim was wearing the papoose holding Mingyu when we stepped off the train, into the chilly air and gray skies of the most populous city of central China.

"Follow me," Lim said, holding a bottle for Mingyu. It was a short walk to the edge of the Yangtze, a wide river, its steel-colored water bisecting Wuhan. Walking across one of the many bridges connecting the two sides of the city, I saw boats of all shapes and sizes making their way up and down the river, looking like toys from our vantage point. An occasional foghorn interrupted the sound of the wind. Tall buildings were crammed together on both sides of the river, coming close to the edge.

Lim took me on a quick tour of Wuhan, which contained many lakes, parks, historical sites, temples, and commercial areas. At noon, we bought a backpack for me to use. I stuffed it with essential items and left everything else in my suitcase which we chucked in a dumpster. I wanted to mail my suitcase home, but Lim was sure the government would intercept anything mailed to my US address and would then know we'd been in Wuhan.

I shook off lamenting the loss of shoes and clothes I'd been attached to during our walk to a motorcycle rental office where Lim picked out a silver and gray model with saddlebags. He was able to squeeze my backpack into one of the saddlebags; his own small bag and supplies for Mingyu easily fit into the other. We were on the road less than ten minutes after stepping foot in the rental agency, Lim carrying Mingyu in the papoose, me on the back. After a few minutes I became worried my wig would fly off, so Lim pulled to the side of the road where I removed it.

Unable to easily converse over the loud drone of the engine, I took in glimpses of scenery as we rode through crowded city streets to less densely populated roads and eventually into the hilly countryside, all the while trying to keep my face obscured against Lim's back. In an hour we were on a winding mountainous road, surrounded by greenery. The road was almost ours alone, with few other travelers in either direction. Although Lim hadn't been there for years, he remembered all the turns onto the narrow, unmarked roads. Finally, my throat dry, dust in my eyes and hair, we arrived at a street with several wooden houses in disrepair. Lim drove past the houses, made a left down a gravel driveway, and came to a stop in front of a small wooden dwelling surrounded by terraced land on which grew trees I didn't recognize.

My ears buzzed from the silence when Lim cut the engine. I took a moment to look around before he grabbed my hand and helped me off the motorcycle. My legs felt weak momentarily. When Lim removed his sunglasses, I noticed that from the dust or emotion, I wasn't sure which, his eyes were wet.

"This is where I grew up," he said. "My parents grew lychee nuts and rambutans. I wonder if someone is living here now."

As he spoke, the door of the house opened and a small boy came out, followed by a young woman, probably his mother. She and Lim began talking in Chinese. As the dialogue continued, Lim remained expressionless. At last, the woman and child returned to the house.

"She and her family have rented this place for over ten years," Lim said. "The government moved them here from a farming area close to the Yangtze that is now under water because of the Three Gorges Dam."

"I heard about that, the huge hydroelectric dam across the Yangtze that's caused the river to rise."

"Right. Millions of people like her were forced to move because of it. She knows nothing about who lived in the village before her, or about the flu epidemic. The recent coronavirus epidemic, she said, bypassed this area. All the houses in town are occupied, many by families who moved in after her. She knows of several older people who she thinks lived here a long time. I asked her about Jiang Ma, a family friend who was a little older than my parents. Apparently, he survived the epidemic because, according to her, he still lives in the same house."

"You should be able to learn what happened to the town during the flu epidemic from him," I said, hopeful Lim would find out details about his parents' last days which, while painful, might settle questions still lingering.

"I hope he can tell me where my parents are buried. But before I visit him, I want to show you something."

Lim took my hand and led me down a path toward a small building the size of a toolshed. He pushed the door opened and led me inside. "The tenant gave me permission to look in here."

The light coming through the single window and open door illuminated a collection of tools and farm implements. Wooden boards were stacked in a corner. Lim moved the boards, then lifted a trap door in the floor, reached into the dark space below, and smiled. "They have not been moved."

He pulled out a carved wooden elephant six inches high, then a carved wooden panda the same size, and set them down. I could tell he was choked up when he spoke. "My dad made these for us. The panda was for Ting, the elephant for me. I cannot explain how much we cherished these. We were not allowed to bring what they called personal items when we left for our Olympic training, so we put them here for safekeeping. Ting will be so happy to see her panda again."

"They're beautiful," I said, noticing the intricate detail of the carvings. "Your dad must have been exceptionally talented."

"Yes, but he never had much time to carve things, something he loved to do. There was always too much to do around here."

We walked back to the motorcycle, and Lim fit the wooden statues in one of the saddlebags. Moments later, we were on the road again, going up and down a series of dirt roads. Lim stopped in front of a small wooden house, similar to the others we'd seen, and again helped me off the motorcycle.

"I hope he is home," Lim said as he walked up to the front door. "I see his bike." He pointed to an old one-speed black bicycle leaning against a wooden fence. Lim knocked loudly on the door and waited. Sadly, there was no answer. After several more knocks with no response, Lim decided to wait.

Mingyu started crying, and Lim checked his diaper. "Dirty again." He laid a blanket on the wooden porch of the house and changed his nephew's diaper. After washing his hands under a nearby spigot, he fed the baby cold rice and tofu, followed by a bottle of formula.

"It's beautiful," I said, surveying the mountainous landscape, the lush greenery growing over large rocks, interrupted by manicured crops growing on terraced fields. The air smelled fresh, cleaner than in any of the cities I'd visited. "I didn't think you could get away from large crowds in your country."

"Here, where I grew up, you can be alone if you want. I did not appreciate that until I left."

Lim jumped up and began waving his arms wildly. In the distance, an elderly man pushing a wheelbarrow, wearing a pointed bamboo hat, a white shirt and black pants, was walking in our direction. When the man was fifty yards away, he put down the wheelbarrow handles and stared. The smile of recognition crossed his face before he yelled, "Chen Lim! Chen Lim!"

Lim returned the greeting. "Ma Jiang! Ma Jiang!"

Leaving the wheelbarrow where it had landed, Jiang ran toward Lim as Lim ran toward the old man. They met closer to the wheelbarrow than the middle and hugged. Jiang reached up high and tussled Lim's hair like a parent would do to a child. They spoke excitedly, back and forth, in Chinese. All I could do was watch.

"I almost forgot," Lim shouted to me after several minutes had passed. "Jiang speaks English. We can all talk." He introduced me to his old neighbor and presented Mingyu as "Xia."

Jiang invited us into his house where we sat on cushions arranged on the floor of the main room. His English was good in terms of vocabulary, but his accent was so heavy, I couldn't understand a lot of what he said. He insisted on serving tea and went to the kitchen.

Lim filled me in on what they had spoken about. "Jiang told me I still look young even though my hair is gray. I told him I went to a costume party and sprayed my hair this color. He laughed. Then he told me of all the new things that have happened in the area over the past years. Many new people live here now, and the village population has grown by thirty. It is more modern now. They have electricity and cell phone coverage."

"What about the flu epidemic and your parents' graves?" I asked.

"He did not mention any of that, but I will ask him."

Jiang returned with a pot of tea and three cups of different shapes and colors. "I apologize for my unsightly tea service," he said. "I am most embarrassed."

Lim and I both assured him that his teapot and cups were quite charming. Subsequently, Lim got down to business while Jiang poured.

"The reason I came here was to try to find my parents' graves," he said.

Jiang stopped pouring and looked at Lim. "Graves?"

"Yes, do you not remember? They died during the flu epidemic."

"Flu epidemic? We recently had a coronavirus epidemic, but our village was spared. I am confused. I thought you wanted to visit your childhood home and see some old friends. You know, next to your parents, I probably spent the most time with you and Ting."

"I remember. I have not forgotten you teaching us how to play mahjong."

"Yes, and badminton. Remember, we played right out there," Jiang said, pointing out the rear window.

"How could I forget? I wanted to see my old house and old friends. But really, I came to see my parents' graves."

"I don't know of any graves. The last I heard, and that was three years ago, your parents were both still alive."

I could see Lim was getting agitated. I think we were both wondering the same thing: this guy, as charming as he was, seemed to have lost his marbles.

"Do you remember the flu epidemic ten years ago that killed most of the people who lived here?"

Jiang looked puzzled. Then he spoke slowly, cautiously. "I do not know what you were told, but there was no epidemic. Some people have moved away, and a few have died of old age or illness over the years, but no great sickness. It was about ten years ago that they took your parents away."

Lim was speechless. He stood up and paced. When he found his voice again, he was animated. "Took them away? What are you talking about? Are you saying they are alive?"

"I believe they are. About ten years ago, they were arrested. They were taken to the Masanjia Labor Camp."

Lim froze for an instant, then exclaimed, *"Wode tian na,"* and collapsed on the pillow next to me, head in hands. I held his arm and tried to console him, but he was beyond comforting. His shoulders and chest heaved as he shed silent tears. Finally, he lifted his head.

"Why were they arrested?"

Jian looked uncomfortable. "It is not your fault. Or Ting's. Your parents wanted to bring you back home. They thought they had made a mistake when they let you go. Your letters upset them. They worked you so hard, you were missing the joy of being children. But you were both big stars. People thought you would get Olympic gold for China. The government did not want to miss that opportunity, so they refused to let you return home. Your parents tried very hard to get you back, even talked publicly about it. First, they were told they could not visit you. Then they were arrested, accused of being *Falun Gong*. Everyone knew that was not true. That was an excuse."

"It is important you do not tell anyone you saw us today. The police are looking for us."

"I know," Jiang said, smiling slyly. "In addition to cell phone coverage, we get satellite internet and TV service here."

"So, you know we need to leave the country."

"That would be a good idea. And I know Xia's real name."

"I am very glad I was able to see you, but we had better leave now," Lim said.

"I understand. My brother's son moved to Wuhan a few years ago. He has a small business, shipping clothing and cosmetics made locally down the Yangtze to Chongqing. I am sure he would be happy to put the three of you on a boat if that would help."

"Thank you, but we are not going in that direction."

"I wish you safe travels."

We both hugged Jiang and started back to Wuhan, the news of his parents weighing heavily on Lim's mind. I knew he was thinking about trying to free them, but he couldn't. Time was running out.

CHAPTER 33

Once we reached the outskirts of Wuhan, Lim found a side street where I put on my wig and reapplied my pink lipstick. It was there that I asked what Falun Gong was. Lim explained that it's a modern spiritual movement promoting breathing exercises and movements based on ancient Chinese teaching, but also follows a set of teachings and meditations on a path to salvation. The government outlawed the practice of Falun Gong, wanting the citizens to be loyal to the Communist state only.

We returned the motorcycle to the rental office and walked to a main street where Lim found a respectable hotel. He negotiated the payment and registered using a fake ID while I stood back. The room on the third floor was nicely appointed with a queen size bed, desk, flat screen TV, and small bathroom. No sooner had I locked my electronic devices in the safe than there was a gentle knock at the door. I was filled with apprehension when Lim opened it, but relaxed upon seeing a hotel porter wheel a crib into the room. Lim changed Mingyu's diaper and dressed him in a pink butterfly outfit.

It was still daylight when we went for a neighborhood stroll, ducking into a small noodle shop to get something to eat. The noodles tasted delicious, a testimony to the chef, or the fact that I was starving. The steam from the noodles fogged my sunglasses, so I removed them to see what I was eating. Lim cautioned me to put them back on. I did as he wished, although I felt he was being overly cautious. Mingyu ate some noodles we mashed up and downed a bottle of formula. Lim placed Mingyu in the papoose and we left the restaurant. Shortly after we started walking, Lim grabbed me, spun me around, and gently pushed me down the street in the opposite direction.

"We've been spotted," he whispered. "Stay quiet and follow me."

I'd noticed two men in military-like green uniforms coming our way but had thought nothing of them. Lim walked quickly as he pulled me down an alley. Turning my head, I had barely enough time to see the uniformed men begin to run before the building on the edge of the passageway blocked my view. The alley was crowded with rows of vendors on both sides selling food, clothing, pottery, and electronics. Lim guided me around meandering shoppers looking over the shops and stalls. With the strength of Superman, he jumped onto a table in one of the merchant's stalls, lifted me, and planted me on top of a cement ledge overhanging the alley. "Lie down flat and don't move till I come back for you." He was still holding Mingyu in the papoose when I heard him jump down and take off running.

My heart was racing while I flattened myself out and slid forward on top of the cement overhang. Decorative ironworks along the front partially hid me from the passersby below. Within seconds, I saw the two officers running after Lim, pushing people out of their way. After they passed by, I lifted my head. Lim was far ahead of them, but I worried when I saw a steel barricade extending across the alley several yards in front of him. I held my breath as he approached the obstacle, then exhaled when he jumped over it easily, never slowing down. He disappeared into the crowd before the officers came upon the barricade and stopped. They spoke to each other briefly before they ran to one end and squeezed around it. Lim was already long gone. The officers took off in pursuit once more but soon stopped and came back in my direction. I stayed low until they passed by me again. I thought of Mingyu. He might have been a little shaken up at the bumpiness of his papoose journey, but I was sure Lim would do what was needed to keep him safe.

It was dark and cold outside; the cement ledge I waited on was hard. I wondered how long it would be before Lim came back to get me. If he ever did. Maybe he would be pursued by others, others who might catch him before he could return to me. This wasn't the situation I'd expected to wind up in. I realized how utterly crazy I had been to ever consider participating in this risky caper. I broke into a cold sweat. Terrifying thoughts flew around me. There was no way I'd be able to find our hotel. I didn't even know the name of it. My passport was in the secure holder under my clothes, but I was being hunted by the Chinese police. Or military. Or whatever they were.

My best chance would be to reach an American Embassy. I needed to find the closest one. How would I do that? Would it be safe to use my cell phone? Assuming I survived, could I retrieve the recordings Daisy and I had risked so much to obtain? Then there was my mom. I hadn't called her since leaving Xi'an. Without me to help, what would happen to her? Those concerns were running through my mind when something tugged at my right foot. I held my breath as my muscles tightened. Tears welled in my eyes—tears of relief—when I heard the soft cooing of an infant, followed almost instantaneously by Lim's voice. "Everything's okay. I'll help you down."

Lim guided me while I pushed myself backward. When my legs were dangling off the edge of the overhang, he pulled me gently, caught me in his arms, and slowly lowered me to the ground. Truly a Superman maneuver. He jumped off the table he'd been standing on and with Mingyu between us, hugged me gently, explaining that he'd been able to outrun his pursuers easily. Mingyu seemed to have enjoyed the adventure, especially going over the barricade.

"We need to be very careful now," he said. "With cameras catching our images almost everywhere we go, we need better disguises to evade the government's facial recognition software. It identifies faces by several measurements, relying heavily on the eyes and mouth. They can often apprehend people within hours. From now on, we need to hide or disguise what we can. A small distortion can make a big difference."

Lim used his phone to locate a party and costume supply store within walking distance, where he bought three fake mustaches. Nearby, we found a drug store where he purchased surgical masks, weak reading glasses and a bag of cotton balls. Upon leaving the store, Lim and I each put on a surgical mask. "We should wear these whenever we can when we're in public, but remember, they can slip off or be pulled off. Sometimes, police will order everyone to remove them, so we need to be prepared."

In an alleyway, we took off our masks. Lim attached one of the mustaches, covering his upper lip. We both put cotton balls between our gums and cheeks on both sides of our mouths to deceive the facial recognition software. Then we put the masks on again. At night, when we couldn't wear our sunglasses, Lim would wear his fake glasses and I'd wear the reading glasses.

We returned to our hotel where Lim walked in alone and scanned the lobby. Seeing nothing suspicious, he waved me in, and we went upstairs to prepare for bed. Lim determined that in a pinch, we could break the large window in the room, drop to the cloth awning two stories below, and descend one floor to the street. Using our sheets as a rope, he thought it would be easy. I hoped it wouldn't come to that.

Looking in the mirror, I saw the alteration in the corner of my mouth created by the cotton balls, then removed them. It would take time to adjust to the feel of them in my mouth when in public. I turned on the TV and was greeted by pictures of Lim, Mingyu, Daisy, and me. Lim translated as he listened. There had been many tips to the police, with sightings of us in Beijing, Shanghai, Xi'an, Chongqing, Chengdu, and Wuhan, in addition to a host of other cities I'd never heard of. Exhausted, I got into bed. I felt comfortable with Lim. The way I suspected married people felt after a few years. I was happy being in the same room with him, eventually falling asleep to the drone of the newsreader while Lim watched with rapt attention and listened for strange noises in the hallway. The next thing I remembered, the door to our room slammed shut. I jumped up and grabbed a sheet, ready to use it as a rope, before seeing Lim, fully dressed, holding Mingyu safely in the papoose. A savory smell filled the room.

"Breakfast," Lim announced, holding up a bag. "Steamed turnip cakes. I hope you like them."

"Well, I guess it's about time I find out," I said. Turns out they were surprisingly good, although I would have preferred a nice bowl of oatmeal with brown sugar and raisins. Mingyu ate a piece of the cake soaked in formula before Lim put him in the crib.

"We can catch a train to Shenzhen this morning," Lim said. "We should leave in an hour."

"How long will it take to get there?"

"Four and a half hours. We will be there this afternoon."

"Finally," I said, "we'll practically be in Hong Kong."

"We will be close, but getting through border security will not be easy. You need a passport, but you cannot use either of the ones you have. You would be arrested immediately. Mingyu and I only need Entry-Exit Permits to get through border security. I have several fake permits for myself, but Mingyu does not have one."

"Uh-oh. What are we going to do?"

"We have to become outlaws," Lim said, smiling.

"I thought we were outlaws already."

"You are right. I almost forgot," Lim said, a smile still on his face. "Do not worry, I have made arrangements for us to get through the border. But we will have to wait here a little before we leave to catch our train. What do you think Bonnie and Clyde would have done if they had to wait around in a hotel for an hour?"

"I don't know, but I'm much too nervous to even think about it."

"Do not worry," Lim said. "I have got this, as you Americans say."

Lim stood behind me and massaged my neck. Then my shoulders. That's all it took. I melted in his arms. We got under the covers and made love after Mingyu was asleep. Shortly after, we ventured out of our room wearing our updated disguises, which now included a mustache, cotton balls, and masks.

We didn't catch the train Lim had planned on, but we made the next one without incident. Once seated, I did my best to act relaxed, like we were a couple of friends traveling with an infant to Shenzhen. Or an elderly man with his daughter-in-law and granddaughter. Lim kept Mingyu's face hidden as much as possible.

Every person who walked by on the long trip presented a new threat. I observed our surroundings carefully while avoiding eye contact. At least ten women noticed Mingyu and tried to pick him up or touch his face. Lim calmly told them that his granddaughter was very ill with something contagious. Worked like a charm. Once we reached our destination, I followed Lim off the train and out of the station.

Smaller than the major cities I'd visited, Shenzhen was still sizable. The air was dirty, but far cleaner than Beijing's. The skies were gray, and being in southern China, the weather was the warmest I'd felt on the trip. No one took note of us when we got into a DiDi car. Lim spoke to the driver, and we rode along crowded streets, over several bridges, and past numerous tall, modern buildings. Many bore the logos of companies I didn't recognize, but some I was familiar with, such as the telecommunications giants ZTE and Huawei. Our driver stopped in front of a tall modern building, all glass, steel, and cement.

Inside, the lobby was furnished with black and white sectional sofas and glass coffee tables. Lim spoke to a man behind a counter who made a phone call while I sat on one of the couches, Mingyu on my lap. After a short time, Lim turned and signaled me to follow him. Moments later, we were in an elevator on our way to the seventeenth floor. The doors opened and we walked out, facing a long hallway.

Lim removed his mask and sunglasses and knocked loudly on one of the doors halfway down. A thirtyish Asian man wearing jogging clothes answered. He and Lim hugged. I removed my shades and mask and watched, noticing an uneasiness in Lim's friend. After Lim introduced me, he and his friend began to speak in Chinese, once again excluding me from the discussion. The conversation quickly became heated, with Lim becoming angrier than I'd ever seen him, the other man appearing apologetic and obsequious.

Lim turned to me. "It looks like we're what you call 'fucked.'"

"What's happening?" I asked.

"My friend was going to get us into Hong Kong in the back of his truck, which has a false bottom. There is a hidden space under the bed, plenty big for all of us to fit in. He has used that truck many times to take people across the border. Nobody has ever been suspicious. Now, with all the publicity around us, he refuses to do it. He is afraid of being caught."

"No wonder you're so upset. What do we do now?"

"There is not much choice. We will not be allowed through a checkpoint. We could try to find a hole in the fence that separates China from Hong Kong. That means going over very rough terrain."

"Do you know your way?"

"Not at all. There is no way I am taking Mingyu on a dangerous expedition like that. We could get lost, be without food and water. Makes no sense."

After all that had transpired, planning, studying, touring the facility, taking videos, getting Daisy out of the country, being chased by police, disguising ourselves, traveling so far, getting so close, and now this. I couldn't believe our mission would end here because Lim's friend was such a chickenshit. I was close to losing it.

"That leaves one option," Lim said.

I gained my composure and was at full attention, as hope made a much-appreciated appearance. "What's that?"

"Snakeheads."

"What?"

"I am not crazy about the idea, either. But I see no other way."

"I wasn't criticizing your idea. I just have no clue what Snakeheads are."

"No clue?"

I laughed. We had a thing or two to learn about each other's cultures. "'No clue' means no idea, or I don't know. In other words, I don't know what a Snakehead is."

Lim laughed. "You Americans. I probably know more about your country than you know about mine."

"I don't doubt that."

"We have a history of people from China trying to get into Hong Kong, back when it was British. Many poor people wanted to go there for better jobs, but the British did not let them in. Similar to the way your country tries to keep out Mexicans."

"I didn't know that."

"Similar to coyotes, the people who help Mexicans get into the US illegally, there were people in China who helped their countrymen cross into Hong Kong. For money. Many of these people were in gangs and became known as Snakeheads. Currently, there is less demand for getting across the border illegally since China owns Hong Kong and issues passes. But there is still a trickle of people who are ineligible to get those passes, so the Snakeheads still smuggle people across. These

Snakeheads are not the best people you will meet, but we are going to have to trust them."

Lim's friend had disappeared into a back room. I was full of questions. I desperately wanted this to work, but I was wary. "How do they sneak people in? How do we contact them?"

"I know some people who know some people who know some people."

"Now you sound like an American."

"See? We are not all that different. My friend said we can stay here until we make our arrangements."

"That's the least he could do."

"No, he could have done less than that. He could have told us to leave, or even called the police."

I laughed. "That's another one of our expressions. 'Least he could do.' That means someone should do at least that. Any less than that would mean the person's a real jerk."

"Then I agree. That is the least he could do. But he is a jerk anyway."

Lim made a series of phone calls. As usual, I didn't understand a word of the conversations. At last, he was done. "We are in luck," he said. "We can leave tonight, and they take bitcoin. We should leave now. We need to be at the coast at 7:00 p.m."

"How about telling me the details?"

"I will tell you on the way. First, we have to get to the subway station. It is a good fifteen-minute walk from here."

We headed for the door, put our masks on, and grabbed our things. Lim yelled "*Zaijian hundan*" to his ex-friend, who remained out of sight. Once we were outside and had put on our sunglasses, Lim took a moment to orient himself before leading me through streets, which became increasingly more crowded.

As we walked, we found that we had to push our masks to the side when we spoke, so the other could understand. Lim explained that the people who would be taking us to Hong Kong, while not exactly reputable, were known by friends he trusted to be reliable human smugglers, not only taking people to Hong Kong, but to America and Europe. They charged a lot of money and knew that reputation was important in this corner of the underworld. During the two-hour boat ride, we would be in a small compartment below the deck.

We arrived at a subway elevator which took us down to the station level. There we were confronted with security, where we placed our bags on the belt feeding one of the x-ray machines. My pulse quickened once I saw two guards dressed in black with "SECURITY CHECK" written in white lettering on the back of their uniforms. Still wearing sunglasses, I kept my head down to avoid the ever-present cameras, passing signage in English and Chinese posted on the walls. Once through security, the tension in my muscles, which I hadn't noticed before, relaxed. Then it was down the escalator to a busy station. Lim bought two subway tokens, each looking like a green coin, in a machine with a touchscreen.

The entrance to the train area was almost exactly like BART's, where traffic through waist-high partitions is controlled by panels jutting out at ninety degrees from either side, retracting when a token is passed over the detector. We proceeded through and stood in a short line before a bank of glass doors to wait for our train. Looking around, I saw signs with clear directions, and monitors with up-to-the-minute information on trains. By the time our train arrived five minutes later, the line behind us had grown. The glass doors opened in sync with the train doors, and we entered the subway car. The seats, all lining the perimeter, were occupied. Having to stand was the least of my problems. Hours later, after four transfers we arrived at our destination, Bao'an station on the eastern coast of Shenzhen.

It was dark, but the streets were lit. Lim had memorized directions to a tea shop on an alleyway off a busy street and gave Mingyu a bottle on the way. Upon arrival, Lim spoke to a man behind the counter who disappeared through a curtain. A young man with spiked hair appeared shortly, wearing a black shirt and cargo pants. The shirt was unbuttoned, revealing a red and black snake tattoo on the left side of his chest. He and Lim spoke before he scanned a QR code on Lim's phone, authorizing payment of one and a half bitcoin, or approximately ten thousand dollars at the going rate.

Lim directed me to hand the tatted man my passport, which I did. The man took it behind the curtain, then returned a few minutes later and handed it back. Lim showed me where a new China exit stamp and

Taiwan entrance stamp had been placed. I returned the passport to its holder, happy that this detail, which I hadn't thought about, had been taken care of.

Next, the young man led us through sparsely traveled dark streets and alleyways, to a highway bordering the water. An expressway loomed over us, the rhythmic sounds of the shoreline interrupted by honking and occasional screeching tires above. The smell of diesel fuel mixed with ocean decay permeated the air. We walked along the dark shoreline, brightly lit tall buildings always in view. Although my feet were tired and my backpack got heavier with every step, I resisted the temptation to complain. I knew it wouldn't help.

In a dark area, our escort came to a stop. He held up his cell phone and briefly turned on the flashlight, blinking the light three times. Out of the darkness came an inflatable dinghy rowed by a man in a yellow shirt. He tied the oars together, then jumped off into a foot of water, as he held a rope attached to the dinghy. The man spoke quietly to our escort, then to Lim.

"We will get a little wet," Lim said. "Don't worry, I'll make sure you're safe."

I wasn't so sure, but I had no choice. Wearing the papoose with Mingyu securely inside, and lit by the quarter moon, Lim removed his shoes and placed them in his bag. Following his instructions, I took off my shoes, put them in my backpack, and handed everything to him. Still carrying Mingyu, he slung my backpack over one of his shoulders and picked up his and Mingyu's belongings in his left arm. He entered the water up to his ankles, turned, and held his right hand out to me. I took a deep breath and grabbed the extended hand.

With the yellow-shirted man holding the dinghy, Lim helped me to an aluminum seat, big enough for one person, at the front of the boat. He handed Mingyu to me, then rolled himself aboard and sat on the air-filled bow, facing me. Mingyu cried out for a moment when Lim grabbed him and returned him to the papoose. For a moment, all was quiet, save the rhythmic sound of waves hitting the shore. The man in the yellow shirt gave the boat a push, then jumped onto the seat behind me and began rowing through the black water, flickering reflections of the moonlight bouncing off the waves. Lim held one my hands. "Don't worry, we'll be on the big boat soon," he reassured me several times.

It seemed like a long time, but it was probably only a few minutes, before I saw lights ahead of us. The form of a boat, a trawler close to forty-five feet long, took shape. Our rower turned the dinghy around and directed it to the side of the larger boat, near a four-rung rope ladder hanging down, and secured our small vessel. Lim stood, miraculously maintaining his balance, and spoke to a crew member above us on the trawler. The man reached down, took the load Lim was still carrying, and placed it on the deck. Lim held Mingyu high in the air and the man grabbed him. Then Lim took my left hand, wrapped my fingers firmly around the rope ladder, and climbed up the ladder ahead of me, into the trawler. Once on board, he reached down, took my free hand, and helped me up. I stood motionless for a moment and took a deep breath, the first time I remembered breathing after getting on the dinghy. Lim retrieved Mingyu from the crewman and returned him to the papoose, as the yellow-shirted man climbed aboard. The whole operation took less than five minutes, but the tension exhausted me. Before I could gain my bearing, Lim and I put on life jackets which were handed to us, and followed one of the crewmen down a steep staircase to a small room, a cupboard really, scarcely big enough for us to sit in. Mingyu started to cry when Lim carried him into the space and sat on the floor. I stood frozen, unsure I could sit in this tiny space with a crying baby for two hours.

"We'll suffocate in there," I yelled.

A strong push down on my shoulder, followed by an abrupt kick forward sent me into the room. With a thud, the door was shut, and all went black.

CHAPTER 34

"Stay calm," Lim said.

The smell from the gasoline engine permeated the space. Mingyu's crying pierced my ears. The floor was wet. My back hurt from being shoved into the cubicle, a condition that wasn't helped by the cramped quarters. I removed my mask, thankful I could still breathe, but worried that the baby's crying would use up the small amount of oxygen that much faster. I heard the floor above creak between Mingyu's screams, as the three-man crew walked around on deck. Muffled voices I couldn't understand, and occasional laughter wafted through the ceiling.

"Don't worry about the oxygen," Lim said. "Air is circulated through this room with a pump. These guys may be criminals, but they know what they're doing."

"I'll be glad if we get there alive. This makes my coach flight to Beijing look like a piece of cake."

"Piece of cake?"

"Another American expression. I guess it doesn't make any sense, but it means 'easy to do.'"

"I think Mingyu finally exhausted himself. If he sleeps for the rest of the trip, it should be a piece of cake," Lim said.

"Any ideas to make the time fly by?" The rocking of the boat was making me nauseous. The last thing I wanted to do was throw up. Maybe if I kept my mind off my queasiness, I could keep from vomiting. I didn't think barfing in this small room would serve to cement my relationship with Lim.

"I have an idea," Lim said. "So many American movies are banned here. You can tell me about some of them."

"What movies were banned?"

"I do not know. They were banned." Lim laughed. "Just kidding, I know the names of many of them. You have a movie about Winnie the Pooh that cannot be shown here."

"You want to hear about Winnie the Pooh?"

"No, not that one. What about *Avatar*? Did you see that?"

"Yes, I watched it a few months ago on Amazon. That's our big internet site like Ali Baba."

"I know what Amazon is."

I felt a slight twang of discomfort since I'd seen *Avatar* with Gabe, a detail I saw no reason to mention. I described *Avatar*, *The Da Vinci Code*, *The Departed*, *Seven Years in Tibet*, and *Captain Phillips*. I was in the middle of recounting *Red Dawn* when the boat come to an abrupt stop and bumped backward.

"I think we are here," Lim said.

Retelling old movies had made the time pass quickly. Mingyu cooed. Lim and I were silent, listening to the heavy footsteps approaching. I hoped they were the footsteps of our crew, and not Hong Kong security. The door to our compartment flew open. Light from a flashlight was the first thing I saw. For several moments, that's all I could see as my eyes adjusted to the light. To my relief, I recognized the voice of one of the crewmen. I wanted to jump out, but my body was stiff and contorted. Lim, holding Mingyu, climbed over me. He stood up outside the small room and spoke to the crew. I stretched my legs as far as they would go into the space vacated by Lim. Then I turned onto my hands and knees, crawled out, and stood in the cramped space between the stairs and the cubicle.

I realized that we had pulled up to a pier, overhead lights illuminating the trawler. "We are here," Lim said to me, smiling. "Welcome to Hong Kong."

The crew led us off the boat, past rows of assorted sea craft including yachts, cabin cruisers, and junks, towards two uniformed officers guarding the gate to the outside. Lim advised me to keep my head down when we passed under the overhead cameras. Upon reaching the exit, one of the crew members gave the officers some cash, and we walked away from the dock, onto a sidewalk by a busy street. Lim spoke to the closest crewman who pointed in the direction of distant lights.

"Just because we are in Hong Kong, you cannot let your guard down. We still need to wear our masks," Lim told me. "There are cameras everywhere here, too, and you can be sure that since Hong Kong is part of China now, they are looking for us here. The legal system here is more like in your country, so in theory, you have more rights in Hong Kong than in China. But if the Chinese government wants you, they will go outside the official laws here to get you." Once our masks were back in place, Lim waved his arms and a cab pulled over. "We can take this cab. It's a long walk."

"Where are we going now?" I asked, as I followed Lim into the cab.

"Tomorrow is a big day. In the morning, you will leave on a small cargo ship for Taiwan. In the afternoon, Mingyu and I leave on a much bigger cargo ship for Oakland. I want to stop by the port now to make sure everything is in order."

"How well do you know the people you've made these arrangements with?"

"I have known one of them for a long time. He has helped several people in our organization escape to avoid arrest. He also arranged for Ting and her children to go to America. I am following the same route she took."

I realized this would be our last night together. For a long time, if not forever. I wondered if Lim was thinking about that.

By the time we reached the port fifteen minutes later, it was 10:00 p.m. We got out of the cab and Lim settled the bill. Bright lights lit up piles of forty-foot long cargo containers of all colors, many with logos or writing on the sides. Even at this late hour, the port was humming with activity as cranes stacked containers onto two huge ships. Lim explained to me that since most people in Hong Kong spoke Cantonese while he spoke Mandarin, he would mostly use English.

I followed him into the main office, where he asked to speak to the supervisor in charge of loading the Oakland-bound ship.

"He not here," said the young woman. "He here at eight tomorrow morning."

"How about his first assistant?"

"He outside loading. Wearing red hat."

We walked outside, where we each put on a hard hat taken from a stack near the door, and looked around. Lim held Mingyu close. Most of the men were wearing black or white hats. I spotted a red hat and pointed to it.

"That is him," Lim said and took off running. By the time I caught up with him, Lim was deep in conversation with the man in the red hat. Lim turned to me. "Everything is set for tomorrow. Your ship will be arriving shortly. They will unload it and begin loading it for the trip to Kaohsiung, Taiwan. I will bring you here before seven in the morning and make my final payment at that time. You will need to get in the special cargo container with air holes that will be waiting for you. You only need to stay there until a little after the ship takes off at nine. Once you are on the open sea, the crew will let you out. It should be around ten. After that, you can do whatever you want. They have an extra cabin for you to stay in. You can sleep there or walk around the deck. They serve meals in the main room below deck. Not fancy, but it will get you there."

"Sounds a lot better than a Chinese prison."

"When you get to Kaohsiung the next day, let Daisy and Ting know you are okay. I also want you to try to call me. I do not know if I will be able to get phone calls. I should be on the open seas by then. If we do not connect, send me a text and an email. I am fairly sure I will be able to receive email. Let me know you are okay."

"Not that there's much you could do if I'm not."

"Probably not, until I get to Oakland. But I will not be able to relax until I am sure you are safe."

"Don't forget to message me back. I need to know if you're both okay and on your way. In fact, with access to the internet, you can send me a message every day. It's not like you'll have anything else to do."

"I will be very busy feeding Mingyu and changing diapers," Lim said, smiling.

"I know it will be a difficult trip with Mingyu to take care of."

"I love taking care of him. I have a lot to look forward to. Seeing Ting, Kang, and Wang Shu. And you. That is, if you will want to see me."

"Of course I'll want to see you."

"Will you? You will be back in your world. I am sure you will have no trouble finding lots of men, men who understand America much better than me."

"I think you understand America better than most people born there. You understand the value of freedom. You don't take it for granted. You know how cruel life can be when you don't have it."

Our relationship had gone from zero to one hundred in record time. The circumstances that had thrown us together served as a powerful accelerant. I was falling for this guy, hard. Beyond the physical attraction I saw a sensitive, intelligent man who was sturdy as a rock. Even so, our bond hadn't withstood the test of time. I didn't want it to end that night. I wanted to see how we'd feel about each other once we'd spent more time together under different circumstance, in America.

"What do you want to do our last night together here?"

I didn't want to give him an honest answer. There was so much riding on a successful conclusion to our mission. I still had to travel by boat to Taiwan, return to San Francisco, begin organizing the information Daisy and I had gathered, and start the process of helping Lim, Ting, and her children gain asylum. Lim needed to get on a large cargo vessel tomorrow with Mingyu and care for his nephew on the long trip to Oakland. All this was weighing on my mind, but I wanted enough carnal activity with Lim to last me over a month. I wanted some hot sex.

"We should get something to eat, then get a good night's sleep," I said.

"I think we should—how do you Americans say it—fuck our brains out."

"That's what I meant." Lim and I were thinking alike.

CHAPTER 35

Our last night together in Asia was nothing short of terrific. I don't think either of us was disappointed. I know I wasn't. We woke before six, dressed, and had breakfast at a small restaurant near the hotel. Using my iPhone, I took several pictures of Lim and Mingyu outside in the cold morning air to share with Ting when I returned. It was hard to believe I would be back in San Francisco in a few days.

The walk back to the pier took fifteen minutes. It was a beehive of activity; people rushing around, trucks, forklifts, and cranes moving material. Lim found the supervisor he'd asked for the night before. A man of few words, he escorted us to a blue container box, open at one end. Inside was a stack of large gray blankets, the kind used by movers to protect furniture. I noticed a man in uniform with a clipboard several yards away asking workers to open seemingly random cargo containers for him to inspect. I was about to say something to Lim, when he said, "Do not worry about him. He has been paid."

"Get in," the supervisor said. "Make cushions around edges with blankets. When you feel crane lift box, you lie down. Maybe you slide a little. Is okay."

"How much time do I have?" I asked.

"Ten minutes, we load."

This is it. My feelings couldn't have been more mixed. I dreaded being sealed in that box. What if the government inspector decided he hadn't been paid enough? I worried about being lifted by a crane. Maybe the crew would forget about me, and I'd be stuck in the box for the entirety of the voyage. Even if all went well with my travels, I wouldn't see Lim again for weeks. Meanwhile, I was left to worry that he might be caught by the authorities before his ship left the harbor. His voyage was much longer and more dangerous than mine. He could run into a typhoon. What if the crew turned against him? Mingyu would be hard to take care of on such a long voyage. After all that, possibly no one would take our story of Chinese human embryonic stem cell gene editing seriously. There were obstacles we had to get through before I was back home, reunited with Lim and Mingyu, the Chinese program in Fengshou was shut down, and the mission complete.

My eyes teared up when I hugged Lim one more time, kissed Mingyu on the forehead, and kissed Lim again, all under the watchful eye of the supervisor. I arranged the blankets around the perimeter of the container with Lim's help. I wished he could enter the US legally, so he could travel with me and keep me safe. We kissed again, and I sat in the metal box, holding my backpack. Seconds later, the two doors on the end were slammed shut. I heard the sound of metal on metal as the bars sealing the box slid into place. Without the threads of light coming in through the air holes, it would have been completely dark. My heart thumped and I began to hyperventilate as claustrophobia overcame me. I calmed myself by closing my eyes and forcing myself to breathe slowly and deeply.

Feeling shut off from the world, my sense of hearing became keen. Surrounded by activity, with vehicles driving past, people running and walking, workers yelling, engines lifting containers on pulleys, and clanking sounds I couldn't recognize, I sat at attention waiting to be lifted high in the air. I jumped at hearing a loud knock on the side of my container. Someone outside yelled in Chinese, then said in a quieter voice, "Get ready. You next." I lay on my back, with one strap of my backpack over my right shoulder.

I sensed my internal organs pull downward when I was hoisted in the air, reminding me of an amusement park ride, something I never enjoyed, even as a child. I held my breath while I slid around the inside of the container, arms and legs out to keep my body from hitting the sides. My backpack became loose and began sliding all over on its own, occasionally hitting me, but not with enough force to do any damage. The blankets didn't keep me from feeling unsafe and vulnerable, although they did prevent me from slamming into the sides of the cargo box and being injured. It felt like my heart hit my breastbone when the container slammed down with a clang. Then all was still. Minutes later, I heard more clanging noises outside when another container was loaded on top of me and another on top of that. I hoped the walls of my crate wouldn't collapse under the weight.

Despite the cool air outside, the inside of the container was hot and getting hotter. Little light entered through the air holes, as they were now blocked by other containers, I assumed. The air became stuffy, which didn't help with my claustrophobia. I reminded myself that many people had faced a similar situation before me. Ting had survived this with two young children. Lim would be doing it later with an infant. My voyage would be much shorter than theirs.

Three long earsplitting blasts indicated we were about to leave the port. I felt a pull as the ship left the dock. I was on my way, the gentle roll of the ship finally relaxing me. After what seemed like an hour, I heard footsteps, followed by a clanging sound outside the doors to my container. One door, then the other swiveled open, the light momentarily blinding me. Once I could see again, I grabbed my backpack and stepped outside the box, next to a short man with long black hair. Gazing up, I saw I was on the bottom of a high stack of containers.

"You come with me." The man led me around stacks of containers to the perimeter of the ship. The cool air was refreshing, despite the faint odor of burning fuel. The vastness of the gray-blue ocean before me was a welcome contrast to the confines of the container box. The man led me up a flight of stairs to my quarters, a small no-frills room with a bed, desk, small window with a view of containers, and a bathroom. Sitting on the bed, alone, the tension left my muscles. I lay down and relaxed. *Soon I'll be in Kaohsiung, Taiwan.*

The next thing I remembered was waking up on top of the bed, still wearing my shoes. Whatever I'd been dreaming quickly escaped my thoughts as I studied my surroundings and remembered I was on a ship. Noting the dim light coming in the window, I surmised I'd slept for several hours.

I turned on the overhead fluorescent lights and checked my phone. No messages. Of course. I still had to get the Wi-Fi password. After taking a shower, I put on the same clothes I'd been wearing, found my comb on the bottom of my backpack, and tried my best to look presentable. Carrying my purse with my phone inside, I entered the empty hallway outside my room. Downstairs I found two men seated in what appeared to be the cafeteria. I asked if I could get something to eat. They looked at me blankly until I motioned eating, bringing my right hand to my mouth several times. The men smiled and yelled something. Shortly after that, a man in an actual chef outfit brought me a bowl of rice and pieces of meat I couldn't identify in a yellowish sauce. I thanked him and he bowed, not understanding a word I'd said, I'm sure, but probably catching my drift. Whatever it was, the food tasted good. After I finished, I waved at the two men still deep in conversation and left.

I came to a large room where fifteen crew members were singing karaoke. I listened outside the room a few minutes, realizing the back and forth rocking of the boat was making me queasy. Luckily, a young crewman was coming toward me, presumably to sing with his friends. I showed him the screen on my phone, displaying the name of the ship's Wi-Fi network, LiuYifei. I pointed to the blank line for password.

"I do for you," he said. He took my phone and entered the password. After my phone was connected, he handed it back, and I thanked him. He bowed and joined the others singing *Hotel California*. Hearing that made me homesick, even though the rocking of the boat grew more pronounced and I became seriously seasick.

I hurried back to my room, where I threw up in the bathroom. Despite my queasiness, I sat at the desk and scrolled through my emails. I hadn't read them for days. In addition to the usual ads for things I didn't want, I saw several messages from Daisy, one from earlier today. But first, I scanned for something from Lim.

Sixth from the top of the list, there it was. My pulse quickened as I clicked on the message. He and Mingyu had safely boarded the cargo ship, were now at sea out of the container, and walking around in the fresh ocean air. The diapers and formula he'd arranged for were waiting for him when he arrived. There was no phone service on board, but he'd emailed Ting, telling her he was on his way. He looked forward to seeing me when he landed.

I replied that I had recently woken up from a long sleep, had eaten something in the cafeteria, and was now signed into the ship's Wi-Fi network. The moment I hit "send" I imagined Lim returning the kiss I'd told him I was sending him.

Next, I read Daisy's messages. A wave of relief enveloped me while reading about her safe return. She described Ting's tears upon seeing a picture of Lim and Mingyu at the airport and asked when I would return. She had already downloaded the asylum application form from the Department of Homeland Security and was helping Ting fill it out. Her company's HR Department had given her the name of the immigration attorney they used. He dealt mainly with H-1B visas, but Daisy thought he could help Ting or refer her to someone appropriate. Unable to get an appointment for over a month, Daisy was wait-listed for the first cancellation, hopefully in a few days.

I replied to her message, telling her I was on a cargo ship to Kaohsiung, where I would arrive the next day, and should be home the day after that. I told her I hoped she would have an appointment scheduled with the attorney by the time I returned, and we could all visit the attorney together. Then I asked if she'd downloaded the data Lim had uploaded to the cloud.

Another email came from Lim telling me he wished I was there, a photo of his small bed attached. I fell asleep despite my nausea and dreamed of being on board the ship with him.

I woke the following morning to light coming through the window and the same view of cargo containers I'd had the day before. Too seasick to eat, I checked my email. Lim was up already and had taken a tour of his boat's bridge. I realized I was missing the opportunity to see the bridge on my own ship but was too nauseated to talk myself into leaving my room. I asked Lim if he'd told Ting their parents were still alive. He emailed me back that he wanted to tell her himself, in person. An email from Daisy told me that yes, she had downloaded all the data Lim had sent to the cloud. She apologized for not mentioning that earlier.

I passed the time reading ads on my phone for cheap airfares, restaurant coupons, and testosterone boosters before dozing off. I was awakened by a sharp bump as the boat came to a halt. I stuffed my belongings into my backpack, pulled my real passport from the secure holder around my waist, and headed to the front of the ship. Elation is the best word to describe how I felt, looking at the dock, on which I would soon be standing.

CHAPTER 36

I felt so free. Full of energy. The weather was warm, the skies clear. Standing on land at the edge of the inlet into the port, the calm, blue water was only slightly darker than the sky. Boats large and small crisscrossed the water, surrounded by a city that came to the water's edge. I walked toward the tallest buildings and was soon on a busy street with high-rises and heavy traffic. Less like Beijing than San Francisco, the traffic seemed more manageable, with fewer cars and bicycles. Buildings were not quite as high as in Beijing, and sidewalks were a little less crowded and hurried.

I'm ashamed to admit that instead of seeking out an interesting neighborhood establishment, I found a Starbucks. There, I explored my flight options over a cappuccino and pastry. Most flights to San Francisco stopped in Hong Kong. There was no way I was going to stop there and risk Chinese police storming the plane. Neither would I fly Air China.

I located a flight on Eva Airways, a Taiwanese airline, that connected in Tokyo with an All Nippon Airways flight to San Francisco and reserved a seat for each flight. Leaving at 7:00 a.m. the following morning, I'd land in San Francisco eighteen and a half hours later, at 9:30 a.m. the same day. Arriving just two-and-a-half hours after leaving, of course, required crossing the international date line. I emailed my travel plans to Daisy, Lim, and my mother, and reserved a room at a hotel near the airport.

After walking around the city for two hours, I took a cab to my hotel and checked in. The clerk was friendly, spoke English, and looked at my passport indifferently. I went to my room, requested an early morning wake-up call, and showered. Lim had emailed, telling me that he and Mingyu were doing well. He told me not to worry, but his trip was going to take a little longer due to a storm ahead. They would get around it by going north. An attached video of the crew singing karaoke convinced me that he was having a better time on his boat ride than I had on mine. I would have called my mom, but it was early in California, and I didn't want to disturb her. I'd have plenty of time to speak with her during my Tokyo layover.

The morning wake-up call came too soon. It was still dark outside when I caught my cab to the airport, a short ride away. I checked in, passed through security and passport check without a hitch, and boarded the plane. At 7:00 a.m. the plane pulled away from the gate. Ten minutes later, we were in the air. From my window seat, I watched the island of Formosa, now dimly lit by the rising sun, get smaller and farther away during our ascent. I was filled with mixed emotions; relieved to be safely heading home, yet missing Lim and uneasy about his journey to Oakland with Mingyu.

The next eighteen and a half hours passed slowly. First, a four-hour flight to Tokyo, during which I watched a movie. Once in Tokyo for a five-hour layover, I tried calling my mom several times, but there was no answer. Sitting with the other waiting passengers, I began imagining I was amongst Chinese agents, waiting for the best time to run up to me and inject me with poison or slit my throat. My pulse quickened every time someone walked toward me. After an hour spent on edge, I walked around the airport, several times ducking into a restroom and locking myself in a stall for an extended period. I ignored the looks from women waiting in line each time I exited.

At last, it was time to board my final flight. I tried calling Mom one more time as I lined up with the other passengers, but again, she didn't answer. I took my seat, glad to be on the last leg of my trip. I sat between an elderly Caucasian woman and a middle-aged Asian man. I was relieved to see the last name on the man's ticket — Takashimi. Japanese. I doubted he had been sent to kill me.

The time dragged as I watched two more movies and read over fifty pages on my Kindle. I realized I had drifted to sleep when the pilot's announcement in Japanese over the PA system woke me. A follow-up announcement in English stated we were beginning our descent to San Francisco. I was almost giddy with excitement. The touchdown was smooth. Not wanting to do battle, I waited until most of the passengers were off before I collected my backpack and deplaned. I wanted to kiss the ground but instead got in the line for customs. The queue moved along, and I was soon exiting the secure area.

I looked around for Daisy, hoping she had come to meet me, and was disappointed when I didn't see her. I texted her to find out if she was nearby but received no response. There was really no reason for her to meet me at the airport, I told myself. She was no doubt busy, having recently returned from a long trip herself, and was probably visiting her parents. Soon I was on BART heading for home. From the Embarcadero station, I walked to my building and punched in the security code. After hearing the familiar click of the door unlocking, I rushed inside, into the elevator, then down the hall to my apartment. I rang the bell, not wanting to fish in my purse for the key. No response. I knocked as Ebba had, three quick raps, then two slow ones. Ting was sure to be home but would be hesitant to open the door to a possible stranger. I heard only silence. I wondered if Ting and the children were sleeping, even though it was mid-morning. Swearing to myself, I groped through my purse, found the key, and opened the door. The apartment was pitch-black. I switched on the light to a scene that took my breath away.

CHAPTER 37

Now I can say firsthand how horrifying it is to see your home—the place where you should feel safest—ransacked. Cushions thrown on the floor, piles of papers all over the tables, counters, and floor. Computers torn apart. Clothes, books, kitchen contents, piled on top of everything else. Whoever had done this had closed all the blinds. The most bone-chilling vision was a dark stain in the carpet the size of a large pizza on the far side of the living room.

I don't remember how long I stood, staring, before I could move. The first thing I did was touch the dark stain. It was moist, the wetness turning my fingertips red. The red substance had an odor I recognized immediately—blood.

Looking around, I saw more red splattered on the closest wall. Near the red splashes, a section of plaster measuring three square inches had been removed, leaving an unsightly hole. The yellow truck I had bought Kang was crushed, as if stomped on by a heavy boot. Other toys had been torn apart, either for sport or in search of some small hidden object. The computers hard drives were gone. In my room, my jewelry box had been emptied, but my eighteen-karat gold chain was on the floor. Whoever had done this wasn't looking for the usual valuables. They were looking for data. Whatever we had recorded, videoed, or written about. Just when I sensed I was safe, I wasn't.

I scoured every inch of my eerily quiet apartment looking for a clue. I didn't know what a clue would look like, but I didn't find one. I picked up a partially eviscerated couch cushion from the floor and returned it to its rightful place after clearing the papers and books away. I sat, trying to collect my thoughts. My hands were clammy, and I felt shaky all over.

When I had pulled myself together somewhat, I rang the bell to the apartment next door. I didn't know the couple that lived there well but was on friendly terms with them, saying hello when I saw either of them in the hall or elevator. One of the young men answered. His eyes widened when he saw me. He looked like he was trying to speak but was unsure what to say.

"I got home from a trip a few minutes ago," I said. "It looks like something terrible—"

"Have you seen it? OMG, you must have. I don't know where to begin. They removed the crime scene tape earlier today. The cops were everywhere—"

"What happened? Nobody's there. The place has been ransacked. There's blood on the floor."

"I guess you haven't heard. I don't want to be the one to tell you. Daisy . . ."

I was a bundle of nerves and losing my patience. "Daisy what? What happened to Daisy?"

"It was terrible. They took her away."

"Away? Where to? Where is she?" My stomach was knotted up, every muscle tense. "Please tell me she's okay." I started to tear up. I thought she was dead.

"No, she's not okay. Shot right in the chest. My husband was home. He heard it."

I started to cry. "Is she . . . dead?"

"ICU. San Francisco General. Last I heard, she was in serious condition, upgraded from critical."

I closed my eyes and breathed deeply. She was alive. "What about Ting?" I asked. "And her kids?"

My neighbor looked at me blankly. "Who?"

"Ting, the Asian woman who was living in our apartment with her kids for the last few weeks."

"Honestly, I have no idea who you're talking about."

"She probably didn't go out much so maybe you never saw her."

"Well, I don't know anything about her."

"She must have gotten away, then," I said, more to myself than to my neighbor.

"Don't ask me. Maybe she wasn't in your apartment. It's not like the cops found any dead bodies in there that I know of."

"Do you know who did this?"

"No idea. I don't think the cops know either. They were crawling all over this place, talking to everyone, two days ago. Wait a minute. I got a card from an inspector. You can call him." He disappeared for a short time, returning with a card. "Here, take this. If anyone can tell you anything, he can."

I needed to find a place to stay that night, but first I wanted to visit Daisy. I took an Uber to Zuckerberg San Francisco General and found the surgical ICU. I explained to the clerk that I was Daisy's roommate and best friend, and I was sure she'd want me to visit. She told me to wait and returned a few minutes later.

"Okay, she wants to see you."

That's when I knew she was not only alive but conscious and able to communicate. I breathed deeply and followed a nurse to Daisy's room. I felt at home in a pediatric ICU, but a unit filled with big people seemed foreign to me.

Daisy was lying in a hospital bed, her upper body propped up at a forty-five-degree angle. Contents of an IV bag were being pumped into her left forearm. She was wrapped in a hospital gown with the opening in front, revealing a drain protruding from a long, sutured wound under her left collarbone. Tubing from a chest tube was hooked up to a vacuum, keeping her lung inflated. Daisy's right index finger was inserted into a small device for measuring blood oxygenation, and EKG wires protruded from the arm of her gown. The wires disappeared behind a monitor displaying pulse, EKG, respiratory rate, and blood oxygen. Her hair was disheveled, and she had a black eye. Other than that, she looked pretty good.

"My god, I'm so glad you're okay. That's one helluva shiner you've got," I said.

"Bar fight." Daisy smiled faintly. Her voice was weak, but I was happy to hear it.

"So, how does the other guy look?" I asked jokingly, aware the situation didn't call for humor, but she started it.

"Damn it, Rosen, don't make me laugh. Hurts like a bitch despite all the medication."

"Sorry. I just got back, and instead of giving me a big welcome home party, I see you're here. What the hell happened?"

"Fight with the caterer."

"It's no joke. One of our neighbors told me you'd been shot."

"So they tell me."

"You don't remember?"

"Not a thing. I remember being home, talking to Ting about getting everything ready for her asylum application. Next thing I remember is waking up here. My parents were the first things I saw. They were here most of the morning. Left maybe fifteen minutes ago."

"Who did this? Has the bastard been caught? What about Ting? Where is she?"

"Slow down with the questions. Geez, are you this bad with your patients? I don't know much at all. All I know is I got shot. The bullet traveled right through me. The surgeon said it nicked my left subclavian vein, the one that goes under the collarbone."

"I happen to know where that is."

"I suppose they covered that in medical school. It went really close to my subclavian artery and aorta. I'm told I was lucky. Although I had a collapsed lung, it could have been worse. A millimeter one way or the other, and I'd have bled to death right away."

"Sounds like it."

"A detective was here earlier asking questions, but I was no help. He told me they dug a bullet out of the wall, and our apartment was ransacked. Did you see it?"

"Sure did. It's a big mess. Did he mention any suspects?"

"No. He said surveillance cameras in the apartment lobby show an Asian woman and two young children running out of the building. From the description, I'm sure that was Ting and her kids. Less than a minute later, two Asian men dressed in black and wearing gloves ran out in succession. No one in the building recognized them. They're most likely the ones who did it."

"How long are you going to be here?"

"At least two more days, I'm told. I lost a lot of blood, and had some heart problems, so they need to watch me for a few days. If I don't get infected and have no more abnormal heart rhythms, I won't have to stay longer than that. Before I forget, I told my parents you were coming back today. They said you could stay with them. As I understand it, our place isn't habitable."

"That's nice of them. But with the Chinese government still after us, I don't think it'd be safe. Those people are smart. I suppose we should have expected this. I'm sure it wasn't difficult for them to find out where we live from our real passports and visas. I'll bet they're watching your parents' house. If I went there, not only would I be in danger, but they would be too."

"Where will you stay?"

"I think my best bet's to go to a high-priced hotel near union square. They won't give out my room number without my permission. In the morning, I'll get my hair colored again. What do you think I should do now? Blond or redhead?"

"Blond. And get it cut even shorter. I've always wanted to see you in a Mohawk."

"I've got to figure out what to do before you get discharged. At least you should be safe while you're in here." I thought about the previous attack on Kang in the peds ICU. "I'll tell the staff to be sure not to let anyone they don't know come back here, and to call security for anything out of the ordinary." I made a mental note to call the police and request extra security for Daisy.

"Could you call Brian? Tell him I'm okay. I was supposed to call him yesterday. He's probably wondering what happened. I never told him about all the stuff we're involved in. I was going to tell him next time we got together, but—"

"I know. Life got in the way."

"Couldn't have said it better myself."

"I'll tell him you're okay, but you got shot during a home invasion."

"Perfect. Tell him not to come here. I don't want him to see me until I have a chance to wash my hair and, basically, look hot."

"You're so shallow."

"You should try it sometime. If you'd been shallow like me, you'd never have decided to help Ting, and we wouldn't be in this mess."

Daisy remembered there'd been a cancellation with the immigration attorney and she had an appointment with him the following afternoon. She gave me the attorney's name and the street his office was on so I could look him up. On my way out, I asked at the nursing station if Daisy had anything decent to wear when she left. I was told her shirt had been cut off when she arrived, but there was a box of old clothes previously left by patients she could choose from.

As soon as I left, I called Daisy's current love interest and explained that she'd been injured in a home invasion. He was appropriately concerned and wanted to visit. I told him she was okay, but no visitors were allowed. Next, I called the closest police station to request an officer be stationed by Daisy's room. I was told they'd look into it.

CHAPTER 38

After checking into the Hotel Nikko, I went directly to my room, dumped the contents of my backpack on the bed, and connected my almost-dead cell phone to the charger. The events earlier in the day had eradicated any thoughts of food, but I was suddenly famished. I ordered a sandwich from room service—a nice perk of staying in a pricey hotel—then checked the Dropbox account Lim had set up. Empty. Everything had been deleted.

It was almost too much to bear. I tried breathing slowly and deeply to control my anxiety. I still had the data cards in a sock, but all the work Daisy had done to organize it was down the drain, and I wouldn't have time to organize it before I met with the attorney. Not only didn't I know how to download and arrange the information, I didn't even have access to a computer. My hunger was replaced by knots in my stomach. I called the last number I had for Ting. No answer. The knots in my stomach tightened. Then I called Ebba.

"Are you back?" she asked, neglecting to start the conversation with a greeting.

"I returned earlier today. Not what I expected."

"Are you okay? What do you know?"

"I'm fine. I'm staying at the Nikko." I felt myself talking a mile a minute. "Saw the apartment. It's a total disaster. I found out Daisy'd been shot and visited her in the hospital. Miraculously, it looks like she's going to be okay. But she doesn't remember a thing. Neither of us has a clue what happened to Ting and the children."

"Relax. They're okay."

I stopped speaking, letting the good news sink in. "Oh, thank you. I was so worried. What happened? Where are they? Are they with you?"

"They're in the Lafayette Park Hotel. It's a good hotel in Lafayette, a small town in the East Bay near Walnut Creek. They should be safe there. I had to practically tie Ting up before she allowed me to pay for her to stay there."

"Was she in the apartment when everything happened?"

"Yes. And the kids, of course. She and Daisy'd spent hours since Daisy returned, filling out asylum applications for Ting and Lim, describing everything they knew about the Chinese gene-editing program and organizing the images and hours of video they'd retrieved from the cloud. When someone knocked on the door saying he was delivering flowers, Daisy thought it was a surprise from her boyfriend."

"Well, it was a surprise, but not from her boyfriend. Two Asian men pushed their way in. Before they could see her, Ting slipped under a table near the front door. Thankfully, there was a sheet draped over it."

"Before we left, Daisy and I had hidden toys for the kids underneath the sheet."

"It's a good thing you did. How she got her kids under there, and kept them quiet, is beyond me. They were very scared, hearing the men ransack the place. Since Ting hadn't left the apartment in over a week, the men didn't know she was there."

"They closed the blinds, then demanded Daisy turn over all her information and recordings from the trip to China, and asked where Ting and the children were. Daisy said she didn't know, but after one of the men slugged her, she showed them where copies of the recordings from China were downloaded on her computer. The men were speaking to each other loudly in Chinese, so Ting understood everything. They searched Daisy's computer and found Lim's Dropbox account. Ting heard them laugh when they found the password to the account on a Post-it stuck to the computer screen. They got into the account, deleted everything, then removed the computer hard drives."

"While they were doing that, Ting decided this might be her last chance, and ran for the front door with Kang and Wang Shu. She heard one of the men take off after them, but was able to evade him by ducking into a fire exit with the kids. Always concerned about escaping a fire, Ting knew there was an exit very close by, which happened to be in the opposite direction of the elevator. She heard a gunshot as she started down the stairs and grabbed Wang Shu. She and Kang raced downstairs, out of the building. She assumed the men ran the opposite way out of the apartment, past the elevator, until they found a fire exit farther away. That's all the extra time she needed. Ting and Kang ran almost a mile without stopping. When it felt safe, she called me, and I arranged for her to go to the hotel."

Ebba gave me the number of the cell phone Ting was now using. Room service arrived as I was preparing to call Ting. I signed for it and got rid of the waiter in seconds. Sitting at the small desk in my room, I called Ting and listened to her describe the horror of the invasion in her own words. She was certain the men who broke into the apartment worked for the Chinese government. While she was under the table, hearing the men yell, and hearing Daisy get hit, she thought of the safety of her kids. She had stupidly left her gun in one of the bedrooms and heard the men laugh when they found it. Hoping Daisy would be safe, she grabbed her kids and ran. After entering the stairwell, she heard the gunshot and called 911 before reaching the ground floor.

"I so sorry. They shoot Daisy because I run out."

"It's not your fault. I think they intended to kill Daisy all along once they'd gotten all the information she had. They wanted her dead so she wouldn't be able to talk, and they would have killed you and your children, if you hadn't gotten away. If they hadn't seen you run out, they probably would have stayed a little longer and shot Daisy again. So, you actually saved her."

"What I do now? I can stay here few days, but not forever."

"Daisy had made an appointment for you to see an immigration attorney with her tomorrow."

"I have application all fill out, with statement explaining everything."

"Unfortunately, they destroyed everything on the computer. They even erased everything in the Dropbox account."

"Good thing I keep backup thumb drive in pocket."

"You have a backup? How much is on it?"

"Everything. But how we get it to attorney?"

"The appointment isn't until tomorrow afternoon. I'll take BART to Lafayette. I can be there by 1:00 p.m. Tomorrow morning, I'm getting a new look, so don't be surprised when you see me."

My appetite returned, and I ate my sandwich after hanging up. I tried calling my mom, but again, she didn't answer. Next, I made an appointment to get my hair cut and colored at nine-thirty in the hotel beauty salon the next morning. Taking Daisy's advice, I decided blond would be less noticeable than ginger.

At 12:30 p.m. the following day, I emerged with short spikey blond hair, purple lipstick, and new sunglasses. Maybe a bit noticeable, even in San Francisco, but not the typical look of a pediatrician. Too late to take BART, I ordered an Uber. During the ride, I called the attorney's office and learned that the appointment wasn't until 4:00 p.m. I arrived at Ting's hotel around 1:15 p.m.—fifteen minutes late despite my best effort.

The clerk at the hotel front desk called Ting, and after checking my ID per her request, permitted me to go to her room. The fact that I looked quite different than my ID photo didn't seem to faze the clerk. Knocking on the door of Ting's third-floor room, I felt excited. Ting swung the door open, then jumped back and screamed. A second later, she was laughing at herself. I had been so transformed she didn't recognize me at first.

I entered the room and shut the door, then spent longer than I should have hugging Ting and the children. Ting, Kang, and Wang Shu were smiling as they gathered around when I shared pictures of Lim and Mingyu on my phone. The children were learning to speak English, saying "uncle," "brother," "boat," and "coming here" several times. Ting made it clear she was unwilling to leave the safety of the hotel to visit the attorney with me.

I checked my watch. Two-fifteen. "I'd love to stay longer," I said, "but I've got to get to the appointment."

"Here," Ting said. She reached into the front pocket of her pants and handed me a small thumb drive. "Everything we work on is here, asylum applications, edited video with all evidence, is very good, but cannot print documents."

"No problem. I'll have them print everything at the attorney's office. Probably charge a fortune, but it's worth it."

I left, but not before telling Ting, Kang and Wang Shu how happy I was to see them and grateful they were all safe. Downstairs, I waited almost fifteen minutes before catching an Uber, a reminder I was no longer in an urban setting.

On the way to the attorney, I phoned the inspector investigating the case. He was polite but reluctant to say much on the phone, agreeing to meet with me the following morning. Then I dialed my mom. She answered, and I told her I was back from my trip and would try to visit her soon. She asked me where I'd been, her speech noticeably slurred. Not wanting to burden her with details of my trip, I changed the subject. She never asked again.

I arrived ten minutes early at the attorney's office, a richly appointed suite in a modern high-rise building. I felt like I was hemorrhaging money as soon as I walked through the door.

I gave my name and explained I was there in place of Daisy Wong.

"What company do you represent?" the receptionist asked. "I don't see it here."

"I'm not with a company. But I have some documents on this thumb drive that need to be printed. Could you do that before I meet with the attorney?"

"You'll need to discuss that at your consultation."

I didn't have a good feeling about the meeting that was about to happen. At precisely 4:00 p.m., the receptionist brought me back to the office of the attorney, a middle-aged man in an expensive-looking suit with closely cropped, thinning hair. We shook hands, he offered me a seat, and I began to explain why I was there.

"My roommate, Daisy Wong, made this appointment with you because your firm was recommended by the company she works for. She wanted to discuss the asylum application of Ting Chen, a young woman from China. Originally, all three of us were going to come today. Unfortunately, neither Ting nor Daisy could make it, so I'm here alone."

"Why couldn't they come?"

"Two men invaded our apartment while I was abroad. Ting was staying in our apartment and escaped. She's now in hiding. Unfortunately, Daisy was shot."

"Is she dead?"

"No. Luckily, she's okay. Right now she's recovering in SF General."

"This doesn't look good for an asylum case. The government will not give asylum to people involved in organized crime."

"Ting isn't involved in organized crime. These men are from the Chinese government. Ting has knowledge very damaging to China's reputation. In fact, Daisy and I were recently in China gathering information to back up what she knows. The men who shot Daisy were looking for the information we'd gathered. Fortunately, Ting had saved everything on a thumb drive, which I have here. It has everything on it. If you could look at the information—"

"I can tell this is a very interesting case," the attorney said in a patronizing tone, "but I don't believe I or anyone else in this firm can help you. We don't have experience with Chinese assassins and such things."

This man thought I was insane. I was about to be bounced.

"I know this sounds bizarre. Perhaps you could verify that my roommate, Daisy Wong, was shot. I have the number of the inspector on the case." I started to look for the card in my purse.

"I'm going to refer you to another attorney who might be able to help." He jotted something on a sheet of paper and gave it to me. "Call him. You can call him any time. He's not very busy." The last remark seemed rather snarky. I sensed that this fancy lawyer was trying to screw with me by recommending a third-rate attorney, but given my desperation, I decided to test this new guy out.

I felt safe in my new guise, and walked back to Hotel Nikko, arriving at 6:30 p.m. after stopping for pad Thai at a local noodle house. Once in my room, I called the recommended attorney, Jonah Pierce. The phone rang once before it was picked up.

"Jonah, here." The voice was husky. I detected a tinge of a New York accent.

"My name is Erica Rosen. Your name was given to me by another attorney who indicated you might be able to help with an asylum case."

"That sounds interesting. Is this for you or somebody else?"

I explained that the case involved Chinese nationals seeking asylum due to having information compromising to their government. They were in danger of being arrested, or worse, if they remained in China. I told him the name of the referring attorney but didn't want to divulge more information without meeting in person.

"Where are you now?" Jonah asked.

"A hotel near Union Square."

"Can you meet me in my office in thirty minutes? It's off Market in the Tenderloin."

Two blocks from Ting's old apartment, I agreed to meet him. It was dark and cold outside. I wasn't going to the best area, so I chose Uber as my mode of transportation. The office was a walk-up above a small liquor store. I stepped over a homeless woman sleeping in the stairwell, all the while wondering if I was making a terrible mistake.

Reaching the landing on the second floor, I saw a door in the dimly lit hallway with a sign reading "Jonah Pierce, Attorney at Law." I wasn't sure if I should knock or just enter. I knocked.

"Come in." I recognized the voice from the phone.

Opening the door slowly, I first glimpsed shelves crammed with books, and tables with piles of papers. As I pushed the door open incrementally more, additional bookshelves and piles of paper came into view. Finally, I saw a man sitting behind a large desk, with a computer monitor and piles of books, newspapers, and documents strewn haphazardly over the surface. He stood and extended his hand, smiling. I had to bend over the desk to shake his hand.

"Nice to meet you, Ms. Rosen."

I tried not to show my surprise seeing a short, wiry man around thirty-five years of age with shoulder-length brown hair and an earring in one ear. Not at all what I had pictured from his voice. He wore a T-shirt and blue jeans. I couldn't see his shoes but suspected he was wearing Birkenstocks. If he could afford them.

"Please have a seat," he said. "Thank you for coming. Before we get started, I think it's fair to warn you that the attorney who recommended me, well, to be honest, he doesn't hold me in high regard. He's my father-in-law, and he occasionally refers cases to me, cases which he thinks are losers. Sometimes he's right, and the cases he sends me are often terrible, with bothersome clients who are hard to satisfy. Now and then, he sends me a gem. A gem he doesn't recognize. I have a feeling your case may be one of those."

"I don't know if it qualifies as a gem, but this is a particularly important case. Not only to the parties involved, but—forgive me for sounding melodramatic—important on a much larger scale." I had a good feeling about this fellow, although I didn't want to trust my intuition on something this crucial. I wanted some indication that this attorney wasn't a total hack. "Do you have experience with this sort of case?" I asked.

"Let me answer that by telling you a little about myself. You can see, I don't have a high-end practice in Pacific Heights. I started off being a journalist and have covered wars in Afghanistan and Iraq. I've done stories on many of the most vulnerable populations of the world, in the Middle East and Asia. My wife, the daughter of the attorney you met earlier, was also a journalist. I met her in Bangladesh over ten years ago while doing a story on the Rohingya persecution. My father-in-law did not approve of our lifestyle, traveling around the globe, reporting from unsafe places. Eventually, to keep the peace, I agreed to go to law school and pursue a career which he would deem respectable and hopefully make enough money to support our family, which at present includes two youngsters. Well, my father-in-law still doesn't approve of me, but I'm committed to the practice of law now. That and food stamps has allowed my family to flourish. Anything else you'd like to know?"

"Have you ever represented a client from China seeking political asylum?"

"One of my first cases as a lawyer was representing a Falun Gong couple who had come to this country illegally because they were being persecuted."

"That's religious persecution," I said. "This is different."

"Why don't you tell me all about it. Then I'll tell you if I think I can help."

"First, can you look at the information on this thumb drive? There are documents and videos here that will be extremely helpful. The woman, Ting Chen, who is seeking asylum with her children and brother, recently escaped from my apartment in San Francisco when two Chinese operatives invaded it. They shot my roommate, Daisy, who is now recovering in SF General. Lucky for me, I hadn't yet returned from China when that happened. I just got back yesterday and got this thumb drive from Ting earlier today. Still haven't had a chance to see what's on it, but I'm familiar with everything that might be there."

"Do you think the shooting has anything to do with Ms. Chen seeking asylum?"

"It has everything to do with her and her children being here, and the information she intends to reveal about the Chinese government. I have an appointment with a SFPD inspector tomorrow to find out what they know about Daisy's shooting. Probably not much, I'm afraid."

Jonah took the device and inserted it into the USB drive on his computer. "Sounds interesting," he said. I couldn't tell if he was sincere.

CHAPTER 39

Once the thumb drive loaded, Jonah scanned the I-589 forms, the applications for asylum Ting had filled out for herself and Lim. After that, he began reading Ting's long and detailed statement about what led up to her seeking asylum in the US.

"She seems quite fluent in English," he remarked.

"She learned to speak in China. However, I'm sure Daisy helped her."

"She was training as an Olympic athlete in China?" Jonah asked, his interest piqued.

"Yes. She and her brother, Lim. He will also be seeking asylum."

"Will be? He's not seeking it now?"

"He's not in the US yet. He's on his way."

"On his way?" Jonah looked exasperated. "What does that mean? It's not like he can walk here."

"Actually, he's on a slow boat from China." I hadn't intended to say something funny, but it came out that way.

Jonah chuckled. "Cargo ship?"

"You guessed it. And he's bringing Ting's youngest child. The other two are with her."

I couldn't be sure, but I believed I detected a subtle eye roll. I needed to keep him interested in the case, at least until we got to the video. Once he saw that, he'd have to believe me.

Finally, Jonah became animated. "Am I understanding this correctly? They forced Ting to carry a baby—one that was genetically engineered?"

"Uh-huh," I said somewhat smugly. I felt like saying, "Told you so."

"Impossible. Aside from that criminal Chinese scientist in the papers a while ago, no one's done that before. That guy seems to have botched it up, anyway. Even if it could be done, there is an international agreement that it shouldn't be attempted."

"Well, they can, and they did. China is only pretending to abide by the agreement. That's why they were so upset with the scientist who announced what he did, bringing all that unwanted attention. Wait till you see the video."

"This is unbelievable. How can this be happening?"

"It's a very secretive operation. All three of Ting's children are the result of genetic engineering experiments. They no longer seem to consider them experiments, though. They believe they have perfected the technique enough to use it whenever they see fit."

"What diseases are they curing?"

"Read on. You'll see that they haven't been interested in curing diseases, although they are starting to work on that now. Their main objective is to produce humans with extraordinary abilities so they can dominate the Olympics."

"Pardon me, but is this for real?"

"Exactly what I thought, at first. It turns out, they've been embarrassed that despite having the world's largest population, their country has yet to dominate the Olympics. They believe that if they produce super athletes, their citizens will be beside themselves with national pride, love for their country, and loyalty to the Communist Party."

"This is really sick."

"Don't I know it. Ting and her brother know it too. That's why they want to expose this operation and put a stop to it."

"What genes are they editing?"

"Keep reading. It should all be explained. If not, I can answer your questions, since I was there. So was Daisy."

"There? Where?"

"At the facility. The facility in China where they do all this crazy shit."

"Is that why they shot Daisy? Do you think they're after you too?"

"Absolutely. The only reason I'm alive is that I hadn't returned yet when Daisy was shot. She got back several days before me."

"Are you worried, walking around in plain sight?"

I took my driver's license from my wallet and showed it to Jonah. "This is who they're looking for."

Jonah studied the picture on my license and looked confused. "Just this morning, I had my hair cut and bleached. I didn't always look like this, like a punk rocker. Look pretty different, don't I?"

Jonah alternated his glance between my face and the picture on my ID several times. "You're right. I'd never recognize you from this picture. This should make you safe, for a while at least. Still, if what you're telling me is true, all of you are going to need protection."

"Agree. We'll have to figure that out."

Jonah continued reading. "Ting was forced to have *three* children?"

"Yes. The first one was more of an experiment to see if they could edit genes at all. Despite having two completely Asian parents, her first child has blue eyes."

"Do you know who the father is?"

"His name is Peng Yang. He was a famous Chinese Olympic athlete, a runner who crossed over to the dark side, you might say. He used to be Ting's boyfriend before he turned into some kind of monster."

"Did he rape her?"

"No, it was all done by in vitro fertilization. The idea is to take children whose mother and father are elite athletes in the same sport and edit their DNA so they will perform even better than they would naturally. In Ting's case, the sport was running. Her second and third child have unusual hemoglobin to give them superhuman stamina. In fifteen years, I suspect her middle child will be a world-class runner, possibly the best in the world. They've put that hemoglobin into children of Olympic speed skaters and swimmers too."

Jonah sat back, a dazed look on his face. "This sounds like a crazy science fiction scheme."

"It is, except for the fiction part. Although they've been successful in some cases, there have also been some horrific results."

Jonah's eyes widened. "Like what?"

"Some babies were so damaged, they died at birth or shortly after. Others survived but have significant birth defects and live in a special building. I didn't see it myself, but Daisy did. There should be recordings on the video. Other abnormalities may show up later in the supposedly successfully edited children. I know Ting's oldest child had an unexpected consequence of the editing."

"The daughter with her in the hotel?"

"Exactly.

"What's wrong with her? Is she deformed?"

"She's a girl."

"My wife would kill me if I dared to laugh at such a joke."

"It's not a joke. Wang Shu is genetically a male. She was supposed to be a blue-eyed boy. But she's a female because of an unplanned genetic mutation. She looks like a perfectly normal little girl, and she'll develop like a normal woman, although she won't be able to have children. Her condition, called complete androgen insensitivity, is caused by a lack of testosterone receptors. It's exceedingly rare."

"Are you saying they wanted to try out the editing technique starting with eye color, something they thought was simple, but wound up messing up the gene for the testosterone receptor?"

"Exactly. But they did succeed with the eye color. She has blue eyes. Impossible for someone who is one hundred percent Asian. Without gene editing, that is."

"How did you and Daisy get involved in this?"

"I first met Ting and her daughter when they came to my clinic to get Wang Shu's school health form filled out. I'm a pediatrician."

"You're a doctor?"

I nodded in the affirmative. Jonah started taking notes furiously, like now he believed I was a solid citizen. Not only was I not a punk rocker, but I held a respectable job. Okay, I'd quit that job, but he didn't know.

"Their visit was fairly routine until the end when Ting told me her daughter should have been a boy according to genetic testing. I thought she might be delusional, but despite my reservations, I had Wang Shu tested for this rare condition. Turns out, she has it. I'd never seen a case of it before, although I'd read about it."

"Then you got involved in her petition for asylum?"

"Not yet. Not until after I was working a shift in the peds ICU, and her son Kang was admitted. Ting wouldn't leave his side. She wouldn't talk to anyone until she saw me. Since she'd seen me before in the clinic, she trusted me."

"Kang was ill? From a genetic engineering mistake?"

"No, he'd been almost killed by a car when he and his mom were walking. Ting was nearly hysterical, saying people were trying to kill him, she was adamant about staff checking the ID of everyone that entered the ICU. I thought she was nuts. That is, until—"

"Until what?" Jonah was leaning forward.

"Until an Asian man came in pretending to be a phlebotomist and tried to kill Kang."

"My god! You're kidding."

"Not at all. Sounds crazy, I know. We had a hostage situation for a while, and the guy got away. We later found that he had taken the ID badge from a hospital phlebotomist—after he killed him."

Jonah looked shocked. "Why? Why would someone go to so much trouble to kill Kang?"

"Because he's living proof of what they've done. Ting was worried they would try to kidnap him and bring him back to China. When they tried to kill him, she realized they'd decided it would be easier to kill him than to take him back. They'll do anything to prevent the rest of the world from learning what they're doing."

"There would certainly be criticism, maybe sanctions. But really, what could the rest of the world do?"

"Kick them out of the Olympics. That would defeat the whole purpose. It would end any hope they had of reigning supreme there, a goal of utmost importance to them."

"This is big. Really big." Jonah continued writing on his pad. "I doubt the Olympic Committee has regulations regarding this kind of gene editing. This is way past doping. I should give them a heads up."

"The good news is they have over ten years to get regulations in place. The oldest of these kids are around four now."

"We'll need a whole lot of proof, needless to say."

"The videos. Also, I have a sample of Peng's DNA. I had lunch with him and collected the napkin he used to wipe his mouth."

"How did you arrange to get into the facility and meet with this guy?"

"Ting's brother is adept at bribery. He arranged for Daisy and me to visit parts of the facility so we could collect evidence. I pretended to be a scientist from Pakistan looking for help in setting up a gene-editing program in Karachi, so I toured the in vitro fertilization and research areas. Daisy, who posed as the future director of residential services in a gene-editing facility being planned, was shown all the housing facilities. We both recorded as much as we could with hidden cameras. In addition, Daisy rescued Ting's youngest child during the tour, and got him to Lim."

"Amazing. Didn't they have security?"

"Tons. But we were able to work around it."

"How?"

"A good plan, guts, and bribes."

Jonah continued reading in silence as I awkwardly looked around the office and checked for messages on my phone. Finally, he looked my way.

"I finished the asylum applications. I need to know—do they have other relatives in China? People who might be punished because of what they've done?"

"Yes, I almost forgot. Ting and Lim had been told their parents were dead, but shortly before we left for the US, he found out his parents are still alive. They'd been sent to a work camp because they tried to take Ting and Lim out of the Olympic training program years ago. Lim desperately wants to get them out of China and bring them here. He plans to tell Ting about their parents when he sees her, face to face. She still thinks they're dead."

"Is there anyone else in China who helped you, that might go to prison because of all this?"

"A couple of people. One of Daisy's cousins. She warned Daisy that her brother, a member of the communist party, had identified Daisy's picture. If she hadn't warned us, I'm sure we would have been caught. I'd be busting rocks with a sledgehammer right now."

"Anyone else?"

"A worker at the facility told me a lot in sign language. I'm sure by now they've reviewed all their camera footage—they have cameras everywhere—and know what she told me. There are two women Lim bribed, and three others who are part of Lim's organization. That's all I can think of."

"Why didn't you leave with Daisy? Why did you risk staying longer?"

"I was going to leave shortly after her, but while I was waiting for my flight, I saw on TV that they were already looking for me. I would have been arrested right away if I'd tried to get on a plane. I should also tell you—" I felt myself blush. I don't know why—I'm not exactly a schoolgirl. "I spent a lot of time with Lim, and, well, Lim and I developed a relationship as we made plans for my return to the states."

Jonah didn't miss a beat. "Are you planning to get married?"

Caught off guard, I stammered. "Well, not now. We didn't talk about that."

"That's okay. If you do plan to get married, it could help his case a lot. Although frankly, if half of what you said can be verified, the case for asylum is pretty fucking strong." His words felt like a set of powerful arms lifting a huge weight from my shoulders. "But first, let me watch the video."

The video Daisy and Ting had put together was ninety minutes long. Jonah and I watched it together on his computer. It started with my recordings, including the various labs, interviews with scientists, and going to lunch with Peng.

Then we saw what Daisy had filmed. Several nice apartments with mothers and their children. Everyone smiling. The Building of Disappointment, more horrifying than I'd imagined, was next. Fifteen infants and young children were in a filthy room, crying and screaming, their beds and cribs crowded together. Two children were thrashing around, tied to their bedframes, appearing to be having seizures. Three toddlers were missing arms. At least one child was blind. Another looked paralyzed, breathing with difficulty, as a rat ran over his motionless arm. Several toddlers had strange growths coming out of their heads or torsos. A man was holding one screaming child down as another injected him with something. A woman behind a desk in the front of the room sat expressionless, studying her cell phone. She appeared to be the only adult overseeing the children's care.

After viewing the facility grounds, we finally saw Mingyu in his crib. We heard Daisy tell her escort she needed to be alone to test the baby. Shortly after that, the screen went blank. I knew there was more on my memory cards that hadn't been added to the video, but this was enough for now.We sat in silence for several moments before Jonah spoke.

"I want to represent you. All of you."

"Wonderful," I said. I sensed an energy coming from him. He was determined to see that justice would be done.

"I'd like to accompany you to your meeting with the inspector tomorrow."

CHAPTER 40

The following morning, I met Jonah outside the San Francisco Central Police Station, a large, modern structure. We agreed that he would do most of the talking; I would only speak when necessary. Shortly after checking in with the receptionist, the inspector I'd spoken to the previous day escorted us to an interview room. A middle-aged man with graying hair and a serious demeanor, he expressed surprise that I was accompanied by an attorney. Jonah informed the inspector that this was much more than a simple home invasion, and he was there to help me explain the background information. First, he invited the inspector to give us all the information he had on the case thus far.

The officer played a video taken from our apartment lobby showing an Asian woman and a small boy I identified as Ting and Kang, respectively, running through the lobby and exiting the building. The woman was holding a girl I confirmed to be Wang Shu. Twenty seconds later, an Asian man dressed in black followed. A second Asian man dressed similarly ran by ten seconds later.

Next, we listened to a 9-1-1 recording made just before the time the woman was seen fleeing the building. The caller had a heavy Asian accent and sounded like Ting. She reported a home invasion at my apartment and said she heard gunfire. Less than thirty seconds later, four calls to 9-1-1 reported possible gunfire in the building.

The inspector told us that police and paramedics arrived within six minutes of the first 9-1-1 call. Two uniformed officers were the first to reach our apartment. The door was open, and Daisy was on the floor, barely conscious. Once they determined the intruders had left, the officers summoned paramedics, who tended to Daisy and brought her to the hospital.

Hard drives of both desktop computers and the single laptop had been removed. The condition of the apartment indicated it had been ransacked. It couldn't be determined whether papers or other items had been taken. The apartment was dusted for fingerprints, but none were identified by IAFIS, the FBI's Integrated Automated Fingerprint Identification System. The police wanted to obtain fingerprints from me, Ting, the children, and Daisy to eliminate ours from those they had collected. A bullet in the wall was all the intruders left behind. Technicians cut out a small section of the wall containing the bullet which was now in the crime laboratory.

"No one in the building witnessed anything," the inspector said. "Nobody we spoke to, and that included people from all the apartments near yours, even knew Ting and her children were living there. There are no leads, although images of the men fleeing the building have been shared with police officers up and down the state." Grainy and taken from a distance, I thought they were unlikely to result in an arrest.

Jonah said, "It appears that you've been doing a very thorough job with the investigation, given your resources. However, this case is much more complicated than you can possibly appreciate. What I'm going to tell you must be held in the strictest confidence. People's lives, including those of my client, Dr. Rosen here, her roommate Daisy, Ting, and her children, are in danger. There is good reason to believe these men will be back with every intention of executing my client and her associates. This case screams for FBI involvement."

"I understand you are concerned about your client and her friends, but it seems these men got whatever it is they wanted, namely the computer hard drives. There is no reason to believe they'll be back."

"I beg to differ. These men are assassins sent by the Chinese government."

"No need to get carried away here," the inspector said, looking more than a little irritated. "Why is it everyone thinks there is a government conspiracy—either involving Washington or a foreign power—when a serious crime takes place?"

"I understand your skepticism," Jonah responded. "But hear me out."

Jonah went on to reiterate all Ting had experienced, the murder of the phlebotomist, the attempted murder of Kang, and the testing of his hemoglobin in my hospital lab. Next, he described the genetic engineering facility I'd witnessed firsthand, the Building of Disappointment Daisy had seen, and the government's goal of creating Olympic champions.

When he had finished, the inspector asked if there was any proof of what Jonah had described.

"I'm prepared for that sort of vetting," he said, retrieving the thumb drive from his pocket and holding it up. "This is all the proof you'll need."

"Leave it here and I'll study it," the officer said.

"Not a chance. I haven't had a chance to copy it yet. This device doesn't leave my sight."

"Okay, I'll copy it." The inspector loaded the drive into his computer. "We might as well watch it together, so you can explain things if I have questions. I hope it's not long," he said as he started the video. The inspector remained quiet for fifteen minutes, sitting glued to the screen. Only after he'd seen the introduction of new genetic material into a fertilized egg, did he speak.

"I've seen this on the news. They say it's a breakthrough that'll allow scientists to cure many diseases. But not for many years, I thought."

"That's right," I said. "The technique shows great promise. But it has fallen into the wrong hands. It's not focused on curing diseases but instead creating babies with unnatural abilities. Because the technique isn't ready for prime time yet, it can create mutations in humans that cause a great deal of suffering as a byproduct. Mutations that can be carried from one generation to the next."

"How can I be sure this video is legit and not some well-designed scam?"

"Watch the rest of the video. Then we can discuss the next steps to take."

The inspector resumed viewing the recording, the expression of skepticism fading from his face. It was replaced by a look of horror when he saw the children in the building housing the unfortunate experimental failures. At the end of the video, he sat for a moment before speaking.

"Quite a story. Quite a story," he mumbled. Looking at Jonah, he said, "Okay, I'll see about getting the FBI involved."

"What about twenty-four-seven protection for these women? Daisy has only the protection of the hospital staff right now. She'll be discharged from the hospital soon, and will have none. Erica, Ting, and her kids need protection now."

"I'll ask about that, but no guarantees. We're stretched pretty thin as it is."

"Kang's medical record contains proof of his abnormal hemoglobin. Dr. Rosen has a sample of DNA from Peng on a napkin. If you compare that DNA and Ting's DNA with the DNA of Kang and Wang Shu, it will prove that Peng is their father, and Ting is their mother."

"I can talk to someone with more expertise about DNA than me."

"Further DNA analysis will show that neither Ting nor Peng carry the abnormal hemoglobin. That will prove Kang's DNA was edited. Lim, Ting's brother, and Mingyu, her younger son, will need protection when they reach Oakland. Once they arrive, Mingyu's paternity and hemoglobin can also be tested." Jonah took in a deep breath as he waited for the inspector's response. I was thankful to have found such an ardent advocate.

"Not asking for much, are you? What you're describing is rather sophisticated testing. We can't do that in our lab, but the FBI should be able to handle it."

"You can see this is going to be an extraordinarily big case. Of national and international importance. It needs to be handled with the utmost care."

"I'll have to speak to my captain and get back to you."

Jonah collected the thumb drive after the inspector copied it. He and I walked to a nearby Peet's Coffee to discuss our next move. It was much closer than his office, and the atmosphere was better. We found a table in the back, away from other customers. I sat facing the door so I could see who was entering. Something I learned from watching *The Godfather*.

"Well, what do you think?" I asked. "Do you think he'll contact the FBI?"

"I think he will. The big question is when. Sometimes these things take a while, but we don't have a whole lot of time, as I see it. You and your friends need protection now."

"Is there a protection service we can hire? I don't have a whole lot of money, but it's easy for doctors to get loans. Even unemployed ones, like me." Then I told him I had to quit my job to go on the China trip.

"It's good you don't have a job. They'd easily find you there. You can't go back to your apartment. I'll give you the names of a couple of agencies that provide bodyguards. Ones that carry weapons. It won't be cheap, but hopefully, you won't need them for long. I'll try to speed things up."

"How will you manage that?"

"My secret weapon."

I looked at Jonah expectantly.

"I have a good friend who's a journalist. He lives south of Market and does a lot of freelance political work. Has a lot of street cred. I'm sure he could get an article into the San Francisco Chronicle. I'll drop by and see him later today, if he's in town, and fill him in."

"I don't think it's a good idea to publish a story about this now. I'm afraid of what might happen."

"I'll ask him to write something up but not print it till we say so. I'll bring it to the inspector and tell him it's about to be published. He'll look worse than bad if he doesn't get moving on this quickly. My journalist buddy can break the story when the time's right."

"Okay. I'm ready for the names of those security agencies."

CHAPTER 41

When I reached my hotel room, I washed my face in the sink, but not before startling myself as I looked in the mirror and saw a strange-looking blond woman with purple lipstick staring back at me. I contacted loan companies I'd gotten solicitations from recently. With just my signature, I could get twenty thousand dollars. I never in a million years thought I'd be inquiring about such a loan, but these were extraordinary circumstances.

While I was arranging for the cash infusion, Jonah texted me the names of three protection agencies. Once I'd arranged for twenty thousand to be transferred to my bank account, I contacted the first agency on the list. I wound up choosing the third because the first two couldn't accommodate the degree of protection I needed on such short notice. The company I hired owned several properties in the area they used for out-of-town clients needing maximum security. We agreed it would be best if Daisy, Ting, the children, and I lived at one of them while under the agency's protection. They would send a car to pick up Ting and her kids in several hours and take them there. Later, they would drive Daisy there from the hospital if she was discharged that afternoon as expected. I would take a cab and use cash. The fellow from the protection agency warned me against using an Uber because it would be possible to track me.

I called Daisy and Ting to update them about the plan. Then I stuffed everything I had into my backpack and checked out. It was rainy and cold by California standards when I stepped onto the sidewalk. Hopefully, the FBI would kick in soon, but until that happened, I would feel safe under guard in the agency's Sunset District house. I was eager to see Lim and have Mingyu reunited with his mother, but there was no way to lessen the time I'd have to wait for that.

It had been a few years since I'd hailed a cab in San Francisco. I took the fifth one I saw on Powell Street. After confirming that the driver didn't look Asian in any way, I gave him the address of my temporary residence. As usual, downtown traffic was slow, the flow of cars obstructed by double-parked cars, buses, and pedestrians. Once out of downtown, the traffic moved better, but I don't remember ever getting close to the speed limit until we were near my destination. Finally, after a forty-minute drive, I arrived at the modest olive-green house in the middle of the block. I paid the driver who sped off, and rang the bell. A muscular man, mid-forties with a shaved head and wearing all black, greeted me. I noticed a holster with a gun on his hip. No fan of guns, I was nonetheless relieved to see the weapon arming someone on my side.

"Dr. Rosen?" he asked.

"That's me."

"Pleased to meet you. Can I see some identification?"

I reached into my purse and retrieved my wallet. "I look different now," I said, exposing my driver's license through the clear plastic window."

"Sure do. But I can see it's you. It's all in the eyes. C'mon in."

The man introduced himself and showed me around the house. Three bedrooms, two baths, with a living room and small kitchen. Plenty big for all of us. Each room was endowed with drab, but comfortable-looking furniture. Every inch of the small backyard could be seen from the living room. Security cameras monitored the entire perimeter of the house, the yard, and the interior. Except the bathrooms. "I can turn the cameras on in there if you want, but most clients don't see the need for that."

"I think I'll stick with what most of your clients do," I said.

"Anything you need, we'll have it delivered. You must stay inside at all times."

"Got it," I said. "Is it okay if I use your computer in the livingroom to do Facetime?"

"Sure. We have a very secure encrypted internet system installed here."

I went to my room and plugged in my phone. I planned on doing Facetime with Lim after Ting arrived. I wanted him to tell her about their parents before she learned it from Jonah or someone else. In the meantime, I downloaded a novel to my phone's Kindle app and began reading while the phone was charging. I had a hard time concentrating. I felt safe for the moment, but my brain was racing in circles of uncertainty.

I must have read and re-read the first two pages of my new book at least twenty times before I heard sounds at the front door. I recognized Ting's voice, followed by the sound of small feet running around, and children laughing and squealing. A man's voice yelled out, "No, you can't go outside," followed by Ting yelling something in Chinese. Although I didn't understand what they were saying, I could tell from the tone that the children were disappointed.

I rushed into the living room to greet them. The children grabbed my legs and hung on. I hugged Ting, bending over Kang while struggling to keep my balance.

"Take a few minutes to get settled," I said. "When you're ready, I'll get Lim on Facetime. Then you can see him and Mingyu."

"That so wonderful. Wang Shu got hand stuck in car seatbelt buckle and has little cut. I take care of that before I see Lim and Mingyu. So excited."

Ting disappeared into a bathroom with the children while I got Facetime up on the computer. My pulse quickened as I entered Lim's number. It had been too long since I'd last spoken to him. So much had happened.

I figured it was morning wherever he was. Maybe mid-day. I wasn't sure how far they'd traveled by now. It seemed like an eternity, but it was probably only seconds before Lim answered. He was outside on a deck chair, and the sun was bright. Mingyu was lying supine on an adjacent chair under a makeshift cardboard shade.

"What is up?" Lim asked, all smiles. From the small amount I could see captured by his cell, it looked like Lim and Mingyu were on an expensive cruise of the Mediterranean. All that was missing was a Margarita with a little umbrella in it.

"While the two of you have been living it up on your cruise, we have had a little more excitement here."

"Oh?" I could see Lim was concerned. "Do you mean there has been trouble?"

"You could say that."

Lim looked confused. "I did say that."

"I know," I said, half laughing. "That's yet another one of our expressions. It's a way of saying 'yes.'"

"You mean bad things have happened?" His eyes widened. "Did something happen to Ting? Or Daisy?

"No, everyone's fine. Ting is in the next room with Kang and Wang Shu. Daisy, she's okay now, so don't worry. But before I got home, two men invaded our apartment, tore the place apart, and, well, they shot Daisy."

Lim gasped.

"She had surgery and is expected to make a full recovery."

"Ting was not shot?"

"She and the kids hid under a table. When she got a chance, she took off running. She carried Wang Shu, and Kang ran with her. They didn't stop running until they'd gone nearly a mile through the city. Really put that blood Kang has to the test. No normal kid that age could run that far, that fast. Unfortunately, the men got away."

"Where are you now? They will come back!" Lim was visibly upset.

"It's okay. I hired bodyguards. People to protect us at a secret location. That's where I am now. I feel very safe." I lowered my voice. "I need to tell you something before Ting comes to talk to you. So, I'll talk quickly."

"I am all ears."

"We needed to tell our lawyer and others about what's happened so we can get government protection and make sure you, Ting, and the children are granted asylum. To make our story as strong as possible, I told them about your parents. I haven't told Ting, but I think you should tell her now, so she hears it from you."

"Hear what?" I heard Ting's voice behind me.

I looked at Lim and shrugged. "Here, Ting, talk to your brother," I said, offering her my chair. Lim had a close-up of Mingyu on the screen. Ting gently stroked the image of his smiling face. She and Lim were speaking in Chinese as I walked into the kitchen. The volume of their speech intensified. Although I didn't understand their words, I knew what was being said. I rushed back in to be with Ting when I heard her break down, crying.

"Ting, it's good news, isn't it?" I said, wrapping my arms around her from behind.

"Yes, yes," she said between sobs. "I so happy. But still, I feel . . . I not know word. Maybe confused."

"I understand. All these years thinking one thing, then finding out something else. Something so important."

"We must get them. Must rescue parents. Here I am, in wonderful free country, and they stuck in horrible prison. I terrible daughter. I so ashamed."

Lim was quiet while I tried to console Ting and convince her that none of this was her fault. She had no way of knowing the truth about her parents before she left China. While I was trying to comfort her, the sound of a loud siren came from the computer, from Lim's boat, to be more accurate. Lim looked around as the blast of the siren was replaced by someone yelling in Chinese over a loudspeaker. The camera on Lim's phone turned to the sky. I heard shouting and loud footsteps, probably from several men, approaching. The sound of someone bumping something, perhaps a chair, was followed by the thudding of feet running away.

"I must go," Lim yelled. I heard Mingyu cry and surmised Lim had picked him up.

"Don't hang up! Don't hang up!" I feared the boat was sinking, or there was a fire on board. My imagination ran wild. But never did I imagine what was actually happening.

The phone was probably in Lim's pocket when the screen turned black. Then, with his voice barely audible, I heard him say, "Pirates."

CHAPTER 42

I froze as I listened to the sound of Lim running and jumping, while others yelled. Not knowing what was happening from moment to moment, I felt helpless while envisioning the pandemonium taking place. I couldn't understand what anyone was saying, and I couldn't do a thing to help. My heart was pounding as if I were there, being chased around the boat, running for my life. I yelled for Lim, but he didn't answer. I was comforted by the sound of his rushing around and Mingyu's crying, verifying they were both alive. I recognized the noise made by a door opening, then closing. Finally, the running stopped. I heard Lim breathing heavily, and the screen became dimly lit.

"I think we are safe now," he said. "Shh-Shh," he whispered to Mingyu, who was still crying.

"What's going on?" I asked.

I barely made out Lim's dimly lit face on the screen. "A boat approached quickly and came alongside our ship. Some of their men may already be on board. Mingyu and I are now in the shipping box we came onto this ship in. It is on top of a tall stack. I climbed up here on the piles of other cargo boxes."

A loud popping noise sounding like gunfire gave me a jolt.

Lim was silent. The muffled sounds of men yelling unintelligibly and more rounds of gunfire kept me in suspense. I repeatedly asked, "What's going on?"

After what seemed an eternity, Lim whispered. "They are looking for Mingyu and me. They speak Mandarin, so most of the crew cannot understand them. I am sure they were sent by the Chinese government."

"Where did they come from? You're in the middle of the ocean!"

"Good question."

"What will you do if they find you?"

"I will use my gun if I have to. I cannot talk much longer. My battery is about to run out."

"You have a gun?"

"Yes. The crew all carry guns. They watched *Captain Phillips*, so they worry about pirates. The captain gave me a gun when we were in waters he thought were dangerous. We are on open ocean now where everyone figured we would be safe, but I kept the gun with me."

"Have you ever used one?"

"No, but I have seen how they work in movies. It looks easy."

"You need training to use them."

"I will not have a choice. *O o.*"

I knew that was the English equivalent of "Uh-oh."

What's wrong?" I asked. Stupid question I realized as soon as I'd asked it. I already knew a lot was wrong.

"I smell smoke."

My heart plummeted to the pit of my stomach. I heard more gunfire. It was getting louder, closer to Lim.

"I love you," Lim said.

I wondered if he meant it, or if those words were just the words of a man facing imminent death. "I love you too," I answered. "Stay safe."

"I have to go. Do not ever forget I love you. Remember that if I never see you again."

The connection was lost. It was more than I could bear, but I didn't have long to dwell on my despair. My cell phone was ringing. It was the inspector.

"Can you get to the San Francisco FBI Field Office on Golden Gate near Van Ness tomorrow morning?" he asked. "There's an agent there who wants to speak to you."

"I'm not going anywhere," I said. Or, more accurately, yelled. I was beside myself. "There are people out there who want to kill me. And my friends. You tell that agent to get over here. Tonight. We're running out of time."

"I'll have her call you."

When the call ended, I froze. Someone was opening the front door.

"Daisy," I yelled, seeing my roommate walk slowly through the door, wearing pants and a stained T-shirt.

I started to run up to her when she held out her right arm, her hand flexed, and shouted, "Don't you dare try to hug me. I'll scream."

"Oh, sorry," I said. "I forgot. I was just so glad to see you. I guess it still hurts a lot."

"Understatement."

"Well, I'm glad you're out of the hospital. It's safe here. I think."

Ting, who had been in her bedroom, came out to greet Daisy and was given the same warning to stay away.

"So sorry," she said. "You hurt." Then she turned to me. "What you yell about with Lim? I hear you yell."

"Sit down, and I'll tell you. Everything's happening so fast."

Ting sat next to Daisy on the couch. "I was talking to Lim. Everything was fine, when suddenly, all hell broke loose. He was running, there was yelling over the loudspeaker, and he took Mingyu into a shipping container. Shortly after, there were gunshots."

Daisy looked horrified, Ting even more so. "What happened?"

"I wish I had better news. They're being attacked by people looking for Lim and Mingyu. Probably sent by the Chinese government. His battery ran out, and I lost contact. I'm so scared."

Ting became panic-stricken. "They're going to kill Mingyu," she yelled. Her head in her hands, she bent over and cried. Daisy put her right arm around her, but Ting was inconsolable.

"We need to stay focused," I said. "We have to do whatever we can to find out what's happening. If Lim and Mingyu are captured, we need to get the government's help to rescue them."

"Rescue not possible," Ting corrected me. "They are assassins. They train to kill everyone. No capture."

She was probably right, but I couldn't think about that possibility. I wanted to—I needed to—believe they would be okay. Captured, perhaps, but alive. Before I had time to think, my phone rang again.

The voice on the other line introduced herself as an FBI Special Agent. "Can I meet with you this evening?" she asked. "The police inspector has filled me in on your situation, and all the players involved. I want to help."

"I hope you can. Conditions have changed from bad to dire. The cargo ship Lim is on with his nephew was attacked by assassins a few minutes ago. I don't know if they are dead or alive right now. There's no time to waste."

"Give me your address. Please."

I handed the phone to the nearest bodyguard and told him to give her the address. Ting went to her bedroom to comfort Kang and Wang Shu, who seemed to sense something was wrong. I broke down and wept.

Now it was Daisy's turn to comfort me. I was ashamed. After all, she's the one who almost died and was still recovering from a gunshot wound. Her right arm was still around me when there was a loud knock at the front door thirty minutes later. A bodyguard opened the door. From where I sat, I could see a middle-aged woman in a black suit with short, wavy brown hair. She showed her badge and credentials to the security guard, who checked them carefully and escorted her in. The sight of her dried my tears. I blew my nose on the tissue Daisy handed me, and we shook hands.

She looked at Daisy. "Are you Ms. Wong or Ms. Chen?"

"I'm Daisy Wong."

"I need to speak to all of you."

Daisy left and brought Ting into the living room. Kang and Wang Shu followed, carrying a toy truck and a doll, respectively. Once we were all seated, the agent began to speak. She was a quick study, appearing to know everything I had disclosed to the inspector earlier. After briefly speaking to each of us privately in the kitchen, presumably confirming we were all in agreement with the facts, she returned to the living room and continued.

"After speaking to you, Dr. Rosen," she said, looking at me, "I inquired about any nautical occurrences in the Pacific Ocean that might meet the description of the recent incident you described."

My pulse quickened, and my stomach tightened. I wasn't sure I wanted to hear what she was going to say next. I glanced at Ting, who sat staring, motionless.

"The Coast Guard in the Seventeenth District which covers the Alaskan maritime region, received a Mayday call from the area southwest of Eareckson Air Station, located on an Aleutian Island close to Russia."

"You think it might be Lim's ship?" Daisy asked. She was the only one of us who could speak.

"It's too early to tell, but it could be. We have a Coast Guard ship heading in that direction now, but it will be hours before it reaches the signal source. Eareckson is no longer an active air station, but it houses private aircraft. Two small planes have departed in the last ten minutes or so to look for the ship. They should reach the area a half-hour from now."

"What do we do now?" I asked, finding my voice.

"Regarding the ship situation, right now we wait. Once they have more information, I will be notified. Until then, there is much to talk about. I'm glad you hired bodyguards. I realize this must be a financial burden, and I would like to offer you federal protection, but that will take a while to arrange. Federal Marshalls sometimes provide security, but that's usually for witnesses of crimes involving the drug trade, terrorism, and high-level domestic criminals. Your case, while compelling, involves a foreign government, yet wouldn't be considered terrorism. I think the best strategy will be to expose the whole operation quickly, removing the motive for assassination attempts."

"I'm all for that," I said. Ting and Daisy nodded their agreement.

"First off, I want to arrange for all the necessary DNA testing. I have collection kits with me for samples from you, Ms. Chen, and your children, to be compared with the sample Dr. Rosen obtained from the purported father, Yang Peng. All I need is a cheek swab from each of you, if you agree."

"Yes, I agree," Ting said.

"I will ask the lab to rush, but at best, I don't expect to get anything back for several days. Next, I need to address the video. It appears to be a copy of several different recordings."

"Is that a problem?" I asked.

"Only in that the FBI requires the originals. They have people to inspect them and assure they haven't been Photoshopped."

"I have them," I volunteered.

"Great. Meanwhile, I suggest you have your attorney come here to complete your application for asylum and send it in right away," the agent said, looking at Ting. "I will see if there is anything I can do to speed it along. Despite what anyone may say, the USCIS, that's the US Citizenship and Immigration Services, sometimes will rush through an asylum appli—"

The agent was interrupted by her phone, which she answered immediately. All we heard was, "Uh-huh, okay, I see, thanks." All eyes were on her as she put her phone down.

"One of the planes spotted a cargo ship. It's still afloat."

I closed my eyes, an intense feeling of relief consuming me. I assumed Ting did the same.

"However," she continued, "it is heavily consumed by flames and is sinking. A smaller vessel is nearby, turned upside down."

"They need to do something," I screamed. "The plane needs to rescue them!" I wasn't thinking clearly.

"The plane is small, and couldn't possibly carry all of the crew, even if there was a way to get them into the cabin. There is no rescue rope on the plane. That only works with helicopters."

She was right. I was grasping for straws.

"The pilot saw many cargo crates floating. Apparently, they had slid off the ship. She thought she saw three rafts floating near the wreckage."

"Thought?" I shouted. "Can't she be sure? She needs to be sure."

"She's doing the best she can. It's overcast and foggy. With all that debris in the water, and being a long distance away, I'm sure it's hard to see."

"Please tell me, one of them has Lim and Mingyu," I said.

"I wish I could, but I'm afraid we'll have to wait."

CHAPTER 43

The agent collected DNA swabs from Ting and her children, then took the micro SD cards with the original recordings I handed her.

Before leaving, she inspected the house and yard, walked up and down the street, and questioned our security team. "I think you're in good shape," she told me. "The whole perimeter of the house and yard is being monitored, and the security detail appears to be quite experienced."

"When will I hear from you again?" I asked.

"I'll call you when I hear something. Anything."

"Thank you. Call any time. I cannot eat or sleep until I hear something," Ting said.

"Same here," I added.

The agent departed, and we were left with our imaginations. I called Jonah, who said he'd come to the house the next day at 9:00 a.m. After that, we said little. I couldn't wait to hear, but in truth, I only wanted to hear good news. Anything else would be unbearable. Daisy, Wang Shu, Kang, and the security guards ate dinner a guard picked up at a nearby Thai restaurant. Neither Ting nor I had an appetite.

Three stressful hours after the FBI agent left, my phone rang. We all held our breaths as I answered the unidentified number. I recognized the agent's voice immediately, and my stomach twisted into a knot.

"I have some news," she said.

I had difficulty speaking. "What?" I asked, hardly recognizing my voice, which was weak and high-pitched. I put my phone on speaker so everyone could hear.

"The Coast Guard cutter is close to the site of the sinking ship. They deployed a helicopter to inspect the area. It's foggy and getting dark, so there is limited visibility."

I felt myself getting impatient. *Just tell me if Lim and Mingyu are alive. Cut all the other crap.*

"What's left of the ship is still burning. It's doubtful anyone is still on board. Hold on. Someone's on my other phone." She put the phone down, and my chest tightened up so much I could hardly breathe. I heard her talking. "Uh-huh. Okay. Are you sure? Thanks." Seconds later she got back to me. "Three life rafts are floating in the area, with survivors on all of them. At least two bodies, possibly deceased, are floating on debris. They are going to begin a rescue with the helicopter as the cutter approaches. The sun will probably be down completely before they're done, so it's going to be difficult."

"Don't hang up," I yelled. "I'll hold on so you can keep me current with the updates you get on your other phone."

"Okay," she said. "It may be a few minutes."

"That's fine. I've got nothing else to do."

Over five minutes went by before I overheard the agent speaking on the other phone. "I see. Yes. Good news." My heart soared. Then I heard, "Oh, no." My heart sank. I looked at Ting. She was expressionless, frozen as she stared at the floor.

The agent got back to me and spoke. "They have picked up three men from one of the lifeboats and are headed back to the cutter. They are all Chinese, so communication is difficult."

"Do they speak Mandarin or Cantonese?" Ting asked, looking up. "Anyone who speak Mandarin, except Lim, they are Chinese murderers."

"I didn't think to ask. They probably don't know, anyway." She paused. "Now I'll tell you everything they said. I'm not going to hold anything from you." She paused again. "The helicopter pilots didn't see a baby."

Ting began crying. "That doesn't mean anything," I said. "Just because they didn't see a baby when they flew over, doesn't mean there isn't one." Ting continued sobbing. It was impossible to comfort her.

"It'll be at least ten more minutes 'til I have any more information. They're going to drop these three men off on the ship and immediately go back for more."

I managed to say, "We're holding."

After an unbearable period of silence, we listened to the agent's footsteps as she walked away from the phone, then returned. She took a few audible sips of a beverage before her other phone rang again, and she answered. "Uh-huh. Speaks English. Doesn't know. Oh, good."

Back on my line, the agent told us they had picked up three more men from the first life raft, emptying it. One spoke English well and explained they had been attacked. Four armed men on a small, very fast vessel, came to their ship. Three tried to board, but only two were successful. The cargo ship sailors gunned down all three who tried to board, but not before two of their own were shot and killed, and the attackers had started a fire in several places. The man remaining on the small vessel sent a missile into the side of the cargo ship, making a hole. It is sinking slowly. A shipping crate fell on the small boat, capsizing it, with the fourth man still on board. He never left the boat and is presumed dead. The names of the deceased cargo ship crewmates are Tom and Shum."

I wasn't ready to hear the names when she blurted them out, but once done, I let out a deep breath. I felt guilty at being happy Lim wasn't one of the two men killed, aware that the deaths were tragedies for their families. Yet my guilt was overshadowed by my relief, believing there was a good chance Lim was still alive. Maybe, Mingyu too. Looking up at Ting, I saw tears streaming down her face.

"Thank you," I said. "If those are the only dead from the ship, that means Lim is alive, on one of those boats."

"I see no reason to think otherwise. You need to remember, though, the weather is inclement, and the rafts may not hold up. But there is reason to be hopeful."

Her statement dampened my optimism, but I still felt like I was crawling out of a very deep hole. "We'll continue to hold."

After another twenty minutes of silence, the agent's other phone rang again. We all froze as we listened to her side of the conversation. "Uh-huh. Good. Chen Lim. You certain?" My heart soared. "Great. Does he have a baby?" After a pause, her voice dropped, and she said, "Oh." The single word and the flat expression said it all.

Ting became hysterical.

The agent came back on my line but it was difficult to hear her over Ting's crying. I didn't blame Ting, but I wanted to hear what the agent had to say. "Chen Lim is on the helicopter. One of his arms is broken, but he appears unharmed otherwise. They also have two other men. I'm terribly sorry, but there is no baby. I told them to ask what happened to him. They will call back once they learn anything."

"Thanks," I said. "I'll hold."

We listened to Ting cry uncontrollably for another fifteen minutes. Kang and Wang Shu tried to comfort her, then began crying and screaming themselves. I worried that the neighbors might call the police. At long last, I heard the agent's other phone ring. "Uh-huh. Great news. Why didn't you call before? I know, but I've got people here, waiting. Okay. That's fine."

She came back to my phone. "Another man on Mr. Chen Lim's boat had the baby. The baby appears to be fine."

I had to grab Ting and shake her. She hadn't heard a thing. "Ting! Ting! It's okay." I grabbed her face and forced her to look at me. "They have Mingyu! He's alive. He's fine. Now listen, you need to listen with us. Sit down."

Ting looked dazed as she wiped her tears away and sat next to me on the couch. Her children similarly quieted down and sat at her feet.

"We're all listening," I said into the phone.

"Mr. Chen is on the cutter now. I was told that after the fire broke out, he left the shipping crate he'd been hiding in with his nephew. When he and a group of the sailors were getting on the lifeboats, an attacker they thought had been shot dead got up and came toward them, pointing his gun. Mr. Chen wanted to stop the attacker, but not wanting the baby to be hurt, he handed him to a man who was about to get on the lifeboat. Then Mr. Chen climbed a stack of shipping crates and jumped on the gunman when he got close enough. The gunman was knocked down, and his head hit the deck so hard, he died. Or he died of his previous wounds. Unclear. But the man had no pulse. When Mr. Chen got on the lifeboat, the water was choppy and the boat unsteady. The man holding Mingyu was at the opposite end of the boat, so Mr. Chen thought it would be best if he kept the baby. He asked the man to put Mingyu under his shirt to keep him warm. That's why no one saw the baby."

"I wished they'd told us about Mingyu earlier," I said. "Would have been easier on all of us."

"I appreciate your frustration, but they were so busy they forgot to call."

"Poor excuse, in my opinion, but fortunately, we're too happy at the moment to dwell on that. Now what? What's going to happen to Lim and Mingyu?"

"First, they will rescue the remaining sailors. Once they're all on the cutter, they'll be taken to a hospital in Kodiak, Alaska, to be evaluated. After that, the cargo ship crew will be flown back to Hong Kong. I'll make sure Mr. Chen remains in Kodiak until we can arrange for him to be transported here."

I wondered how long that would take, but I was ecstatic. I tried calling Lim's phone, hoping he still had it, and it miraculously had some juice. I got his voice mail. The greeting was in Chinese. I left a message, doubting he would get it. But it was wonderful to hear his voice.

CHAPTER 44

I fell asleep waiting for Lim's call. When morning arrived, I was too busy to worry about the lack of a phone call. I helped Ting get the kids dressed and fed. Then I changed the dressing on Daisy's wounds, front and back, and assisted getting her clothes on. She still had pain and reduced mobility of her left arm. Another call to Lim's cell phone reached his voicemail.

I attempted to call my mom, again with no answer. It was a bit early, although she was usually up by this time. I'd been so caught up in the events swirling around me that I'd pushed her difficulties to the back of my mind. That needed to stop. Once Jonah arrived, my day would be frenetic. I decided to call my mom's friend. If my call woke her up and she thought I was incredibly inconsiderate, so be it.

She answered on the first ring. Then she unloaded. Where had I been? My mom was in the hospital being evaluated for her decline in mental function. Since she now required someone to care for her 24/7, they were looking for a bed in a memory care facility for her. I knew that was a euphemism for a place to warehouse demented people until they die. My heart sank. My brain was ready to explode with questions. Angry no one from Adult Protective Services had notified me, I called the hospital my mom was in and, after being transferred several times, got the name of her attending physician. I called his office but reached his answering service. I left my cell number and explained that I was a physician and needed to speak to him ASAP about my mother, Maya Rosen.

Jonah arrived at 9:00 a.m. sharp, turning my attention from my mom to the task at hand. We crowded around him as he booted up his laptop and began going through the applications for asylum and supporting statements Ting and Daisy had worked on before the attack. Jonah edited every document as we proceeded, adding his lawyerly advice often. Five hours later, we were mentally exhausted but done. Jonah left to send the completed applications and affidavits by overnight mail to the USCIS processing center in Nebraska. Next, he planned to drop a copy off to his journalist friend, and another to the FBI agent at the San Francisco FBI field office, hoping she would make good on her offer to expedite it. On the way back to his office, he would go by the local headquarters of our congresswoman and leave a confidential copy there, urging the staff to forward it to their boss immediately so she would be in the loop if we needed her help.

I spent the next hour cruising the internet, searching for pediatrician jobs in the area. I perused popular sites used by doctors looking for permanent jobs as well as temporary fill-ins for doctors taking a vacation. The Kaiser Permanente site alone had several listings for positions in the area. It would be easy to find work as a pediatrician, yet I thought about giving up medicine. Now that I'd tasted the life of intrigue and suspense, I considered pursuing a career in the FBI or CIA.

My phone rang. I was excited until I saw the call was not from Lim, or my mom's doctor. I recognized the name, however. It was the journalist Jonah had mentioned. I answered.

"As you are aware, Jonah has shared your story with me," he began. "This is big. I want to do a story with pictures, everything."

"I'm not sure that will be a good idea at this time."

"Look, Jonah wants me to do this. I'll have the article in the can so I'll be ready to send it off when you and your friends are comfortable. You may need this. Don't underestimate the power of public sentiment."

"I suppose it will be okay if you come here alone and make sure no one is following you."

"I need to bring my photographer. Jonah knows him and trusts him. I want lots of photos. Especially of the kids."

"Wait a second."

I checked with Ting and Daisy, then with the security team. All approved of the idea, so I gave him the green light.

"We'll be there in an hour."

I spoke to Jonah, who was enthusiastic about the upcoming interview with the journalist. He suggested getting an SF Giants cap and T-shirt for Kang, an American flag T-shirt for Wang Shu, and a shirt with the Golden Gate Bridge for Ting, things to make them look like gung-ho Americans. I told him Kang had a Giants T-shirt, but it was at our apartment. Jonah didn't want to go there, but he volunteered to pick up the needed items at a nearby shop that sold touristy things.

I was the only one with extra clothes, the ones that had been jammed into my backpack in China. I ironed what I had and gave Daisy a pair of clean tan pants and a blue blouse to wear. The top buttoned down the front, allowing Daisy to put it on without too much discomfort from her injury. Jonah came by with a cap and T-shirt for Kang, and T-shirts for Ting and Wang Shu. Once the sales tags were removed, the cap and T-shirts were on, and everyone had washed their faces and combed their hair, we sat on the living room couch, ready.

One of our security guards answered the knock at the door, and we waited silently. I heard the journalist and his photographer introduce themselves. The guards had them empty their pockets and open the photography equipment case. Seconds later, I heard a light slapping sound as the guards patted the men down. Finally, our visitors were allowed into the living room.

Jonah greeted his friends, then made introductions. The journalist, a tall, thin man with curly brown hair and tortoise-shell glasses, had an engaging smile. He handed me his card, and asked the photographer, a stocky man with short red hair and a beard, to get us ready for pictures.

The redhead moved the single lamp in the living room closer to the couch. "You guys look great," he said. "Everyone's gonna love you. Cute kids melt hearts. Always a great recipe for success."

"Let's get pictures first before I interview you and tire you out," the journalist said. "Then my photographer can sit by and take more candid shots. That always seems to work best."

The next hour was spent posing while the photographer did his job. He took pictures of each of us alone and in almost every combination of grouping possible. It was getting late by the time he was done. I checked my phone. Still nothing from Lim or my mom's physician. We spent the next two hours talking to the journalist, filling him in on details not covered in the material Jonah had given him. He must have said, "This is really big," at least twenty times, Jonah always remarking, "Told you so," afterward. Kang and Wang Shu had fallen asleep on the floor by the time he finished. We all went to sleep right after Jonah, the journalist, and the photographer left.

The next morning Kang and Wang Shu were complaining. The first time I'd heard whining in Mandarin. Not that I blamed them. We were all tired of being cooped up inside for days.

By the time Jonah called at 9:00 a.m., he had already called the USCIS office in Nebraska, and our congresswoman's office in Washington, D.C., where our representative was currently located. He hadn't expected any action on their part yet but wanted to direct their attention to our problem. He'd also spoken to the FBI agent, who claimed to have run against a brick wall while attempting to get security for us. She was, however, expecting to get the DNA results later that day, having badgered the lab into expediting the samples.

After explaining all of this to me, as an afterthought, Jonah asked, "How are you all doing?"

"We're fine but going a little stir crazy. I think we all would love to be able to go outside, go for a walk, anything. It's like we've been quarantined. We want to get back to a normal life. I still haven't heard from Lim, so I'm concerned about that."

"Once they've finished questioning him and decide he's okay, they'll let him call. Should be soon. Meanwhile, stay here, and try to stay calm. I'm trying to get this resolved ASAP."

"I know you are, and I really appreciate all you've done."

"I think it's time I called WADA, the World Anti-Doping Agency."

"They should be very interested in this," I said. "I wonder how they'll respond since this isn't exactly doping."

"It may not be doping, but genetic engineering falls under their purview. It turns out they're trying to stay ahead of the cheaters. They don't believe there has been any genetic manipulation involving Olympic athletes yet, but they understand it's just a question of time."

"From what I've read, they're considering partial or complete sequencing of athlete's DNA early on and comparing it in the future to see if there's been any manipulation. As the cost of sequencing goes down, that approach will be affordable. But it won't detect embryonic gene editing because the athlete's DNA sequence won't change over time. They'd have to test the parents. If they are alive and they know where and who they are."

"I could see how that might make for some embarrassing discoveries down the road," Jonah added. "Like if an athlete's dad isn't the biological dad."

Jonah promised he'd call when he heard anything new, and I decided to pass the time playing with Kang and Wang Shu. They knew enough English now that we could communicate sufficiently to play Hide and Seek. I was hiding, curled up in one of the bathtubs, when my phone rang. *Damn, now I'm going to lose.* Sure enough, Wang Shu ran into the bathroom and excitedly yelled that I'd been found, as I glanced at my phone. A number I didn't recognize, from area code 907. I pressed the answer icon.

"Bonnie, this is Clyde."

I was almost speechless. "Lim! I've been dying to hear from you. Did you get my messages?"

"Sorry, my phone is on the bottom of the Pacific Ocean. It fell out of my pocket when I got into the life raft. Did you hear about that?"

"Yes, I heard you jumped on one of the attackers, got in a lifeboat, and were rescued by a Coast Guard helicopter."

"Then you are caught up. Except for the part where I broke my arm when I jumped on the guy. Sorry I could not call you earlier, but I didn't have access to a phone."

"I have so many questions, I don't know where to start. How are you? How is your arm? How is Mingyu? Where were those guys from? How did they get to your ship?"

"Whoa. Let me try to answer you. I am fine. My arm is in a cast. Both bones in my forearm broke, but the doctor expects it to be fine once it heals. Mingyu is happy and healthy. He got a few scrapes and scratches, but nothing serious. Now about the men that attacked us."

"Are you sure they were there to kill you?"

"Me and Mingyu, yes. I heard them shouting our names to the sailors, asking where we were, but no one gave us away. The guy I jumped on, I looked through his pockets before I got on the life raft. He had pictures of the two of us."

"Oh, my god! How in the world did they know where you were?"

"They probably questioned everyone working the docks in Hong Kong. They have ways of getting information they want."

"Where did the boat come from?"

"I am not sure, but it appears to have come from one of the tiny uninhabited islands, either American or Russian, south of the Bering Strait."

"Where are you exactly? When will they send you here?"

"I am on an Alaskan island called Kodiak. There is a Coast Guard base here. They are sending all the sailors they rescued on the ship back to Hong Kong tomorrow."

"What about you?"

"Good question. They want to send me to Hong Kong, too, but I have been telling them I refuse to go there."

"They'll kill you if you go back. You need to ask for asylum. We've been working with an attorney here. He's trying to get asylum for you, Ting, and the children. Call him right away."

After I gave Lim the number, he said, "I will call him first chance I get. Right now, however, I have to go. They will not let me stay on the phone. Love you."

There it was. He said it without being under the threat of impending death. My heart melted. "Love you too." I meant it.

As soon as I disconnected, my phone rang again. I answered.

"This is Dr. Blaine. I'm the neurologist who's been taking care of your mom."

"I'm so glad you called." A thousand questions rushed to my head. "I've recently returned from an overseas trip, and now I understand my mother is hospitalized. What's going on?"

"I'm afraid I don't have good news for you. She is declining neurologically, but we have her on medication that may be helping. She can no longer live independently."

"How can you be so sure?"

"She was visited by Adult Protective Services and found to be unable to care for herself properly. She won't be able to live in her apartment again, even with an attendant. From what I gather, her decline seems to be fairly rapid for her condition."

"Are you saying she has Alzheimer's disease? She's not even sixty years old. Have you looked for other things, like a nutritional deficiency, depression, or reaction to medication?"

"In addition to her cognitive issues, your mom recently developed motor problems."

"Motor problems? Like she can't walk? Did she have a stroke?"

"We did a panel of tests. I was waiting to get the results before calling you because my suspicion was high. I got the results back earlier today."

"What tests? What's the result?"

"I think you should sit down."

After all I'd been through, I was sure I could take some bad news about my mom. I was getting impatient, being strung along by this doctor. I sat down. "I'm sitting now."

"Since you're a physician, you'll understand the significance of what I'm going to tell you."

Get on with it already. "Please, just tell me."

"Your mom has Huntington's Disease. Confirmed by genetic testing."

His words knocked the wind out of me. Took me completely by surprise. I couldn't speak.

"Are you okay?" Dr. Blaine asked.

"No question about it?"

"None, I'm afraid. Is there anything you want to ask me now? Anything I can do to help?"

"I need to go." I disconnected the call and sat as the information took residence in my brain. Now I understood why the doctor had taken his time disclosing my mother's condition. She had a hopeless, incurable, neurodegenerative disease that would leave her a vegetable before she died a horrible death. But that wasn't all. The disease is inherited, and I had a fifty percent chance of meeting the same fate.

CHAPTER 45

I couldn't sit there in a stupor all day. I took a deep breath, preparing to stand. Halfway through exhaling, my phone rang again. My favorite FBI agent. I pushed my latest problem aside. There was no way I could deal with it now.

"I've got good news," she said. "The DNA results are back. They confirm Ms. Chen is the mother of both children, and Mr. Yang is the father."

Exactly the results I had expected, yet I was surprised at my reaction. I was repulsed, nauseated, thinking about that monster Peng being the biological father of these two adorable children, and probably Mingyu. I knew it all along, but this underscored that fact.

"I'll tell Jonah," I said. "This evidence should help our case."

"Absolutely. We have also reviewed all the medical information available on Wang Shu and Kang. Everything you told us about Wang Shu's condition and your observations about Kang's hemoglobin has been confirmed. We have scientists now sequencing the segments of Kang's DNA involved in hemoglobin synthesis and will compare them to the same areas in Ms. Chen's and Mr. Yang's DNA. Hopefully, that study will be completed by tomorrow."

"What about Lim?"

"I've arranged for him to sign a copy of the asylum application your attorney filled out. I expect to receive a scan of the signed document soon, which I will forward to the USCIS office."

"Have you spoken to anyone there? Are they rushing the process?"

"I'm told they are hurrying it along, but it doesn't look like it's going to be any time soon. Instead of taking many months, it may get through in several weeks, which is not good enough. I'll try putting more pressure on them. I'm also trying to arrange Mr. Chen's transportation here. With the baby, of course. I'm not finding the Coast Guard to be very cooperative."

"This is not progressing nearly fast enough," I lamented.

"I know. Hang in there. I'm doing everything I can."

I called Jonah to let him know of the DNA results. He said he would pass the information on to his journalist friend, so he could add it to his exposé. Other than that missing data, the piece was ready to go. He planned to have dinner with him that night at John's Grill near the Chronicle office to read through his article.

"By the way," Jonah said. "I called WADA and spoke to someone there who was very interested in what I had to say. If our government isn't interested, at least the Olympics Committee is. I've been trying to speak to someone high up in our congresswoman's staff but keep running into dead ends. If she was made aware of what was going on, I'm sure she'd do something, but I doubt she's getting the message. If I don't hear back in a few days, I'll fly to DC. I'll speak to her directly if I have to camp out in her office. I'm still hoping Plan A, government action, will work."

"What's Plan B?"

"Release the article and have public opinion turn the wheels of justice. Meanwhile, I'll keep you posted."

"Call me when you hear something. Anything. I'm so tired of being cooped up here."

The next phone call I received was from a company selling solar panels. It was a relief to receive a call requiring such little mental energy. Nevertheless, I disconnected the call after five seconds.

I got back to searching the internet for jobs, now looking for positions in Hawaii, Colorado, and New York. I had no intention of moving, but I needed to keep my mind occupied. I didn't want to think about my mom, Huntington's Disease, or my future. I needed to get tested myself. That would answer the question looming large—had I inherited the disease, meaning my life would be cut short, and any children I might bear would have a fifty percent chance of inheriting it, too, or had I completely dodged that bullet? My phone rang. Irritated, I checked the caller. Jonah.

"Got some news already?" I asked.

"Listen," he said in a hushed voice. "I can't talk for long. There are two Chinese guys with guns in my office looking for information about your whereabouts. Someone at WADA must be a spy for the Chinese government. No other way they could know about me. I got them to let me use the bathroom. I keep a phone in here, but I've got to make it quick. They're trying to get me to give up your address. I'm a lawyer, not a navy seal. I don't know how much longer till they start torturing me, and I tell them. You need to get out of there. Tell the bodyguards to find you a new place. They're coming. Gotta go."

I allowed myself a few seconds to process this information before I sprang into action. I told the security detail what had happened. They called 9-1-1 to inform the police two armed men were holding an attorney, notified the FBI agent of the latest development, then began making arrangements for a new safe house while I told Daisy and Ting. Kang and Wang Shu began whining; I could see they were becoming Americanized. Within minutes, we had packed our belongings and were riding in two cars to a new safe house, this one in Daly City. I wasn't fond of Daly City on account of the fog, but I didn't mention it.

Used to the vagabond lifestyle by now, it didn't take long to get settled in our new abode. The bodyguards secured the premises and enabled the surveillance system in minutes. Feeling completely helpless, I hoped Jonah could escape his captors unscathed. It was only a matter of time before the Chinese hunted us all down and killed us. I made a unilateral decision. It was time to enact Plan B.

CHAPTER 46

I had put the journalist's card in my wallet after the interview. I fished it out and dialed his number. My heart pounded as the phone rang. Three rings later, he answered.

"This is Erica Rosen," I said.

"How are you? Anything new?" he asked.

"I want you to release the story. Now." My voice was shaking.

"You sure?"

"Absolutely. They've got Jonah. They're trying to get him to disclose where we are."

"Holy shit! You'd better get out of there. Have you called the police?"

"Yes, the police and FBI have been notified. We've already moved to a different location, so we're safe for now. I hope Jonah's okay. I feel so terrible getting him involved."

"Don't worry about Jonah. He loves this kind of shit. Lives for it. Hang tight. There's gonna be a shit storm when I release the story. Meanwhile, I'll see what I can find out about Jonah."

I waited fifteen minutes before opening my San Francisco Chronicle Twitter feed. I began reading. Tomorrow would be a "Spare the Air" day, meaning no fires in fireplaces allowed due to air pollution. Traffic in the Tenderloin area was being diverted on account of a "police incident." I wondered if that had something to do with Jonah. I hoped so. The City

Council had approved a plan to install bathrooms and showers for homeless people on Market Street. Oakland International Airport Terminal 2 was being evacuated in response to a terrorist threat. A Chinese plot to genetically engineer human embryos for the purpose of producing super athletes has been discovered. More to come. My pulse quickened.

"Ting, Daisy, come here," I yelled. Ting and Daisy ran to me and I showed them the Twitter message.

"Woo-hoo," Daisy shouted.

Ting stood silently for a few moments, then spoke. "What now?"

"I'm not sure," I said. "This is all new to me."

I turned on CNN. All I saw were more pundits haranguing about the sorry state of our nation's politics.

The journalist called. My voice shook as I answered the phone.

"He's gonna be okay," he said.

"What do you mean, 'gonna be?' What's going on?"

"Jonah's a bit banged up. It appears our Chinese friends decided their powers of persuasion were limited to brute force. They tried to beat your location out of him, but since he didn't know, he had nothing to tell them. Unfortunately, they didn't believe him. He appears to have at least a broken rib and a busted nose and is on his way to the county hospital. Beat up, but conscious and talking. The Chinese guys didn't give up easily. One was shot and killed. The other suffered serious injuries but was apprehended alive. I don't have any more details. Have you seen anything about your article yet?"

"There's a little information on the Chronicle Twitter feed."

"Don't worry, more will be out soon."

"You think we're safe now?"

"Not yet. Not till the whole story's out. I'm sure they've got more guys here who will continue to look for you. Don't tell me where you are. I don't want to know. They might come after me next."

"I'm sorry."

"No apologies, please. This is what I do. Now hold tight and watch the news."

It took all of three hours. The San Francisco Chronicle was given credit for breaking the story. I'm sure the editorial staff was proud. It all came out. Everything. The plot to genetically engineer human embryos to produce super athletes, so China could dominate the Olympic games and show their people, as well as the rest of the world, that their way of government was the best. The elaborate facility set up for this purpose, where women were forced to have engineered babies. The collateral damage in the form of genetic mistakes that had resulted from their experiments. The attempt to kill people wanting to expose the operation and destroy evidence by assassinating two adorable genetically engineered children, one three years old, the other five months old. Sympathetic pictures of Ting and her children splashed on the screen, followed by pictures of Mingyu taken in China. A brief video of the young victims living in the Building of Disappointment was shown. The public reaction was immediate, and it was forceful. I love the American people.

Laboratory analysis confirmed that Kang's hemoglobin gene was different from either parent's, providing irrefutable evidence of embryonic stem cell gene editing. After three days of this breaking story dominating the news, Jonah thought it was safe for us to be interviewed.

We agreed to a press conference at a secure site in San Francisco, admitting only credentialed members of the press. Ting wouldn't allow Kang or Wang Shu to be included but brought them with us to stay in a nearby room under guard, away from the press. She didn't want to be far from them.

The press conference was as one might expect. Jonah, wincing from his painful rib fractures, his face badly bruised, and a bandage over his left temple, insisted on being there. He, along with me, Daisy, Ting, the FBI special agent and members of the San Francisco Police Department stood at the podium. Lights flashed in our eyes every time a photographer took a picture. Members of the press clambered for our attention. The conference began with a narration of the events by the FBI special agent. She concluded by announcing that moments earlier she had learned the second Chinese assassin had expired in the hospital without gaining consciousness.

A member of the SFPD announced that ballistics matched the bullet removed from the wall in our apartment and the bullet removed from the body of David Fang to a gun found on one of Jonah's attackers. This was followed by questioning and the release of more video excerpts from our China trip. After forty-five minutes of grilling from the press, we ended the event. We had gotten our story out. If the Chinese government understood anything, they would know that killing us would no longer serve any purpose. Pandora's box, with all the ugliness they had tried to suppress, had been opened.

It didn't take long for our congresswoman, as well as many other members of the House and Senate, to weigh in on the outrageousness of the events. They swore that China would be punished with sanctions, they would be disqualified from future Olympics, and Ting and her family would be granted asylum. She would be reunited with her brother and youngest child immediately. Keeping them separated had been an inexplicable error. Behind the scenes, they began negotiations with China to send Lim and Ting's parents to the US along with two people who had helped us in China—Chan Wen, the deaf janitor, and Daisy's cousin, Lan. The members of Lim's organization who had helped us had been secretly contacted, and each had refused to leave China, where their work was far from over.

Daisy, Ting, her children, and I moved back to our apartment after crime scene cleanup experts thoroughly cleaned it and made it livable again. I was constantly receiving phone calls, either from government officials, law enforcement officers, or journalists. Most of my time was spent on the phone or meeting with people. I had no time to get myself tested for Huntington's Disease, but that could wait until the pandemonium was over. It's not like I could have done anything about it anyway. I hadn't yet decided how to tell Lim about that major glitch but would need to tell him soon. I wished I had the results already, but even if I'd been tested as soon as I'd learned about my mom, I doubted I'd have the results back yet.

Lim and Mingyu arrived at SFO on an Air Alaska flight the day after our congresswoman sprang into action. Ting and I were waiting in front of a large contingent of reporters. Kang and Wang Shu stood with their arms wrapped around Ting's legs. With tears in my eyes, I watched Lim as he walked past the TSA personnel, towards the waiting crowd. He looked handsome and fit, despite the cast on his right arm. His left arm was wrapped around Mingyu, who was smiling and kicking his legs excitedly. Lights flashed, and cameras clicked as the moment was recorded by the press. There were a few awkward seconds when he handed Mingyu to Ting while whispering, "Ting, I think he needs to be changed," before we embraced. Once in his arms, I felt safe, warm, and joyful, all at once. I had no doubt he was the one for me, and I knew then and there that I wanted to spend my life with him. If I could. The life of adventure my father had led wasn't for me. Lights continued to flash, and cameras continued to click, but I didn't care. We kissed long and hard, while Ting stood next to us, sobbing with joy as she hugged Mingyu.

After several emotional minutes, Lim whispered, "I have had a lot of time to think. I want us to get married and make a cousin for Mingyu."

My eyes filled with tears, from joy or a feeling of dread, I wasn't sure which. *If only it were that simple.* I didn't respond.

NOTE FROM THE AUTHOR

Word-of-mouth is crucial for any author to succeed. If you enjoyed *Unnatural,* please leave a review online—anywhere you are able. Even if it's just a sentence or two. It would make all the difference and would be very much appreciated.

Thanks!
Deven

ACKNOWLEDGMENTS

Writing, by its nature, is a lonely vocation. Most writers, especially those who write fiction, need to constantly question themselves. Is the writing clear? Is it interesting? What about inconsistencies? I have relied on the feedback of others to answer those questions.

First and foremost, my critique group deserves a standing ovation. As I type this, I am on my feet, clapping for the members of my group, George Cramer, John Schembra, and Jim Hasse. Each of them is a writer in his own right (look them up and check out their work). Thanks, guys!

I appreciate the very helpful input (and virtual wrist-slapping) of my editor, Violet Moore (Livermore, CA). Thanks, Vi, for your insight and overall pickiness.

Much thanks to others who have read all or parts of this novel as I was working on it. A big thank you goes to my brother Seth Greenberg, who was always full of suggestions. Others deserving thanks include (in alphabetical order) Linda Laviolette, Yimei Mao, Jen Petersen, Celia Silverman, and Suzanne Spradley.

I appreciate Reagan Rothe, David King, and the staff at Black Rose Writing for getting this thing into print.

Of course, this work wouldn't have been possible without Google. Countless searches and Youtube videos helped me accurately portray many of the scenes. Two books I relied heavily on for getting my facts straight are *A Crack in Creation: Gene Editing and the Unthinkable Power to Control Evolution* by Jennifer A. Doudna and Samuel H. Sternberg, and *Young China: How the Restless Generation Will Change Their Country and the World* by Zak Dychtwald.

My biggest thanks goes to my husband, Glen Petersen, who read and offered feedback on my work, encouraged me, enabled me by giving me time to write, and brought me coffee in bed every morning. It doesn't get better than that.

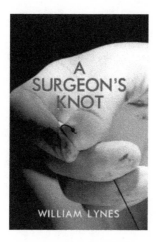

CPSIA information can be obtained
at www.ICGtesting.com
Printed in the USA
FSHW011542041120
75457FS